HEROES LIKE US

HEROES LIKE US

THOMAS BRUSSIG

TRANSLATED BY JOHN BROWNJOHN

FARRAR ■ STRAUS ■ GIROUX ■ NEW YORK

Farrar, Straus and Giroux
19 Union Square West, New York 10003

Copyright © 1996 by Verlag Volk und Welt GmbH, Berlin
Translation copyright © 1997 by Verlag Volk und Welt GmbH, Berlin
All rights reserved
Distributed in Canada by Douglas & McIntyre Ltd.
Printed in the United States of America
Designed by Abby Kagan
Originally published in 1995 by Verlag Volk und Welt, Germany, as
Helden wie wir
First Farrar, Straus and Giroux edition, 1997

Library of Congress Cataloging-in-Publication Data
Brussig, Thomas, 1965–
    [Helden wie wir. English]
    Heroes like us / Thomas Brussig ; translated by John Brownjohn. —
1st ed.
        p.   cm.
    ISBN 0-374-16983-7 (alk. paper)
    I. Brownjohn, John.   II. Title.
PT2662.R87H4513   1997
833'.92—dc21   97-16652

CONTENTS

HEROES LIKE US

KITZELSTEIN

I could claim to have been brought into the world by an entire armored regiment. *Lumbering in the direction of Czechoslovakia on the night of August 20, 1968, Soviet tanks passed a small hotel in the village of Brunn, where my mother, then more than nine months pregnant, was spending her maternity leave. Engines roared, tank tracks jingled on asphalt. Panic-stricken, I pierced the amniotic sac, slithered down the birth canal, and landed on a living room table. Darkness and pandemonium reigned, tanks rumbled past, and there I was. An evil stench filled the trembling air, and the world into which I emerged was a political world.*

You see, Mr. Kitzelstein? I'm so fully aware of my historic responsibilities that I've already begun to write the story of my life, though I have to confess that two whole years of endeavor have failed to get me further than the first paragraph. What I had in mind was an autobiography in which, while treating my person with due reverence, I would present a firsthand account of recent events in Europe that put me in the running for both the Nobel Prize in Literature and the Nobel Peace Prize (to acquaint you right away with one of my salient characteristics: megalomania). Who knows how much longer I might have toiled at my autobiography if you hadn't called me to request an interview on behalf of *The New York Times*?

How did I manage to topple the Berlin Wall? It's a long story. First, however, let me dispel a few misapprehensions.

I had hoped that my role in the events of that night would remain unrecognized a while longer, but I underestimated the persistence of American investigative reporters. When the Wall was suddenly no more, people rubbed their eyes and came to the conclusion that they themselves must have demolished it. That myth would not endure for long, I knew. They had to be somewhere, these people who had breached the Wall, but where? More realistic observers came to the conclusion that no such people existed. So who was responsible?

At this stage, recollections of Günther Schabowski's press conference surfaced. The myth that Schabowski had proclaimed the Wall open suited me admirably because it discouraged inquiries in my direction and enabled me, firmly intent on the Nobel Prize that was my due, to press on with my autobiography in peace. Besides, I always knew that if I confessed, I could dispose of the press conference myth with relative ease. One has only to listen closely to what Schabowski said at the time. When confronted by journalists and bombarded with questions about the flood of defectors, he granted the latter right of direct passage into the Federal Republic, probably because it irked him that the rest of the world should be gloating over television pictures of miles-long lines of cars at the Czech–West German border. His sole concern was to render the exodus less sensational. Although it's true that one hour later the West German Bundestag deputies interrupted a debate to rise and sing *"Deutschland über Alles,"* nothing had happened as yet at the Wall itself—except that a large crowd of curious, expectant onlookers gathered there. And then I appeared on the scene. You told me on the phone that you'd stumbled upon me while analyzing some videotaped material. Why should I deny it?

Yes, it's true, it was me: *I* toppled the Berlin Wall. Ah, but if that were all, as it would seem from the effusions of historians and journalists: "The end of divided Germany," "The end of the European postwar era," "The end of the twentieth century," "The end of the modern age," "The end of the Cold War," "The end of ideologies," "The end of history." They're like the brave little tailor—seven at a stroke— but shall I tell you what really happened? The world is entitled to my story, especially since it makes sense.

The story of the Wall's end is the story of my penis, but how to embody such a statement in a book conceived as a Nobel Prize–worthy cross between *David Copperfield* and *The Rise and Fall of the Roman Empire*? I've spent two years vainly seeking a solution to that problem. Now do you see why I find your appearance so timely? I mean, if I can't write about my dick, I'll talk about it. My remarks won't be youthful rodomontades, either, but pieces in a mosaic of historical truth, and if you don't want to leave any loose ends you must not mind if my recollections become a trifle dick-heavy at times.

That I should be recounting the story of my dick to you, of all people, is a tribute less to your investigative flair than to your business card. How many people get the chance to unbosom themselves to a *New York Times* correspondent, and where, I wonder, will you feature someone with my claim to fame—"The end of the modern age," "The end of history," etc.? On page one, of course, where else? What a prospect: I, the terminator of history, on page one of *The New York Times, the* mouthpiece of the world's liberal conscience (I'm never at a loss for such verbal gems).

It will, in fact, be my second page one appearance. Why? Because the *NBI,* or *Neue Berliner Illustrierte,* East Germany's best-selling weekly magazine, featured me on its front cover at the age of nine. That was in my third year of school, when we acquired a new principal who considered leisure activities worthwhile only if pursued on a team basis, and, since participation in team activities was statistically recorded, made it his objective that one hundred percent of his pupils should engage in them.

My purely emotional inclination was to join the Sailing Club, but my mother ("I know what conditions are like afloat!") didn't want me going anywhere where I could get my fingers crushed or ripped by splinters. I was well aware that wounds inflicted by wood splinters could result in blood poisoning, amputation—even death. It was routine procedure at home to fear the worst and issue solicitous warnings about it, and my mother was never more profoundly solicitous than when telling me something for my own good. My upright, authoritarian father was uninterested in trivialities. He very seldom addressed me, and then as succinctly as possible, for example, "Tuck your shirt in!" or "Quiet!" or "Hurry up!" For the rest, he was a man who spent his evenings vegetating in front of the TV set, the legs of his sweatsuit rolled up and his feet in a bowl of cold water.

"Do what you like, but you're not going sailing!" So sailing was out; instead, I joined the Young Scientists' Club. It was customary to unload the tedious job of running such clubs on the youngest teacher in any specialty, so the Young Scientists were supervised by a twenty-seven-year-old physics teacher named Küfer, whose sizable bald patch had, he claimed, been occasioned by "excessive brainwork." I had no idea what physics was and vaguely surmised that youthful scientists kept guinea pigs or hamsters. Herr Küfer, who didn't know what else to do with us, enlivened our meetings by projecting educational films on the Great Depression and the Spanish Civil War in reverse. The effect was unforgettable, for instance when mounds of rubble suddenly became puffballs of dust and transmuted themselves into buildings, or when aircraft, seemingly fitted with magnets, collected the bombs that came floating up toward them from below . . . (Küfer was fired a few years later, one of the grounds for his dismissal being that he had bred pacifist sentiments by running war films backwards.)

Then I saw a TV documentary in which particularly noisy streets were flanked with three-foot concrete walls to form baffles. Because the word "physics" occurred twice in the program, I asked Herr Küfer how baffles functioned. Gratefully seizing upon my suggestion, he proceeded to expound the theory of acoustics. Within a few weeks the Young Scientists' Club had developed an "experimental acoustics set" and displayed it at the local Masters of Tomorrow Exhibition. But it didn't end there: we won a place at the district level and were thereafter chosen to participate in the regional exhibition—and I was appointed to run our stand! A third-year student versed in experimental acoustics! What would my father say to that—a father who thought so little of me that he couldn't even muster the energy to complete a scathing sentence like "Pah, that boy will never amount to anything!"? He merely made a dismissive gesture whenever he got to "Pah, that boy . . . ," nor did he ever utter my name aloud. It's a fact: I never once heard my name on his lips! Although no boy should be saddled with a name like *Klaus* (rhymes with "mouse" and "house"—cute, yes?), I was somehow hurt that he completely eschewed it. I now resolved to call at his office so that, duly chastened, he could introduce me to his colleagues with some such words as "This is my son, who tells me that he has just been appointed to run an exhibition stand devoted to some scientific subject of which I, alas, am entirely ignorant . . ."

I had never visited my father at his office—he worked at the Ministry of Foreign Trade—but the city map indicated that it was twenty minutes away by U-Bahn—our subway. The security guard looked up the number of my father's office in several different directories. My first name is bad enough, but my surname—*Uhltzscht*—is a downright disaster: it always has to be spelled out and is quite unpronounceable, certainly at the first attempt (I've won bets with it). I still recall the guard's moist enunciation of the name: he showered the glass partition with spittle every time he uttered it. "No," he said, "no Uhltzscht. We don't have any Uhltzscht here." That was his initial response, and he stuck to it: he'd never heard the name and couldn't find it listed anywhere. Thoroughly disconcerted, I went home.

When I asked my father at supper where he worked, he muttered something about a "branch office." I retired to my room feeling dismayed, if not shocked. A *branch* office . . . of *course*! At last I had a solid reason for my father's continual ill temper: shunted off to a *branch* office, he'd been denied a great and glittering career. An outsider sentenced to work in a ministerial outpost, he must be inwardly as lonesome as a lighthouse keeper and eaten up with disappointment at the malevolence of those who had callously banished him to such a backwater. My father was the biggest shit I'd ever met, admittedly, but that was no reason to think ill of him. "Aha! Who forgot to draw the curtain again?" It could only have been me, but which curtain did he mean? I emerged from my room to find him dramatically pointing, with an imperious expression, at the undrawn curtain of the shoe closet. Ah well, now that I knew he'd just come home from a *branch* office, I saw him in quite another light. I drew the curtain, he removed his shoes, opened the curtain, put his shoes on the shelf, drew the curtain again, and regarded me with scorn: *It's as simple as that!* When I finally told him that the Young Scientists' experimental setup had been nominated for the regional exhibition—when I at last announced *proudly* that I, a nine-year-old, had been appointed to run the exhibition stand—do you know how he responded? He tweaked the front of my shirt and said, "Let's hope you've learned by then to do all your buttons up."

Forget it. The exhibition was scheduled to open with a tour of the stands by sundry "important government representatives," and ours was on their official itinerary. I was prepared for the occasion by my principal and some people I didn't know, who kept impressing on me how honored and privileged I was. You may be sure, Mr. Kitzelstein, that my shirt was correctly buttoned when the time came. Of the event itself I remember only that my stand was visited by a gaggle of fat, perspiring men. I didn't get far with my presentation, which I'd learned by heart, because one of the men, presumably the most important, cracked a joke—one that I didn't understand and recognized as humorous only because the members of his retinue vied to see who could produce the most ingratiating laugh. A brace of press photographers clicked and flashed; the joker patted me on the back and said, "Carry on." The whole performance had lasted two minutes at most.

I was featured in the next day's *Berliner Zeitung*. My mother promptly bought thirty copies and sent me out for another ten. A few days later came my appearance on the front cover of the *NBI*: I, a nine-year-old, on the cover of our biggest illustrated magazine, alongside one of the most powerful men in the land! The phone never stopped ringing: "Was that really *your* Klaus . . . ?" "Is it true that Klaus . . . ?" "To think of your Klaus with . . ." My eager-beaver principal held a school assembly in my honor. Heads turned wherever I went. "That's him!" people whispered. For the rest of my time at the school, a framed copy of the *NBI* cover hung in the lobby. By the time *Trommel,* the Young Pioneers' newspaper, followed suit and belatedly devoted a full-page article to me, my mother was so blasé that she bought only eight copies.

My dearest ambition was being fulfilled. I wasn't a failure after all: that cover picture proved it. I, a Young Scientist and Master of Tomorrow, had appeared on the front of our Democratic Republic's most widely read magazine. The editor must have known why he'd put me, of all people, on his cover. Wasn't I the most promising Master of Tomorrow—wasn't I a Nobel laureate-to-be? Such was the roseate cloud on which I floated through my daily life. The future Nobel laureate was well behaved, the future Nobel laureate serenely drew the shoe-closet curtain, the future Nobel laureate listened when other people told him things. What could possibly go wrong? Sooner or later streets would bear my name. I started to keep a diary. Although my entries were largely addressed to posterity, I always—and, I felt, to my great credit—had a few words to spare for my fellow mortals.

And my mother! At last I could look her in the eye! No, they had not been in vain, those eight years of professional advancement she had sacrificed to my upbringing. She had not only brought up an ordinary, well-behaved, industrious, clean, clever, and altogether presentable son; she had reared a future Nobel Prize–winner. I was the product of eight arduous years during which I had been persistently enjoined to "complete your sentence" (incomplete sentences were ignored) and forbidden to play any but educationally worthwhile games such as Scrabble. Although my mother sanctioned an occasional game of jackstraws, Parcheesi and old maid were out, not to mention go fish, that *ne plus ultra* of intellectual hebetude.

Thanks to the cover picture, I also became my own composer of headlines. When I'd spent an agreeable afternoon with my pal Bertram, I expected page two of the morrow's *Neues Deutschland* to read KLAUS AND BERTRAM HOLD AMICABLE MEETING, and when I waited, impatiently clicking my fingers, for the teacher to let me answer a question, YOUTHFUL SCIENTIST WOWS CLASS.

It went on like that for years—until I came face-to-face with an original copy of the West German *Bild-Zeitung*. I had occasionally seen reproductions of *Bild*'s front page, so I wasn't wholly unprepared; moreover, one of our women teachers often referred to Western "tabloids." Having deduced from the context that a tabloid was a species of newspaper, I was expecting something out of the ordinary— something that resembled a newspaper but was, in fact, an insidious and subversive *tabloid*. As for the headline . . . But first, before I disclose those unforgettable words, I must pay tribute to the presentation: such big, bold letters—letters that might have been hewn from a boulder, letters that suddenly brought the term "*block* capitals" to life! The headline would have been sensational enough had it only read WORLD ENDS TOMORROW! but it was more horrific still: POLICE ROCKED BY SEX SCANDAL! How *frightful*! That the police, those guardians of the law and protectors of honest citizens, who labored day and night to maintain peace and good order, should be pilloried in such a fashion! Did these Western rags stop at nothing? Why did they agitate against the police? The police were crime-busters, so anyone who abused them must be in favor of crime. And why should they be charged with sexual delinquency, of all things—was there nothing a Western editor wouldn't stoop to? What worried me, as a thirteen-year-old, most was the thought of being awarded my Nobel Prize at the very moment when I happened to be afflicted with a hard-on. What then? Would I be the subject of a headline such as SEX MANIAC DISGRACES NOBEL PRIZE CEREMONY?

That apart, I wanted my name, unappealing though it was, to appear in print as often as possible. I wrote letters to the editor and entered competitions. My desk—I'd had one of my own since first grade—was never without a stack of postcards. I combed every available periodical for quizzes, with the result that I've never met my match when it comes to answering questions like "How many grooves are there on an LP?" The second tactic I employed to keep my name before the public was to contribute to the correspondence column in *Trommel*, though I also wrote to nearly every paper that published readers' letters. I had an opinion on every subject and the ability to express it in a printable form. I kept a record of my published utterances and suspected skulduggery when I remained unpublished for six, eight, or even, on one occasion, fourteen weeks. Bumptious little beast that I was, I thought no end of my letters to the press and read them aloud to my mother—though only, of course, if they were published. This was the real thing! How could I have doubted it? *Childhood is a time devoid of doubt.* Ugh, an aphorism slipped out! I detest aphorisms, especially my own, but they do have the desired effect on fat-assed, corpulent listeners: *Mm, interesting, never looked at it that way before . . .* I've been an experienced aphorist ever since my letter-writing days. Aphorisms are forever escaping me—they flow from me like diarrhea.

Where was I? Oh yes, childhood and doubt. *Children must believe what they fail to understand; once doubt creeps in, they cease to be children.* Aphoristic, right? A sure thing for publication in the concluding section of correspondence on the subject "Too young to be an adult? Too old to be a child?" *Adolescence is the age of doubt; when doubt ends, so does adolescence.* There's mental diarrhea for you! Not an ounce of weight or substance, but my brain is awash with such aphoristic nonsense. It's a wonder I can speak at all for the clamor of the aphorisms in my head: "Hey, say me out loud! Make me up! Make me sound witty! You want to be famous, don't you?"

I'd like to be able to open my mouth, just once, without feeling that I'm speaking into a microphone. And now you and your tape recorder are here in front of me, the terminator of history, and I have an opportunity to appear on page one of *The New York Times.* You realize what you're doing to me? I could talk as I have always wanted to, talk as if issuing a press release or making a personal statement. I could summarize, announce, evaluate—but casual chitchat can prove disastrous. You were still busy adjusting the controls when I was flirting with my page one syndrome, and what did I come out with? Resentment and insecurity. No wonder I've produced only one paragraph of my autobiography after two years' cogitation.

So what choice do we have but to carry on as before? Allow me to preserve the illusion that we're still at the voice-test stage—at least pretend to twiddle a knob from time to time—and I'll go on speaking until I'm through. It'll be the most celebrated voice test in human history—which is saying something, because, while we're on the subject of celebrated voice tests, I'm reminded of Ronald Reagan and his heartfelt announcement that he'd just signed a bill for the nuking of Russia. That's just the way we'll handle it, too: I'll be able to say anything that comes into my head without having it pinned on me afterward—this will only be a voice test, after all. But believe me, I wouldn't be speaking at such length if I didn't have to. I'm not chatting at random; I'm making every effort to answer your original question and keeping that end in view at all times. Anything you may at first find puzzling will be explained in due course, because all the threads of my story came together on that fateful, historic night. *I* did it—yes, but who was I? Well, to put it in a nutshell and acquaint you with the central theme of my remarks: I was running away from my dick, and when the Wall happened to stand in my path—

What, changing the tape already?

THE LAST OF THE DOG-PADDLERS

really did come tumbling out into the world and onto a living room table in the village of Brunn, not far from the Czech border, "in the absence of trained personnel" (my father's pedantic circumlocution for "without a midwife"). My parents' home at that time was an old apartment on Pfarrstrasse, in the Lichtenberg district of Berlin. I was four years old when we moved from there to an eighteen-story high-rise beside the Magdalenenstrasse subway station, immediately opposite the Ministry of State Security. The neighborhood was known as Frankfurter Allee Süd, or FAS for short. Don't expect me to have formed any opinion worth mentioning about our new abode, not at that age. I only know that I found it exciting to ride the elevator. I didn't have to go to kindergarten, so I remained at home, blissfully playing with my crayons and producing pictures that never failed to send my mother into raptures. She beamed, she laughed, she *praised* me, and when my father came home after work she would exuberantly show him my "paintings." He showed no interest in them, however, and I always got the feeling that they weren't what he expected of me. I attributed his habitually surly manner to his job, which had something to do with "foreign trade." I had some very definite ideas on this subject. Anyone in "trade" had to be a trader, in other words, a kind of street trader, and that I had considered the cruelest of all occupations ever since witnessing a pathetic spectacle at the Christmas market: a shivering cotton-candy vendor with his frozen fingers wrapped around a mug of hot coffee. It seemed clear to me that traders were bound to be morose because of all their hardships and privations. While I was plying my crayons, my father was compelled to stand on a street corner with his teeth chattering, soaked to the skin. No wonder he never came home in a paternally jovial mood: "Well, well, and what has our little treasure been up to today?"

Being an enthusiastic listener to my fairy-tale records, I was forever aware of the fate of Hansel and Gretel, whose woodcutter father, like mine, performed an arduous job in order to support his family. When I overheard my mother talking on the phone—"No, I don't really want to send Klaus to kindergarten"—I was utterly dismayed and horrified because I thought a kindergarten was a garden to which parents sent the Hansels and Gretels of today.

I'm not sure if I ever had a *formative* childhood experience, but I certainly know which one left the deepest impression on me. It was when my father had a fight—or, to be more precise, when he fought *for my sake*. Imagine: my father, that paragon of law-abiding probity, actually *fought* for me, even though any child knows that fighting is wrong. What happened? He'd taken me to the opening of a new playground, and a little girl ran into the swing I was sitting on. It wasn't my fault—I simply swooped down and collided with her. A strange man, presumably her father, reached me in two strides and shook me in a fury until my father came and wrested me from his grasp. A scuffle ensued. They grabbed each other by the lapels and exchanged menacing glares. I sensed that a great deal of raw strength was involved, and that the situation was *serious*. They pushed and shoved each other across the sandbox, faces contorted with rage. Never having seen my father in such a state, I felt frightened for him. Eventually the other father tripped him up and laid him flat on his back. That done, he kicked sand over him with the point of his shoe. My father scrambled to his feet with a muttered "Come along!" We didn't exchange a word on the way home. If only it hadn't happened, I thought. He, who had a hard enough time as a street trader, had actually been hurled to the ground on my account! Showered with sand, too! What now? Would I be sent to the kindergarten after all?

I regret to say that I also maneuvered my mother into a situation where she had to cast decorum to the winds and stand up for me. I've heard the story retold so often, I can hardly distinguish between it and my own recollections of the incident. I was five years old and had gorged myself on strawberries, a circumstance I owed entirely to the fact that, in the course of a Sunday outing, my mother seized the opportunity to buy three baskets of strawberries from a roadside stall. These she put in the trunk of the Wartburg, where—what with the trip there and back, the summer heat, and the cobbled streets—they turned into a memorable mush (I still associate it with the word "biomass"). We didn't have enough sugar to make jam out of it—that's right, it wasn't a Sunday outing, it was a Saturday, when the stores closed at midday, and she couldn't have bought any sugar the next day either— so our only recourse was to eat the strawberries "quite spontaneously." (Splendidly spontaneous, weren't we? We made Sunday excursions on Saturdays, and, if no alternative presented itself, polished off as many strawberries as we could manage.)

That night, when I couldn't sleep for itching and my mother had vainly examined me and my bed for bugs, she diagnosed hives, an allergic reaction to the nettle family of plants, to which, she claimed, strawberries also belonged, and called the local emergency room to ask if the appropriate antidote was available. My father had drunk a glass of wine that night—I already mentioned how law-abiding he was, didn't I?—so it was legally impossible for him to drive us to the hospital. My mother took a taxi and did what she always did: she *admonished* me. "You mustn't scratch, Klaus, be brave, scratching will only make it worse, scratching doesn't help, it never has, you'll only break the skin and let in the bacteria, and it'll become all inflamed, so grit your teeth and think of something nice, besides, it'll soon be better . . ."

I continued to wail, beside myself with despair, until the cabby growled, "Go on, let the poor kid scratch." My mother told him she knew best. "I've had medical training," she said. The cabby pulled over and stopped. "And I've had it up to here," he retorted, whereupon my mother lost her temper. "Shut up and take my son to the emergency room at once!" she yelled at the top of her voice.

My key experience, maternally speaking: Mama yelled only when her son—me!—had to get to the emergency room. Yes indeed, I'd seen it for myself. When *her son* had to get to the emergency room she abandoned her good manners, her self-control, her composure—in short, *everything*! Where is it still to be heard, the cry of a desperate mother? In southern Italy? In films of unbridled passion? What was more, her selflessness (not to mention her spirit of self-sacrifice) was ever-dependable: even when I was nineteen and had both arms in plaster casts for six weeks, she wiped my bottom for me—no kidding! I was as helpless as a two-year-old, so how would I have coped *without* her?

Oh, Mr. Kitzelstein, why can I never speak of my mother without a mixture of gratitude and remorse? I was the one that blighted her career, there's no denying it: when *I* turned up she had to discontinue her medical training. She never mentioned this, of course, nor even hinted at it; she made such sacrifices in silence (except for an occasional slip of the tongue about "what might have been"). I must have been ten before I realized that *I* had deprived her of a medical degree. In default of that, she became Lichtenberg's sanitary inspector, and she *delighted* in her work. She had her own specialty, a white uniform, an office, a telephone, half a dozen women assistants, and innumerable calls to make. Actually, "sanitary inspector" is an inadequate description; my mother was a *goddess of hygiene.* She inspected railway station urinals, cafeteria kitchens and snack bars, cold-storage depots and municipal swimming pools, food stores and public baths. Better known than the mayor of Lichtenberg himself, she was blessed with an abundance of the personal qualities normally exclusive to the protagonists of thirteen-episode soap operas. Her reliability, her competence, her commitment, her incorruptibility! My mother's most spectacular initiative was to enforce a fourteen-month closure of the tropical section of the Berlin Zoo by insisting that visitors to the zoo be specially shielded from falling bird shit. I once saw her in action, by the way, and what can I tell you? She was perfection! Generations of sanitary inspectors will have to measure their achievements against hers!

Oh, God, Mr. Kitzelstein, we won't get anywhere like this. Isn't there any way of talking about my mother without immediately singing her praises? Can I never do justice to her without delivering a eulogy? You think I'm being sarcastic? That's a relief.

If my father was a skunk and my mother the opposite, I'm logically and emotionally bound to describe her as a *good* woman—GOOD, know what I mean? I sense that I must now look facts in the face and recount an anecdote that illustrates my worship of the lesser evil. What else could I have done but exalt my mother into the diametrical opposite of my father? Oh, it's all so hopeless . . . "It can't have been *all* bad," to cite a phrase employed by East German heroes like us when we don't know what else to say about our former Republic. But there must also be something unequivocally nice to be said for my mother. Even if I'm not giving her a chance, I'd like at least to *seem* as if I am. Let's see if I can associate her with three undeniably favorable characteristics or memories. *Three,* no less! The world is welcome to know that mine are the remarks of an ungrateful son who feels a warm glow when he drags his parents through the mire!

Well, as I already mentioned, I once saw my mother in her sanitary inspector's incarnation. I was in second grade when the classroom door opened in the middle of a lesson and two women appeared on the threshold. They were dressed in angelic white, and one of them was my mother! Stationing herself in front of the class like a kindly storyteller, she informed us that there were noxious little creatures called lice that bit and stung and concealed themselves in children's hair or laid their tiny eggs in it. However, we could consider ourselves fortunate that she had come here today to inspect our heads and find the said lice. It wouldn't hurt, so we mustn't be frightened. She was a kind of doctor, but not the kind that comes armed with a hypodermic syringe. Still in storyteller's vein—and what child doesn't love a storyteller?— she explained that no little boy or girl can help having lice.

Any one of us could be infested with them, so we mustn't poke fun at those who were, and anyone that did so would merely be showing what a very stupid child he or she was. We were to play together as usual and need not steer clear of the children in question, because they would be treated that very afternoon. The treatment, which was altogether painless, entailed washing their hair once "with our secret formula."

This speech left us all yearning—I nearly said "itching"—to be infested with lice. Like treasure chests and maps, secret formulas loom large in an eight-year-old's imagination. We simply *had* to have lice! Anyone who did would be a hero, an initiate, a veteran of the secret formula. We jumped up, crowded around my mother and her assistant, and expectantly proffered our heads. "Have I got some?" "How about me?" "And me?" My mother fended off the rush, sent us back to our places, and proceeded with her inspection—from which our teacher, incidentally, was not exempt. None of us qualified for an application of the secret formula, as bad luck would have it, but every child was favored while being examined to a nice, *personal* remark: "What a pretty barrette you've got!" or "How did you get that nasty bruise?" or, in a whisper, after a glance at a notebook, "Are you *sure* fifteen minus six makes eight?"

Everyone envied me my kindly, friendly, clever, important mother, the mistress of the secret formula and most painless doctor far and wide—indeed, I envied myself! It was an unsurpassable performance, and I have never felt, to this day, that infestation with lice is in any way discreditable.

Another of my mother's truly meritorious attributes was her *knack of entering rooms*. She was, without exaggeration, a queen among room enterers. The procedure began when she gently depressed the handle, simultaneously pulling it toward her to avoid making a click. Then she opened the door a crack and peered around it with the delighted curiosity of a child peeking at presents under a Christmas tree. Finally, having devoted two seconds to a panoramic survey of the room, she *smiled* and opened the door wide enough to admit her entire body. Wonderful! That was how she entered my bedroom every morning to wake me; how she entered the classroom for louse inspection; how she entered *every* room, period. She was so good at it, she could have made it her profession. She could have advertised in the local paper: *Room-entering carried out, charges by arrangement.* My father, on the other hand, opened every door as if liberating a bunch of hostages. A resounding crash, and there he was. I could never tell, when he came home from work, if he had merely opened the front door or kicked it in. But my mother . . . It goes against the grain to denigrate such an expert at entering rooms. I'm not worth the spittle I deserve to be showered with!

Third, she had the knack—sometimes, not often, just now and then, but still—of getting to the heart of things with a clarity and simplicity that seemed quite at odds with her nerve-racking, debilitating disposition. Her resigned verdict on the modern age, uttered during a TV talk show only a few weeks ago: "Nobody's got a clue these days." Then she switched the television off. She also summoned up enough irreverence to dismiss television audiences as the "square-eyed masses" or declare that selfishness was the hardest enemy of freedom to cope with. It took me years to fathom that observation and incorporate it in my private archive, my Thousand Wise Sayings.

Oh, Mr. Kitzelstein! Every remark she made was a maxim—a *maxim,* you understand? The only words worth uttering were statements of principle. Quite merciless in that respect, she hammered them in like tent pegs. The three words she would have taken with her to a desert island were BELIEVE YOU ME! I still have a vivid recollection of her anti-jeans campaign. *What's so chic about them? Sooner or later they give you varicose veins, and then you can forget about chic—believe you me! Pants, in particular, should be loose and airy. Whether they're cotton or not, sweating into them will give you eczema. And the smell! It beats me why people squeeze into such tight pants. How do they expect their digestion to function normally? And as for men! What they're doing to themselves! Recent research indicates . . .* Did I know why America had lost the Vietnam War? Because no country could ever win a war with *jeans cripples*!

My mother also disapproved of tattoos. Soccer players, too: *Grown men, and they have nothing better to do than run around after a ball. Honestly, I don't know . . .* But her deepest hostility was reserved for people who neglected to wash. "He was *un*washed . . ." She could infuse those words with such indignation and despair that she evoked a wave of sympathy, just because an *un*washed person had crossed her path. "It's really not expecting too much of people, not these days, to buy themselves a bar of soap and at least keep their *bare essentials* clean." Who could quarrel with that?

My mother's interventions on behalf of our household's hygienic concerns were also preceded by the words "It's really not expecting too much . . ." or "I'm really not asking the impossible, but . . ." At her insistence, for example, we were armed against the threat of squalor with a *second* vacuum cleaner in case our big industrial-strength machine had to be sent away for repair. The war of aggression she waged against microbes was quite unforgettable. Every "crack" in the kitchen and bathroom was "sealed" lest microbes should "nest" or germs become "deposited" in them. No meal at a restaurant was complete without the comment "I'd rather not know what the inside of *that* kitchen looks like!" I was early enough acquainted with terms like "bodily orifices," "infections," "antiseptic," and "tincture of iodine" to gauge the risks of being born on a living room table, especially on a summer's night in the country, where flies abounded— and "no one knows where they've been." The very thought makes me feel uneasy. Had I, who could never "bide my time," brought my mother to the verge of "no, I'd rather not think about it"? Did I already have her on my conscience, even at a stage when I barely existed? Whatever the truth, she didn't go back to work afterward. She abandoned her medical studies, exempted me from having to go to kindergarten, and wiped my little nose for me whenever it ran. Was I worth it?

What would I be without her? I have only to recall my school enrollment day. We children were shepherded into the assembly hall and told to sit down in the front few rows while our parents took their places at the back. I then became acquainted, for the very first time, with the problems posed by my name. The schoolteacher who was dividing us up into classes and reading out our names from a list—reading itself was an almost superhuman ability in my eyes—came to a sudden stop. "Klaus Uh . . . Uhl . . . Ultschl . . ." she said falteringly. Not realizing that my name was harder to decipher than all the rest, I failed to grasp that she meant me and remained seated. She showed the list to the principal, and together they pieced together some name that bore a vague resemblance to mine. I continued to sit there until I heard my mother discreetly calling me from the back row: "Klaus, they mean you." At that I stood up and came forward, fully aware that, but for my mother, I would never have risen to my feet and been enrolled, thereby disqualifying myself from attendance at school and sentencing myself to perpetual ignorance.

But why hadn't the teacher known my name, when she knew those of all the other children? They and I were different, I assumed. They were bound to be kindergarten children, every last one of them, and so undiscriminating that they came when called by any old name. If asked whether I regarded conditions outside my home as "squalid" and considered myself a cut above the rest, I would naturally have replied in the affirmative (and I still, in my heart of hearts, feel the same). What confirmed my suspicions was that the other children spoke a language entirely foreign to me. Hitherto shielded with care from the sweepings of the gutter, I had now entered an environment in which Berlin dialect was spoken. Impeccable standard German was *de rigueur* where I came from, but this? I shuffled from foot to foot, unable to understand a word. I was totally bemused when a boy came up to me and, after uttering a series of sounds which I now know meant "Wipe this muck off my shirt, or my mother will give me hell!," turned his back on me. A cryptic but friendly-sounding remark followed by an abrupt about-face? Being unfamiliar with this ritual, I didn't react. It wasn't until the boy rounded off his mysterious performance with the word "Asshole!" that my face lit up. At last! At last a word I recognized: *Asshole*!, an allusion to the "little oven door," as my mother termed it, but what did he mean? Why mention the little oven door in such a context?

I was always expected to recount such incidents at supper, the forum for *events of the day* and the meal we shared every evening, as befitted a proper family. My father was in the habit of wordlessly tossing a second slice of bread onto my plate, and my mother's "You want to grow up big and strong, don't you?" left me with no choice but to butter and eat it. At one stage I gave up helping myself to bread altogether because I knew in advance that another slice would be forced on me. There was a time when the very act of swallowing food filled me with mortal dread. Ever heard of asphyxia by *bolus,* Mr. Kitzelstein? Didn't *you* have a mother who sometimes read you excerpts from her medical dictionary? We have a network of nerves in the larynx that can bring on reflex cardiac arrest if the esophagus becomes clogged, and a strict interpretation of this fact—and my mother's interpretations were never less than strict—dictated that every morsel of food I ate was potentially lethal. Was my father trying to kill me by forcing me to eat more than I wanted?

No, please don't laugh! I was seven or eight years old, an age when children are entitled to feel afraid of ghosts or thunderstorms, and food-induced asphyxia seemed to me as common a cause of death as wood splinters or a failure to wash properly. What intensified my fear of death was that I nearly always ate dry-mouthed, so I swallowed my food in lumps that clogged my gullet and put me in dire peril. Why drymouthed? Because whenever I was taken to task, obliged to justify myself, or pinned down in some way, my salivary glands packed it in and compelled me to ingest my food in lumps. In *lumps,* when any blockage of the esophagus could spell instant death!

One evening, when I was summoned to supper in the middle of watching a courtroom drama on television, the transition between that American trial and the scene at our supper table was imperceptible. I, the accused, sat facing my parents, who played the roles of district attorney, presiding judge, and all twelve jurors. Sometimes my mother would put in a good word for me, sometimes she or my father would drop the charges against me—sometimes, even, the hearing would end in an acquittal—but I was always the accused on trial for his life. Because my father so seldom addressed me directly he had to cross-examine me through my mother and always referred to me as *he* (he never uttered my name, or did I mention that already?). "So," he would say, knife poised, looking around to indicate that the proceedings had opened, "and who forgot to lock the front door again today?" At some stage it became second nature to me to visualize my misdemeanors posted up on walls: *Wanted, dead or alive, for failing to lock the door of his parental home* . . .

She, plaintively: "Eberhard . . ."

He, stubbornly: "How many more times must we . . ."

She: "He didn't mean . . ."

He: "That's no . . ."

She: "It won't happen again . . ."

He: "I've heard that one before . . ."

Sentence wasn't passed off the cuff, Mr. Kitzelstein. Oh no, they deliberated first, quite openly and in my presence! And at such length! There was nothing arbitrary about their kind of justice. It was meted out with such care that I couldn't but take their accusations to heart, especially since leaving the front door unlocked was a serious offense. There were individuals known as burglars, after all: masked, unshaven men carrying flashlights and huge bunches of skeleton keys and sacks bulging with silver candlesticks. That was terrible enough, but what rendered such people really sinister in my eyes was that they burgled houses although burglary was *against the law.* What sort of men could they be if they didn't shrink from breaking the law? *I* still feel I've been caught *in flagrante* if I even see a notice board prohibiting something! I failed three driving tests because the sight of a distant NO

ENTRY sign sent me into a panic each time, and when my mother lectured me on the perils of sex, prefacing her remarks by citing the words found on warning notices, "Parents are responsible for their children," I was afflicted with near impotence for the next four years. If I cross the street against the light, I half expect a bullet in the back. No one could accuse me of disrespect for the law, but those burglars! They were not only lawless but—it was better to be prepared for the worst—possibly *tattooed* into the bargain! Anyone forgetful enough to leave the front door unlocked was virtually inviting such creatures into his home!

My one consolation was the big office building across the street, the Ministry of State Security. Where could a person feel secure if not opposite the Ministry of State Security? I was still a little boy frightened of the dark, but I didn't dwell in a gloomy forest, I was lucky enough to live within hailing distance of the ministry responsible for the security of the state. In an emergency I could call for help, and the State Security Service would hear me and come to my aid. It was years before my view of the Stasi changed; at first I genuinely revered it like some big, anonymous guardian angel. Being as scared of burglars as I was, I thought it unforgivable whenever I forgot to lock the front door. And because I myself thought it so, I was never punished unjustly. There was only one form of punishment in any case: I had to sit for an hour in the middle of the room and reflect on what I'd done wrong. The only exception was when I came home later than permitted and was punished by "spontaneous nonadmittance," which meant that I had to spend twenty minutes sitting in the hallway (and reflecting on what I'd done wrong). I was never beaten or bellowed at, and even when I *was* to be punished my parents had to arrive at a unanimous verdict, jury fashion, which wasn't so easy sometimes.

She: "Must we always to be so hard on . . ."

He: "Are you suggesting we overlook . . ."

She: "But if he promises never to . . ."

He: "And let him off without a . . ."

But for me, I thought, they would live in perfect harmony. Maybe I really was a pigheaded youngster who didn't know "how fortunate he is" and gave his parents "nothing but heartache," who didn't "listen when told" and could never "bide his time."

Was my father really such a cantankerous man? He had a reason for insisting that the front door should be locked. He only meant well. After all—I'd seen it with my own eyes—he had actually fought in my defense! Could he really be as bad as all that? Had I underestimated him? Perhaps he simply couldn't show his true feelings. What a personal tragedy: he, the breadwinner and protector, misjudged by his only son. No matter how unpleasant his manner toward me, deep down inside he was GOOD. I was overwhelmed by conflicting emotions: I loved him, but I couldn't stand him.

If only it hadn't mattered to me, but it did. If ever I looked up to a person, Mr. Kitzelstein, that person was my father. He wrought signs and miracles that never failed to fill me with awe. At some stage in the evening the front door of our apartment would open with a crash and my father would materialize as though emerging from the fourth dimension —unlike my mother, who always took so long to insert her key in the lock that I had time to come prancing out of my room to greet her. Or take the way my father used to sit watching TV with the legs of his sweatsuit rolled up, sloshing his feet in a bowl of water. It was good for smelly feet, I learned. Sheer magic: my father could transform ordinary tap water into a deodorant! He gained in importance from day to day. When I grew up, would I be able to open the front door as quickly? Would I, too, suffer from malodorous feet? And what about his beard? Although he shaved every day, it always grew back. Or take driving a car. Quite apart from a manifest ability to reach the pedals with his feet, he always seemed to know which one to depress. The car stopped whenever necessary and, as I saw it, *he* was responsible! The car obeyed his will! And the way he *coordinated* several procedures at once! He could, for instance, sleep and snore simultaneously! And as for *nose-blowing* . . . I had to unload my nose into a tissue which my mother thrust in my face with the words "Blow your little tooter," whereas *he* performed solo with a handkerchief the size of a pillowcase. My father's nose-blowing technique? I can keep silent no longer! Once he had draped the handkerchief over both hands and buried his nose in it, an acoustic phenomenon rent the air. I'm tempted to say that he *bellowed* into his handkerchief, but *can* you bellow through your nose? No matter. He also tugged at it as if wrenching it off, and, when the noise subsided, inspected the contents of his handkerchief like a Gypsy reading tea leaves . . .

But even years later, when I myself could conceive of someday having hairy legs like his, my father remained an enigma to me. Or can you explain what goes on inside someone whose whole attention is focused on the door of a bus when he runs to catch it? My mother would try to catch the driver's eye and call out "Thank you!" if he waited for her. Did my father, who never said a thank-you, believe that he had mastered destiny by willpower alone? It occurs to me that he never uttered the words "The driver waited for me," whereas my mother never said, "I only just caught the bus." Did he feel like a lone warrior forging a path through the wilderness?

I could talk about my father *ad infinitum*, simply to avoid having to come out with the most important fact of all, namely, that he had written me off as hopeless. Whatever I said, thought, felt, wanted, believed, wrote, gave, or asked for—whatever I *did*—I could hear his unspoken verdict: "Typical!" I never made a blunder, however small, without involuntarily thinking of my father, who had always known that I would perpetrate it. He could give me looks that would have withered flowers. He could, when checking into a hotel, engage the receptionist in an argument about incorrectly installed fire extinguishers that lasted longer than the sum total of his conversations with me in the entire decade of the 1970s. What did he want of me, for God's sake? Can't anyone tell me how I should have behaved and what I could have done to establish some kind of rapport between me and my demoralizing father? I would gladly leave no stone unturned, even on the ocean floor, if I thought I could find the answer. What did he expect of me? *Where did I go wrong?* These questions still hang like millstones around my neck. It never crossed my mind that he might, for some reason, have *envied* me.

When I attended swimming lessons with my class in second and third grade—a period when my mother taught me all I would ever know about athlete's foot—our swimming instructor divided us into non-swimmers, dog-paddlers, intermediates, and swimmers. I was wholly unamused by this system of classification because I myself was a dog-paddler— and remained so. The other dog-paddlers rose to become intermediates and swimmers. I alone made no progress, and one evening, when my father looked at my mother across the supper table and asked "How is his swimming going?," I was compelled to answer, truthfully, that I was "the last of the dog-paddlers." Even though there were still three non-swimmers, which meant that I wasn't the worst in the class, no admission could have been more shaming. I mean, try saying it yourself: "I'm the last of the dog-paddlers" or "I'm the only dog-paddler left."

Imagine how a dog-paddler would have fared when the *Titanic* went down: he thrashes around in the Atlantic for a hopeless half minute before ignominiously drowning. Not so the non-swimmers. Knowing what awaits them, they sit in the saloon in their dinner jackets, drinking the bar dry and puffing at their cigars until, having dispensed a last, fat tip, they sink serenely below the waves—with style! The intermediates manage to keep afloat until they're rescued. As for the swimmers, *they* can't drown because they're unsinkable; they go on swimming until they reach land. What I mean is, the world is divided into gallant failures, triers, and experts on the one hand and dog-paddlers on the other. Dog-paddlers are the ones who strive in vain, and I'm one of their number. No wonder my father thought me a flop. How would he have felt if his colleagues had asked him over lunch—I'd discovered by then that foreign traders and street traders were not the same thing, though my grasp of world price indexes was still shaky—how would he have felt if asked how his son's swimming was coming along? "He's the last of the dog-paddlers" would have been the honest answer, but how could he be expected to admit such a thing? If I put him in embarrassing situations of that kind, no wonder he never spoke to me. He would treat me quite differently, I was sure, if he felt I'd wised up at last—if it made him proud to be my father. It was only natural, therefore, that I set off at once for the Ministry of Foreign Trade to break the news of my prestigious appointment to run our stand at the Masters of Tomorrow Exhibition. I craved his respect. No longer the last of the dog-paddlers, I was a Master of Tomorrow. As such, I wanted him to parade *me* proudly before his colleagues, head erect and hand on my shoulder.

▪ ▪ ▪

So, Mr. Kitzelstein, this might be the moment to initiate you into the metaphysics of my soul, and I can't think of a better way of doing so than to remind you of my name: Klaus Uhltzscht. That says it all. I couldn't have a more appropriate name—the most infelicitous, ineffectual flop of a name imaginable. Take "Klaus," for a start. I still can't understand why it ever became popular. It sounds so priggish, so boring! What, I ask you, could be more banal? When I complained about it to my mother she spent five years rubbing my nose in every eminent Klaus she could think of. A pretty meager haul: Klaus Feldmann, Klaus Mann, Klaus Kinski. I mean, if Thomas Mann called his son Klaus, there *had* to be something wrong with the name. "But it's such a *nice* name," she kept insisting.

Fine for her to talk! She has a wonderful first name. Hers—and I say this without a hint of sarcasm—is the most wonderful name any woman could wish for: *Lucie*. Soft and mellifluous—not a common name, but not ostentatiously exotic either. Lucie . . . If I were her, I'd have a whole drawerful of T-shirts emblazoned with "Hurrah, my name's Lucie!" But Klaus . . . Your name is Oscar—like to swap? Oh well, forget it. As for my surname, it reminds me of my father. Why? Because *Uhltzscht* embodies two sounds associated with him in my mind: *Uh,* the groan he uttered whenever he heard about another goof of mine, and *ltzscht,* the contents of his footbath landing in the kitchen sink. An innocuous association compared to what follows, for *Uhltzscht* contains the seeds of disaster. You only need look at that poor, lonely vowel laboring under the weight of all those consonants. Already *in extremis,* the luckless "U" is loaded down with more and more of them.

My mother brought me up on the same principle: her demands on me were endless, and the product of them is sitting here, moist-eyed, before you. The disastrous thing, you see, was that I mistook solicitude for affection. So did she. My father had given up on me; my mother hadn't given up on me *yet*. He thought me a failure; she did not. But what if she were to change her mind? Anxious not to let that happen, I became precisely what my name suggests: *Klaus* epitomizes my fanatically good behavior (it's exasperating but true: my childhood was a superabundance of good behavior), and *Uhltzscht* my strenuous efforts to do anything, anything at all, rather than disappoint my mother.

"Notice anything, Klaus?" she said one day as she entered the bathroom, where I had just done my number two. What did she mean? What *should* I have noticed? Had I committed some sin of omission? She usually walked in with a beaming smile, but she wasn't smiling now, she was frowning. Why, what had I done? "Don't you notice anything?" she asked again, cocking her nose and sampling the air a couple of times. "It *smells* in here!"

I never gave my mother another chance to complain of my bowels, but at what cost! How could any boy attain true manhood if doomed to feel ashamed even of his very own, self-produced excrement? From then on, I flushed as soon as I heard the plunk, simultaneously rising to my feet because I couldn't bear being splashed. I also lifted the seat because I had no wish, in the event of a second visit, to sit on a seat besprinkled with droplets. What a sight: bent double with my pants around my ankles, I manipulated both flush and seat behind my back. I would gladly pay any blackmailer good money for the negative of such a photograph.

But there's more: for reasons I myself don't understand, I

carefully drape toilet paper over any john seat whose principal user is not an intimate acquaintance of mine. This is an invariable procedure. I never rely on the paper overlays provided by better-class public conveniences or airlines; they can *slip*. I tear up all the paper and flush it away with the rest of my business—provided the outlet cooperates. I've caused hundreds of blockages in my time, but I persevere as obsessively as any serial killer. Every time I undertake a trip back to Eastern Europe I travel equipped with several rolls of the wherewithal to block the drains there as well. Sooner or later I'll be arrested at the frontier: "Out of the car, please. Three days ago you entered the country with four rolls of toilet paper; now there's none. Where's the paper now?" Where indeed? In fifteen blocked toilets—yes, *fifteen,* for even my number ones are performed in a sedentary position, which is why I'm so extravagant. I never *stand* to pee—God forbid! I might *miss*! I remain my mother's son through and through, even in the most squalid Romanian railroad station. I would never use a *urinal,* either, I'm far too shy. No, I take refuge in a cubicle, resolutely plaster the seat with paper, sit down like a good boy, and—on one out of every three occasions— leave behind a clogged toilet bowl. My mother never had to repeat her veiled admonition, much to my relief, and if compelled to do so she would have prefaced it with *Klaus, I'm really not asking the impossible, but . . .*

To think that I always felt so emotionally torn! To think I always believed that, not being a genius, I was a failure! Can you understand how wonderful it felt to be featured as a Master of Tomorrow on the cover of East Germany's most widely read magazine? To get myself talked about as a *Cover Picture* destined for greatness as a Nobel laureate?

This did not, however, mean that I was exempt from renewed affronts to my dignity. One night, while lying in my double-decker bunk at summer camp, I listened with bated breath to a conversation between my twelve-year-old peers, who were pursuing to its logical conclusion the idea that every birth must be preceded, some nine months before, by the procreative act. They devised the most charming scenarios: *I was conceived on a romantic summer's night*—*I'm the product of spring fever*—*My parents made me in a snow-covered chalet*—and so on. The other boys could luxuriate in such flights of fancy, whereas I found it hard to accept that my parents had copulated at all, let alone with each other.

I would not have become the person I am, Mr. Kitzelstein, had I not gone regularly to summer camp. I was thrown into a renewed turmoil every year. The human condition proved to be even more shocking than I suspected. Every time.

It was impressed upon me before my first trip, at age seven, never to open my suitcase unless absolutely necessary, and then only in such a way that "no one" would be able to see into it. (So much emphasis was placed on this "no one" that I at first thought its contents were off-limits even to my own eyes.) The night before I left, my father took it upon himself to school me in how to hold the lid of the case open with one hand while rummaging in it with the other, the important thing being not to make the crack too small because that would only whet the other children's curiosity. I was also to keep the case locked at all times. This was the first occasion on which my father had devoted any time to me; summer camp was clearly a serious matter. It didn't surprise me in the least to be conditioned like someone doomed to spend three weeks among thieves and ruffians. After all, the world seethed with dangers of which burglars, tattooed men, and candy-poisoners were doubtless only the tip of the iceberg. On the one hand, I considered myself too old to cuddle my Teddy bear; on the other, I shuddered at the prospect of exposure to a world in which burglars were rife. I must never accept a piece of candy from a stranger because it would be poisoned. I was terrified of dying in a road accident, not to mention from bolus-induced asphyxia and wood splinters.

If only 50 percent of my belongings were pinched, I could always lose the other half myself. I was a notorious and legendary loser of things, and my losses were a regular topic of conversation at supper. I even lost things that had hitherto been considered unlosable. I lost my sandals although I was wearing them, I lost the contents of my schoolbag although it was on my back—I even lost a tooth without noticing it. If a boy like me went away for three weeks, what, my parents speculated, would my return portend? Would they then learn the true meaning of the phrase "He possessed less than nothing"? But, as I've already said, I was trained as if about to brave an underworld in which I would have to defend my goods and chattels. And, sure enough, my initial reaction when assigned to a group of strange boys the next day was wary in the extreme. How many of them merited my mistrust? Every last one?

Then came my life's most terrible experience to date: being parted from my mother.

She accompanied me to the buses that were to ferry us to the camp. The thought of farewell tears had never entered my head, but when she introduced me to my group leader and expressly instructed her that I must never eat tomatoes or strawberries because they brought me out in hives, when she handed me the spare key to my suitcase, when she bent down to give me a farewell hug and rested her cheek against mine, I was overcome by blind panic. *What were we doing?* How could I exist without her, my source of guidance and praise, protection and consolation? What did I amount to without her? Who else would stick at nothing to ensure that I was taken to the hospital in an emergency? This mother who knew all about me, who was always there for me, who had done, was doing, and would do anything and everything for me—was I to exchange her for a stranger? For a woman I'd never seen before, a woman who'd had to check my name off on a list? Oh no, a few farewell tears weren't enough. I wept like a gusher, dementedly hoping throughout the bus ride that the driver would relent and take me back where I belonged—back to my mama, my own, dear, darling mama! My paroxysms of grief persisted even when we reached the summer camp, and I didn't stop sobbing until the last bus had driven off.

Where was I? Alone in a hut with seven other kids, all of whom were probably thieves. Or, if not thieves, undoubtedly neglected, or they would have clung more tightly to their mothers and bidden them a more dramatic farewell. I was *different,* I could sense it.

When it came to sleeping arrangements—we slept in double-decker bunks—everyone naturally tried to get an upper berth. Although I managed to secure one, someone had claimed it by the time I returned to the hut after an absence of two minutes. I told him the bunk was mine; he said it was his. He was a friendly type, the kind that always picks sides for team games. Before we could come to blows he made a suggestion: The upper bunk would belong to whichever of us could pee the farthest. He said it in a quite unspectacular way. Was this how all disputes at summer camp were settled, I wondered. The one who peed farthest could sit beside the driver, the one who peed the farthest could help himself to the biggest slice of melon . . . If that's the system, I thought, I'd better go along with it.

The word quickly spread: "Hey, everyone, they're going to have a peeing contest!" I'd obviously embroiled myself in the kind of duel that didn't happen every day. Besides, it seemed that I was the only one who didn't know the game. Was it really as obscene as it sounded? Would I really have to handle *it* in the presence of others? I'd already done so once in the day-care center of the Centrum Department Store, where my mother had deposited me for an hour while buying Christmas presents. There, for some unknown reason, I was befriended by a girl a year or so older than myself, who crawled behind a big wooden crate and offered to show me "hers" if I would show her "mine." In all innocence, I consented. That record still stands: no girl has ever asked to see my dick after an acquaintance of less than two minutes. When my mother collected me and I told her all about it on the way home, she promptly turned back, grim-faced, and gave the day-care supervisor a piece of her mind— she even waited for my girlfriend's mother to turn up and castigated her, too. She also took me to task at supper that night: Hadn't it occurred to me that we were doing something "nasty" if we had to go and hide for the purpose, and didn't I realize that I mustn't take part in "that sort of thing"?

And now? Was a peeing contest *that sort of thing*? I couldn't back out, I knew, but what attitude should I take from the moral and sanitary standpoint? What had I let myself in for? Wouldn't anyone help me? Where was I?

"Come on," my opponent said amiably, and went behind the hut with me. The other kids followed. One of them drew a line on the ground with his foot. My opponent dropped his pants. So did I. We took up our positions side by side.

"Ready?" he asked.

I: "Mm."

He: "With hands or without?"

I: "I don't mind."

He: "Okay, with."

He took hold of himself. I followed suit.

He: "With or without foreskins?"

I: "I don't mind."

He: "Okay, without."

The sun was shining. We blinked in the glare.

He spread his legs a little wider. "Ready?" he asked.

"I guess so." I said.

He arched his body, thrust out his hips, and pissed into the middle distance. Not a chance, I thought, not against a fire-hose jet like that . . . It took me a while to get going, and even then I had to take care not to widdle on my toes.

"You lost," he said in a conciliatory tone, when we'd finished.

Funny kind of game, I thought.

One of my life's peculiarities, Mr. Kitzelstein, is that I can—today, at least—read some meaning into everything that has ever happened to me. I'm almost embarrassed, my life is so devoid of mysteries and unsolved questions. Try to visualize the impression made on me by that peeing contest. It was an hour or two before I grasped its full implications, but when I did I was abruptly overcome with horror. What a sink of iniquity I was immersed in! My father had taken so much trouble to forewarn me against the criminal types I would encounter at summer camp, but all to no avail: I was a victim of their thievery! I'd been robbed of my upper bunk and invited to regain it by participating in a game I didn't know—

unlike those delinquents who didn't turn a hair when parted from their mothers. What sort of person was I to think of playing a game with such children? It was a bad game, true, and it had some connection with my dick. If you were my shrink, Mr. Kitzelstein, we could pat each other proudly on the back: I had used my thing for a purpose other than number one, and lo, it was *wrong*, it was *bad*! I'd become an accomplice of the underworld and participated in its rites! What would my mama think of me? Back home, I kept the story of the peeing contest to myself. After all, I knew what to expect: *And if he'd told you to jump out of the window?* She'd have been right as usual. *What on earth were you thinking of?* Nothing. *Nothing isn't good enough. You must have had some thoughts on the subject. I simply want to know what went on in your head, Klaus.*

My mother, a paragon of predictability. Even her seven-year-old son knew precisely what she would say. While on the subject of my mother and my dick, I've suddenly remembered what she used to call it—no, wait, *guess!* My mother, the linguistic purist *par excellence* who was so insistent on my speaking without a regional accent that I incurred universal suspicions of arrogance, called it my *Puller*—which, being translated, means "piddler." She hacked her way through the linguistic bush like a jungle fighter, nor did she shrink from crawling through the undergrowth of etymology. "Klaus, do you know what 'sympathizing' with people really means? It comes from the Greek, and it means 'feeling with' them." What did that have to do with my *piddler*? A joiner was called a joiner because he joined pieces of wood together, a tailor was called a tailor because he tailored clothes, and your piddler was called a piddler because it piddled.

You didn't make a fuss about your piddler, you used it in the toilet, and only a dirty beast did anything else with it because, as everyone knew, a piddler presented problems of personal hygiene to be resolved by washing your hands after every piddle. It had its own special bar of soap, the Red Soap. (The other bar was known either as the Blue Soap or "the soap for washing your hands with." Once, when I picked up a bar of soap in a department store and saw that the wrapper read "toilet soap," I took this to be a synonym for Red Soap and inferred that the distinction between Red Soap and Blue Soap was universal.)

All seemed clear and logical until, the year after the peeing contest, I returned to summer camp and found myself billeted with nine experts who all referred to their piddlers as "dongs" and discussed the size of their fathers' dongs the very first night! I had firmly resolved never to take part in another peeing contest, but I hadn't anticipated *this*. Imagine *talking* about such things! Who *were* these boys? Where did they come from? My father never exposed his nakedness, and even if he had I wouldn't have peeked! (Of course I would.) What other things did they do at home? I dreaded to think.

So there we lay in our double-decker bunks. I, who had opted for a lower berth to banish all possibility of another peeing contest, was wholly ignorant of my father's penis size. When asked "How about your father?" I evaded the question by mentioning a TV documentary that had featured "naked Africans with things this long."

"How long?!"

"This long," I said, demonstrating.

"That's no bigger than my father's," someone said disappointedly. "Or my father's." "Or mine."

What! Were these boys trying to tell me their fathers were hung like Africans?

I recalled another feature that had struck me. "They were thick, too," I added. "This thick." I spread my thumb and forefinger.

"Just like my father's." "And my father's." "And mine."

I thought hard.

If all those fathers . . . Did *my* father resemble an African down there, too? When I grew up, would I also look like an African? Wouldn't my cute little tassel simply grow in proportion to the rest of me and become a slightly bigger tassel? Would I really resemble those savages dancing around the fire and brandishing their spears? In some dismay, I consulted the occupant of an upper bunk: Would mine become like that, too? "You bet," he said.

Why were they such experts? How did they know? A few weeks later, for the very first time, I used the showers of the swimming pool and found myself surrounded by naked *white men*. The steamy atmosphere was laundry-like. While pretending to look for a free shower head, I surreptitiously allowed my marveling eyes to roam. There they stood with suds oozing down them, puffing and spluttering and thrusting out their chests. I stationed myself next to a man who was pleasurably soaping his impressive equipment with each hand in turn, two strokes with the left, two with the right. It was true: quite ordinary-looking men—men such as I saw in the street every day—had "dongs" like the men of Africa! Of *Africa*! What child doesn't regard Africa as the continent of superlatives? The sun is hotter, the animals more ferocious, the butterflies more colorful, the snakes more poisonous. I had mistakenly believed that African *piddlers* were bigger. And now? African dimensions prevailed in the swimming pool in Berlin. Wonders would never cease.

I broached the subject at supper, that being an occasion on which my father could contribute some personal knowledge. "Will *I* have a big piddler, too, when I grow up?"

My father put his glass down with a crash and regarded my mother with a mixture of triumph and derision: *And that, Your Honor, concludes the case for the prosecution.* I already told you, didn't I, Mr. Kitzelstein, how puny, dumb, clueless, maldeveloped, retarded, undeserving, dim-witted, maladroit, and feeble I used to feel at supper?

"Why do you ask?" Yes, why *had* I asked?

"The boys at summer camp knew all about it, and I saw it myself at the swimming pool."

"Ah, at summer camp." My mother smiled her most condescending, understanding smile. "So the subject interests them, does it?"

"They know about these things and I don't! I want to know about them, too!"

"But, Klaus, we've taken you to the museum *so many* times."

That, believe it or not, was a reference to the statues I'd seen there—those absurdly underdeveloped statues that made the gods look as if they'd just waded out of the Arctic Ocean.

"But theirs are much smaller than real ones," I pouted.

"Really?" she said mockingly. "You pay attention to such things, do you?" What a mother! Her not-so-little son asks her if all men have big piddlers, and instead of disclosing that piddlers are only half the story because, well, bees and ants, for example, the male ant and the female ant, etc., she stalls. My inquiry would have made an ideal introduction to the most awkward aspect of sexual enlightenment—less complicated, at all events, than the How-do-babies-get-into-your-tummy? question. It would have been so simple, but what does my mother do? She counters by lecturing me. She counters with sarcasm. She *counters*, period. But she wouldn't have been my mother if she hadn't added something profoundly puzzling.

"The statues in the museum have such small ones because the sculptors wanted to make the human body look as beautiful as possible. It's what we call the *ideal of beauty*."

What a somersault! I ask for an anatomy lesson and she lectures me on art history. No mention of the fact that ladies advertising in Lonely Hearts columns sometimes use the code word "cucumber" to define their requirements, no allusion to Woody Allen's fundamental discovery of *penis envy in the male*—no, even the ancient Greeks knew that *small is beautiful,* and people still flock to museums in their thousands to pay homage to that aesthetic ideal.

She fetched the encyclopedia and looked up "Greece."

"Here," she said, pointing to a fold-out page of gods and heroes in marble. Sure enough, sprouting from each muscular, athletic frame was a piddler the size of a garden snail.

It was all so plausible: those big things that reminded me of a boxer's snout, and which I still, in my innocence, thought of as *piddlers,* were not only hideous but positively disfiguring, quite unlike the dainty little adornments of the Greeks.

My mother has always acted so damnably innocent. She still says "piddler" to this day; she doesn't think twice about calling her cat "Pussy"; and on one occasion she even put down VULVA when we were playing Scrabble. Oh, Mr. Kitzelstein, the things I could tell you about my mother and the subject of sex! *Sex,* did I say? For her it didn't exist, that word with the splendidly sibilant, voiceless "s," incisive as a whiplash; it never, ever passed her lips. It didn't need explaining to me, that word; I *sensed* what it meant the very first time I heard it correctly pronounced. But my mother, normally such stickler for careful articulation, pronounced "sex" with a voiced "s," in other words, like "zex." This made it sound like *sechs,* the German for "six," and gave birth to such hybrids as homo6ual, 6 kitten, and 6 film. Her weirdest creation, if you really want to know, was "6y"— enough to kill the most hardened sex offender's hard-on.

Then there were the contexts in which she used the word, for instance during the Calgary Olympics of 1988, when we sat up until 4 a.m. to watch Katarina Witt's great free-skating program. Katarina floated over the ice like a princess, smilingly self-absorbed, and everything, but everything, in her program came off perfectly: the ice humbly melted beneath her blades—even the overhead spotlights beamed with rapture and were proud to make her rhinestones sparkle. It was then that my mother thought the moment had come to delve deep into the masculine psyche. "Well," she asked me companionably, "do you find her 6y?"

What on earth was I to say? Was this what Mama had always wanted to know about 6 but had never previously dared to ask: whether I felt like screwing Katarina Witt? Don't get me wrong: I wouldn't have spurned Katarina, but my imaginary harem was incalculably vast, so why single her out as if sex were personified exclusively by well-built, photogenic young figure-skating stars—as if I needed a double Lutz and a miniskirt to put me in mind of sexsexsex? At nineteen I considered myself one of the most perverted individuals on the face of the globe. I thought incessantly of sex; I couldn't suppress the thought; I never thought of Katarina Witt or the checkout girl at the local supermarket—her of the fabulous, bejeaned buttocks—in concrete terms, but only of the sexual phenomenon. My mother would have accused me of being 6ually obsessed had she known my true state of mind. All it took to trigger a whole spate of lecherous thoughts was a sweater with two superbly firm boobs straining against it—indeed, I pictured circumstances in which I could wobble them to and fro to my heart's (not to say, my dick's) content. I could never decide which interested me most, the boobs or the woman they adorned, nor did I know which *ought* to interest me most. And as for *pussies* . . . Once my dick had been inside one, it never wanted to be anywhere else! It had found its true destiny, to wit, finding its way into pussies and rollicking around in them to the gratification of all concerned. But it *shouldn't* have done so—or should it? As the sexual theologian says: What is good for your dick can't be good for *you*.

TAPE 3

ON THE VERGE OF RENAL FAILURE

When Klaus the Cover Picture—that's me—took his Frisbee to the playground, where seven young loiterers clamored to become his Frisbee partner, he gave them a hard nut to crack: only the one who knew most about *compasses, atlases,* and *encyclopedias* could play with him. Compasses were the only subject they could manage, thanks to the Sailing Club and its educational repercussions, but atlases and encyclopedias? I refused to relent and played with none of them: I sent the Frisbee spinning through the air, ran to the spot where it landed, and threw it again. Half an hour of this, and I was worn out. I needed someone to play with after all, but by then the others were playing hide-and-seek. They invited me to join in—the Cover Picture was regarded as a VIP in the playground, as elsewhere—but how could I hope to hide successfully when encumbered with a Frisbee as conspicuous as a marker buoy? Put it down somewhere? What, and have it stolen? Never! I went straight home, where I was—believe it or not—*congratulated* by my discerning parents. Yessir, they actually *praised* their conceited, suspicious, smug, stuck-up, selfish little twerp of a son! My mother was beside herself with delight when I explained my system for choosing a Frisbee partner. Wasn't that sweet of her? And my father! I'd earned his approval at last, just for behaving as if I were surrounded by thieves. Was that all it took? Was it that simple? A Bogart-type father would have taken me aside and snarled, "Listen, kid, everyone needs a *buddy*— someone to throw his Frisbee back at him." And a down-to-earth mother would have laughed me to scorn: "What, back from the playground already? Hey, don't hoard your toys, play with them."

It wasn't a sniveling child that went off to summer camp, not this time; it was a Cover Picture. On the bus trip there I circulated the magazine in a transparent report cover, and loudly proclaimed: "That's me!" And again: "That's me!" And, for the benefit of the last in line: "That's me!" And, to the bus at large: "That's me!" I was instantly offered an upper bunk from which, the same night, I lectured my vulgar, undistinguished hut mates on globe lightning and the Bermuda Triangle. They would be able to tell their grandchildren how, in 1979, they were at summer camp with Klaus Uhltzscht—yes, *that* Klaus Uhltzscht—and how, even at the age of ten, he . . . What joy! Until one of them asked if we'd even seen our parents *screwing*. Suddenly, *I* was the dunce. What was screwing? What were they talking about? Something beastly, beyond a doubt—something these degenerate children knew more about than I, the only scion of a respectable family, the Cover Picture, the paragon, someone they would name a street after . . .

I was duly enlightened: "Screwing means making children," one of the boys explained. Unemotionally, he elaborated: "The father has to stick his pecker in the mother's pussy." What! *Father's pecker in mother's pussy?* Impossible! *My* parents would never do such a repulsive thing! Never!

Not ever! Not in a million years! What sick mind could have devised such an enormity? What sort of parents did they have, these children? Did they really interlock the body parts my father never exposed and my mother deemed worthy of their own, separate bar of soap? How did they think of such things? Why did they spend their time dreaming them up? Didn't they own a TV set?

But what if it were true? What if these children were right yet again? Had my father pissed me into the world? If so, I must have gone whooshing down his pecker into . . . I sniffed my arm. Were traces of pee still clinging to my pores? I went and took a shower right away, even though we were forbidden to leave our huts after lights-out. (In a dire emergency, even I could break a rule.) Imagine: pissed into existence!

One of the boys was still awake when I returned. He explained to me, man to man, that a child starts life in the father, who plants it in the mother's body, where it grows until it comes into the world. He talked of *seed*. From then on, being familiar with the cozy notion that flower seeds were sown in "Mother Earth," I went around convinced that a child originates in the father alone. It was years before I could masturbate for fear of my unborn children's dying screams . . .

I lay awake for a long time, pursuing this train of thought to its logical conclusion: my parents had fucked, and so had my teachers. The whole of humanity was the product of innumerable fucks, and I, Klaus the Cover Picture, the budding scientist who daily drew a little closer to the Nobel Prize for which he was destined, had known nothing about it! If that wasn't a valid reason for doubting the screwing theory, what was? Had prehistoric man voluntarily inserted his primordial pecker in the primordial pussy? Did prehistoric man know more than Klaus the Cover Picture? Hardly! So why hadn't the human race become extinct? Aha! I had shattered the screwing theory! The science of which I was a representative would soon put paid to the superstitious belief that peckers had to be inserted in pussies in order to beget children. A great sigh of relief would go up all around the world: Fucking is out from now on!

I triumphantly asked my mother—though not in so many words—how our ancestors screwed. As rewarding a question as the one I'd asked about penile dimensions, and the answer, Mr. Kitzelstein, was just as exasperating. How had our ancestors contrived the primordial fuck? They often touched each other in the relevant places, my mother told me, especially when cuddling up together in their chilly caves. For the rest, she advised me to consult the encyclopedia. I did so. Fifteen volumes, and not a single reference to screwing or fucking! This I construed as evidence that the pecker-in-pussy theory was an old wives' tale. I mean to say, if it wasn't in the encyclopedia! I struck oil under PREGNANCY and from there found my way via → FERTILIZATION and → SPERMATOZOON to → OVULATION. There were repeated references to → OVULATION but none at all to → SCREWING.

I never had any problem with the theory that human beings are descended from apes, but I steadfastly refused to accept that I was descended from screwing parents. For quite a time—at least three years, certainly—it was one of my secret ambitions to be an adoptive child. I wanted my parents to disclose, at long last, that they had procured me from an orphanage rather than have to fuck each other.

I can't remember how the situation resolved itself, but I probably acknowledged, under the impact of countless sighs and reproaches, e.g., *I only have your best interests at heart* or *We only want what's best for you,* that even my parents had fucked. However, they must have fucked purely because they wanted me. Their desire for a child had overcome their reluctance to engage in the most disgusting activity I'd ever heard of. My father had been understandably reluctant to insert his pecker—if he really possessed one—in my mother's pussy, and my mother can't have been too pleased either, but it was unavoidable. Not only did my mother tongue-lash cabbies and my father fight on my behalf, they had actually *fucked* for me! Although I couldn't do anything about it at this stage, was I to behave as if it didn't concern me? No! Being ashamed—yes, *ashamed*—that my parents had had to fuck for my sake, I felt an urge to repay them and show my gratitude. How could I show myself worthy of such supreme unselfishness, not to say self-sacrifice? If they had taken it upon themselves to fuck each other for my sake, I must become what they wanted me to be. Was that asking too much?

I tried to envision how they'd gone about it. How had they managed to get the distasteful business over and done with? Who had borne the brunt of the performance, my uptight father or my hygienic mother? How long had it taken? A fraction of a second? Several seconds, even? Had they done it in the bathroom? After sluicing each other down under the shower? I pictured my father maneuvering his secret thing into my mother's pussy, not with his bare hands, but with the aid of rubber gloves or barbecue tongs . . . I could see them bravely persevering for twenty seconds—just once and never again! Afterward they must surely have treated themselves to a few weeks' vacation. It never crossed my mind, not for a single moment, that they might have performed the act in bed. The bed was a bastion of hygiene. I never put my pants on a made-up bed, still less sit down on one before I've removed them, because they've been in contact with surfaces on which other people's posteriors have reposed. I preserve my bed's purity at all costs!

You can imagine the monastic atmosphere that prevailed in my home if I tell you that it was Dagmar Frederic who gave me my first—how shall I put it?—my first hard-on. For the benefit of your American readers, Mr. Kitzelstein, I should explain that Dagmar Frederic was a television host, and about as sexy as Nancy Reagan (sexier than that, East German TV never got!). She and O. F. Weitling hosted a talent contest whose title might be rendered into English as *A Mixed Bag*. Well, O.F. rested his paw on Dagmar's hip, very much the professional entertainer, and said, "All right, Dagmar, you can introduce our next contestant." "It'll be a pleasure," she purred.

It was then, as she laughingly echoed O.F.'s tone and glanced at him coquettishly out of the corner of her eye, that my pajamas stirred into life. What had happened? Sure enough, Dagmar Frederic's sidelong glance and dulcet tones were giving me my very first genuine hard-on! What a sensation! It felt curiously hot and titillating, and all at once I grasped what went on between men and women: men were forever trying to do things to which women responded with glances that triggered *that sort of thing*. So *that* was what all those boring lovey-dovey movies were about, I knew it now! But first, in order to examine my tent pole at leisure, I was anxious to disappear into the bathroom without my parents' spotting the tent. Although seated between them on the sofa, I managed to maneuver my erection into the bathroom, locked the door, lowered my pajama bottoms, and marveled. Good heavens! It could elevate itself like a crane, it could grow big and hard. It could even be twanged! I was just about to experiment by suspending sundry objects from it—one of my bedroom slippers, for instance—when my mother tried the door handle.

"Klaus, why have you locked the door?"

Why had I locked the door? Why had I retired to the bathroom to admire my first homemade hard-on? Why hadn't I gone to my room and inspected it under the bedside light? Because I was permitted to touch my thing only for urinary or sanitary purposes. Because the toilet was the only proper place for hygienically delicate procedures. Because my thing had absolutely no raison d'être elsewhere.

I turned on the tap, bravely calling out, "Won't be a minute," but I hadn't the least idea how to make an erection subside.

"Come on, open this door!" my mother called. She sounded stern. "You never lock yourself in as a rule."

I unlocked the door and tried to slip past her, but she barred my path and thrust me back into the bathroom. Then she caught sight of what she wasn't meant to see.

"Have you been playing with it?"

"No!" I protested. "It happened by itself."

"Don't give me that," she retorted sarcastically.

I was burdened with a terrible suspicion: she thought I'd been playing with my pecker! You remember her remark *It smells!* and the effect that had on me? If so, you'll understand why I spent the next few years ceaselessly endeavoring to eliminate my hard-ons—and, coincidentally, compiling sufficient material for a scientific treatise entitled *Erections in Puberty: Methods of Prevention*. Short of preventing erections, I wanted at least to render them inconspicuous, and this, especially in the first year, was doubly difficult because their angle of incidence was never less than ninety degrees and made a bulge in my pants. Gone was my soft little "rabbit's paw" (another of my mother's penile euphemisms); I now had to tote a spear wherever I went. I kept a Rubik's Cube in my pocket to render detection more difficult. I remained seated during intermission at the movies. I joined a chess club, not only because chess, mathematics, and Nobel Prizes go together, but mainly because there was no need to stand up while a game was in progress. I drank as little fluid as possible because I had somehow discovered (or convinced myself) that it would be beneficial to my new aim in life. Any Catholic with my fluid balance would have been sanctified. Mine was a unique case of self-mummification *in vivo*. Not even a renowned ascetic like Mahatma Gandhi had gone to such lengths. I drank so little that my blood count dipped alarmingly; for years I was on the verge of renal failure. In the 2,000 meters I wearily dragged my desiccated body around the track in last place, every inch the last dog-paddler. My popularity took a dive, the more so because our phys. ed. teacher refused to get out the soccer ball "until the last of you comes in." By contrast, my mathematics steadily improved. Mental arithmetic proved wonderfully distracting and effective when it came to combating erections. To begin with, I squared the number 2—did Nobel laureate Albert Einstein ever work out $2^{2.5}$ at the age of eleven?—but later I trawled the reaches above 10,000 for prime numbers.

But school in general . . . The ever-present danger of being summoned to the blackboard, or called upon to rise and answer some question, or told to swap places during a written test to obviate the possibility of cheating, or made to attend the music lessons during which we always stood to sing . . . Then there was *recess*. A hard-on during recess was disastrous. What to do when the bell rang, signaling my departure for the playground with a dick as rigid as a deep-frozen gherkin? And as for phys. ed. classes! The horror of having to do a chin-up and hang from the horizontal bar with my own bar equally horizontal . . .

Above the blackboard in the literature classroom hung an aphorism of the kind favored by men of letters, in this case

Maxim Gorky: *A human being—how proud that sounds!* But I, instead of being a proud human being, was afflicted with erections. I would have felt better standing in front of a monument devoted to a proud human being whose pants displayed the same bulge as mine always did. Maxim Gorky with a maxi-gherkin. The literature classroom did, however, furnish me with another remedy for my problem: imaginary accidents. It was there, when we came to the Cyclops episode in the *Odyssey,* that I had heard about a giant who smashed two seamen against a rock and devoured them. Turning pale, I asked the teacher's permission to leave the classroom for a moment. Only then did it occur to me that I would inevitably expose myself to ridicule, but there was no going back. I rose gingerly, careful not to snag myself on the edge of the desk, but where was my hard-on? Rampant a moment ago, it was now quiescent, and all that had intervened between one condition and the other was a blood-curdling story. Yes, Klaus the Cover Picture had often heard tell of this phenomenon: every persevering scientist's greatest discoveries owe something to chance.

At first I recalled the Cyclops myth in case of need, but when that lost its efficacy, as it gradually did, I devised some horror stories of my own. These I always preceded by banner headlines in the style of Western tabloids: ACCIDENT AT STEEL WORKS: OPERATIVE FALLS INTO BLAST FURNACE!—SAWMILL TRAGEDY: SLEEPING WORKER SAWN INTO PLANKS!—SWITCH-YARD DISASTER: RAILROAD MAN PULPED BY BUMPERS, TRI-SECTED BY CAR WHEELS! Any flight of fancy was permissible as long as it demolished my erections. My most outrageous accident fantasy featured two mangled equine cadavers with outstretched necks and some old women in pink petticoats lying dead on either side of a railroad embankment: PEN-SIONERS' WAGONETTE HIT BY RUNAWAY LOCO!

I spent my entire adolescence trying to banish hard-ons, but with only limited success. When emerging from school after our graduation ceremony, eager for some fresh air, I passed Ilona Pohle in the lobby. Ilona was in my year but in another class, and all I knew about her was her reputation for being the sassiest girl in the school. We'd never exchanged a word before, but when we met in the hallway on the point of going our separate ways, she laughingly bade me goodbye. "All the best for the future, Klaus," she said, toasting me with her bottle of bubbly. "And may you soon get over those troublesome reflexes of yours." Ilona Pohl wasn't my immediate neighbor in class, Mr. Kitzelstein, she wasn't in my class at all, yet even she was acquainted with my most intimate problem! How come, when I'd done my uttermost to keep it a secret? For six long years I'd striven, and my efforts had been as unavailing as any efforts could be. It was the most unavailing thing I've ever done.

There are, as everyone knows, two guaranteed remedies for an erection: jerking off, on the one hand, and cold showers, on the other. Although the brutality of the cold-water method doesn't deter me, its effect is only temporary. As for jerking off, it occurs to me that, as an eleven-year-old in summer camp, I had an older friend named Martin with whom I regularly played chess, to whom I used to lend my *Young Scientist* magazine, and by whom I was one day invited—should it interest me—to watch him produce some sperm. "Oooh yes, let's see!" I said, and waited for him to wring himself out in some way, thereby extruding creatures that bore a resemblance to earthworms or maggots, tadpoles or water fleas. But no, Martin hired a rowboat and took us out into the middle of the lake, where he handed over the oars and instructed me to keep us away from the other boats. Then he settled himself in the bow, i.e., behind me, and got down to work. Once I turned to see him whacking off like a madman. I wished I hadn't! I mean, his hobby was tinkering with *radios*—he'd given me an expert demonstration of how to listen in to the police wave band, and the tone of voice in which he'd offered to show me some sperm was the same as the one in which he'd asked if I'd like to eavesdrop on some police messages. And now this! Martin clearly wasn't performing in the interests of science. He had his head on one side and was strenuously biting his lower lip. There was a problem, it seemed. He took a breather and asked me to put on his ABBA T-shirt, the wrong way round so the picture on the front would be on my back, facing him. I was being abused, Mr. Kitzelstein! He was whacking off at the blonde! Anyway, he picked up his rhythm again, stuck at it, and heralded the finale with a businesslike "Now!" I shipped the oars and turned to look.

Was that it? No water fleas, no earthworms? The substance that was spattering his upper thigh resembled *spit*! Was that supposed to be the fount of life? Nonsense! Where, pray, were the sperm of which my peers were always talking? Where were they, the wiggly little creatures? Well, Mr. Kitzelstein, I was promptly reminded of my original theory, according to which the connection between screwing and procreation was merely a myth. The year before, I had addressed the problem of prehistoric copulation; now I devoted myself to spermatozoa—*if* such things existed. This stuff here proved nothing. I mean, if what had issued from Martin's dick was as lifeless as the glaze on an apricot tart, it wasn't required for the making of children; it merely manifested itself in certain circumstances, like tears, pus, or snot. Its importance was thoroughly overrated, and one day I would announce to everyone that fucking wasn't necessary any longer: they needn't be afraid their species would become extinct because they no longer transmitted those off-white droplets from male to female. What was more, I could finally stop suspecting my parents of having fucked each other.

Deploying all the diplomatic skill at my command, I endeavored to extract an admission from my mother: Had they, or hadn't they? I didn't get far. When I intimated, in carefully chosen words, that I regarded the whole copulatory theory as a myth, now that actually I'd seen some sperm . . .

"You WHAT?" she demanded dramatically, opening her eyes to their fullest extent. Why was she so appalled? I'd only wanted to acquit her of suspected copulation. What had I done wrong? I came out with the whole story. All she said was "We'll talk about this later." Having consulted the encyclopedia in the meantime, I was overcome with self-reproach: sperm was indeed a source of human life, *life like mine*. What had landed on Martin's thigh could have become a *human being*, a Cover Picture like me, a Nobel laureate, someone they'd name a street after. But Martin had never intended his sperm to fulfill its true destiny, the procreation of Nobel laureates; he had assassinated human beings like myself, and I had egged him on and shielded him from view. Far from staying his hand, I had donned his ABBA T-shirt back to front. Martin had exterminated some *fifty million spermatozoa* at a stroke; in other words, he'd murdered fifty million people! What had occurred on his right thigh was comparable, in every respect save that of material devastation, to World War II—and I had helped him! Not only did I deserve to be brought before a court; I should have been tried at Nuremberg!

Later, when my mother carried out her threat and discussed the subject with me, I learned that Martin's was a criminal offense, an act of exhibitionism, and that, having passed his fourteenth birthday, he could be *reported to the police* for it. And I had sat beside him during the perpetration of his crime! I had aided and abetted him! I was in the same boat—actually and metaphorically—as a member of the criminal fraternity! I would come to a bad end. I could already hear the clang of a cell door closing behind me . . .

I saw my first photographs of people engaged in 6 at summer camp—where else? Those little colored prints, whose acquaintance I made beneath the cosmonaut Gagarin's bust in the gardens dedicated to his memory, were crude and had precious little to do with my notions of people procreating: no barbecue tongs, no subdued lighting. Where was the participants' sense of decency? Why did none of them have their faces blacked out? Newspapers daily made it clear that humanity was capable of concentration camps, apartheid, and atom bombs, but not that human-beings-how-proud-that-sounds could bring themselves to put a have-you-been-playing-with-it in their mouths. Had they done so under duress? I looked in vain for the pistol that had been trained on them. Had drugs been involved? Was everyone in the West a drug addict?

The following year, a hut mate who had read a Western sex manual alerted me to the existence of a so-called G spot guaranteed to give any woman an orgasm of incredible intensity in double-quick time. He endeavored to describe the G spot's location, and the next morning I got him to pencil it in on a kind of genital map. This I retained for future reference, feeling like Long John Silver, but before going in search of buried treasure I decided to consult an East German sex primer for confirmation of the legendary G spot's alleged position (or at least of its theoretical existence; after all, Einstein wasn't awarded the Nobel Prize until his theoretical prediction of the curvature of light had been experimentally confirmed).

To this end I procured a copy of *the* East German sex manual, Dr. Siegfried Schnabl's *Mann und Frau Intim.* "Procured" is the right word, because I didn't want to buy such a compromising publication at the corner bookstore, where I might bump into a nosy acquaintance of the Ilona Pohle variety—one who would say, "Ah, what's this you're reading?" and reach into my shopping basket. I was equally reluctant to advertise my interest in such a book to the staff at my regular library—familiar faces all—so I joined another. I joined it, yes, but the female librarian who registered my application asked me, after we'd spent ten minutes filling in forms, "What books would you like to borrow today?" I couldn't bring myself to answer *Mann und Frau Intim.* I was halfway to becoming a man and she was a woman, so she might have found my request offensive. I mumbled something noncommittal and beat a hasty retreat.

I now possessed a second library card, but I still hadn't acquired *the book.* One day, therefore, I traveled by the S-Bahn—our suburban train service—to Nauen, where I could be pretty sure of remaining anonymous. Choosing a moment when I sensed that no one in the bookshop was looking, I took a copy of *Mann und Frau Intim* from the shelf, checked the price, and went to the cash desk with the exact money in my sweaty hand. I deposited the book on the counter facedown, intending my body to shield it from the gaze of the customers standing in line behind me. Unexpectedly, the counter was so low that I had to hug the spine, which was duly inscribed *Mann und Frau Intim,* to my *genital area*! A sex manual fetishist would have behaved in just such a fashion. Could I secretly be one without knowing it? As for expecting the girl behind the counter to handle *that* book, still warm from its contact with my crotch, did that constitute a *prima facie* case of sexual harassment? Cheeks aflame, I paid and scuttled out of the shop. I stowed the book inside two plastic bags, both of which I had tested for opacity in advance.

But *Mann und Frau Intim* afforded no clues to the G spot. Did it, or did it not, exist? Did it exist only in the West? Was the G spot peculiar to Western women? Would the solution of this mystery be rewarded with a Nobel Prize?

Other people were always privy to information I knew absolutely nothing about. Even when something did reach my ears, I was sure to be the last to hear it. I got used to this, though. You simply *know,* sooner or later, that you're the most ill-informed person far and wide. The morning after every PTA meeting my schoolmates knew everything and I nothing. My parents—"Why do you think it's called a *parent*-teacher association?"—actually prided themselves on my ignorance, with the result that I was the last to learn that Herr Küfer, the physics teacher under whose wing I had become a Cover Picture, had blotted his copybook politically. The invariable explanation for his downfall was "Well, there was that PTA meeting . . ." I questioned my schoolmates, my teacher, even my parents, but they all prevaricated: "Well, you know, it was that PTA meeting." "Yes, but what *happened,* exactly?" "I wasn't there myself." The parents of one of my schoolmates evinced the opinion that Herr Küfer had "gone too far." But what did "gone too far" mean? What had he *done?* My Russian-language teacher eventually confided to me, her conscience in turmoil, that it was "that business with the films. You simply can't do things like that, not these days."

Although I never discovered if anything else was involved, the whole atmosphere gave me food for thought. The parents who had driven Küfer into a corner were "associates," the official name for the Stasi employees who abounded in our neighborhood, pursuant to the principle that East German citizens should live near their places of work.

Herr Küfer was subjected to disciplinary proceedings during summer vacation and dismissed. Nobody protested—so far as I, the most ill-informed person, could tell—nor would I myself have protested even if he had gotten me onto a magazine cover ten times over. I considered his dismissal *normal,* and why not? At thirteen, I thought that if teachers and parents failed to protest, being older, more experienced, and better informed, they must know what they were doing. What struck me as sinister, on the other hand, was the fact that nobody *said* anything. I suspected duress of some kind, presumably on the Stasi's part. Such a great big building, and nobody knew what went on there. Everyone spoke of it in whispers. A teacher was fired and no one would tell me why. Ergo, there was something fishy about the Stasi.

I made the Stasi my secret enemy, christened the office block across the street the Ministry of Evil, and shunned the company of associates' children. I spent many hours observing what went on in the offices though a pair of binoculars. I even kept a record of my observations and entered them on a diagram of the façade, noting them down in the relevant window spaces. Feeling like a legitimate descendant of Zorro, I secretly spied on my enemy and nursed my hatred until the hour of vengeance struck.

Or, rather, until the day my father happened on the product of my labors. I don't know how best to describe his reaction. *He writhed in mental anguish,* perhaps—does that give you some idea of it? He had always considered me an imbecile, but those innocent jottings of mine proved that I was far more imbecilic than he'd ever thought possible. Whom had I told about them? Whose idea were they? How long had I been keeping the Stasi under surveillance? Were there any more such records lying around? He just couldn't fathom how a thirteen-year-old boy could be stupid enough, out of sheer boredom, to keep watch on the Stasi and guilelessly commit his observations to paper. Writhing in mental anguish, he told me that if my activities ever came out, he and my mother would be convicted of espionage and sent to prison.

In those circumstances, I discontinued my surveillance of the Stasi. I still didn't like the institution, though. It pursued sinister activities of which I knew only that I knew nothing about them. How stupid I felt—I, the eternal non-initiate! That great big office block stood just across the street, and my ignorance about it was almost total. Other people were bound to know more; they always did. I was sick of unpleasant surprises. Being unable to investigate the Stasi without dooming my parents to imprisonment, I concentrated on sex.

My ignorance of that subject was quite phenomenal. Thanks to my mother's comments on Martin's performance in the rowboat, for example, I believed that jerking off, exhibitionism, and prosecution went hand in hand—until I saw my first *genuine* exhibitionist in a deserted S-Bahn at five o'clock in the morning. Boarding the car half-asleep, I became aware that a grinning six-footer had extracted his massive dong from his fly and was working away at it with a pair of equally massive hands—and all without consulting me first! Martin in the rowboat had been quite another matter.

Sex seemed ever more weird to me. *Weird?* Strike that word: it was *shocking*. After seeing those pornographic photographs I could not but ask myself the same old question:

What is my thing *for*? Not just to urinate with—that was obviously a delusion. Peckers were manipulated, inserted in pussies and mouths, or displayed to others. What else? Eager to know the whole truth, I investigated the subject of perversions. Ah, perversions and I! I, who still, in my heart of hearts, considered the missionary position perverted, now learned of sex with animals, sex with children, sex with great-grandmothers and dead bodies. Help! And those inconspicuous words like *sodomy, pedophilia, necrophilia . . .* Was *philately* a euphemism for *sex with postage stamps*—or at least *sex with stamp collectors*? *Fellatio* sounded like an Italian health resort to be noted for use in crossword puzzles. What else was there? *Anal intercourse! Coprophagy!* The most perverted of the perversions on my list was that relating to the ingestion of one person's excrement by another . . .

By the time I went off to summer camp the following year I felt sure that nothing could shake my composure, especially as my companions weren't the usual blockheads. This was a mathematicians' camp, a *specialists'* camp attended by *my equals*. I owed my selection for it to a school inspector who had been favorably impressed by me while sitting in on a mathematics lesson. ("Cream always rises to the top" was my mother's comment on the news, whereas my father had merely glanced at me over the top of his newspaper.) Seated beside the campfire on our last night, after three weeks spent among other "talented" and "gifted" boys, I felt like a Cover Picture once more. Everything had gone right for me: I was the only one to defeat a grand master at simultaneous chess; as the Lichtenberg team's goalkeeper I had saved a crucial penalty in the soccer final against the mathematicians from Pankow; and my method of solving a geometrical problem had been universally acclaimed for its *elegance*. Quite the Cover Picture, wasn't I?

So there I sat beside the campfire, at pains to strike a pose whose Einsteinian modesty would imprint itself on the memories of my fellow campers. Seated next to me was a teacher with a debonair, sophisticated manner who sold me on the idea of completing my secondary education at Berlin's Heinrich Hertz College, which my mother roundly described as an "elite establishment." He made the same suggestion to two other boys, of whom one wore a perpetual smile and the other picked his nose incessantly. At some stage, while the four of us were chatting by the fire, the teacher asked the smiler what his father did for a living. "He's in the Stasi," replied the smiler. "And yours?" he asked the nose-picker. "So's mine," the latter said casually.

Where was I? Was the world full of associates' children, the ones I did my best to avoid? Why hadn't they said who they were the very first day? Were they here on an assignment? Had I said something incriminating? Had I betrayed someone? It's unfair to hold children responsible for their parents, I know, but that didn't prevent me from doing so.

"And what does your father do?" the teacher asked me.

"My father's with the Ministry of Foreign Trade." The teacher surveyed us uneasily, the smiler smiled, the nose-picker excavated his nose. The teacher rose and brushed some pine needles off the seat of his pants. "Well, I'm for bed," he said, and made himself scarce, leaving me alone with the two scions of the Stasi. What, I wondered, would I talk about with *them*? Perhaps I ought to steer clear of them like the teacher.

It was a fine night. The campfire crackled, sending showers of sparks into the darkness overhead, wavelets were splashing against the landing stage, and the reeds that fringed the lake were stirring in a gentle breeze. I was seated beside a warm fire on a chilly night, and everything, but everything, was so wonderful that even my recent triumphs seemed un-important.

"Come off it," the smiler said to me in a low voice, "your father's in the Stasi, too."

"*No!*" I yelled. "*No, he isn't!*" But I knew he was right. These summer-camp types were always right—always one distasteful fact ahead of me. If *anything* was possible, why shouldn't my father be in the Stasi?

Of course he was! I'd never telephoned him at the office, and the only time I'd gone there the security guard had never heard of him. And do you know what he said at supper when I asked him very, very angrily, "By the way, Father, where do you *really* work?" What a question to have to ask! I mean, was this a sequel to *The Godfather*? A man knocks off for the day and his fourteen-year-old son asks him where he works. My mother winced as if someone had trodden on her toes. As for my father, he stretched, folded his arms behind his head, grinned at me (I positively *detested* him for that grin), and said, "Well, so you've caught on at last." Double-dyed shit that he was, he considered me a failure because I'd bought that foreign-trade job of his and preened himself on having deluded me until I was fourteen. Some family, huh, Mr. Kitzelstein?

I awoke one morning to find a damp patch on my pajama trousers. Fifty million . . . So my time had come at last. Masturbation was the only remedy, but that I rejected on moral grounds. Even at a stage when I examined everything imaginable under a school microscope, I was unprepared to jerk off for research purposes. Sacrifice morality for the sake of knowledge? In a socialist state? Not I! Better to sully my sheets than defile the socialist ideal.

It was only a matter of time before my mother, while changing my sheets, surveyed the results of my latest wet dream and said, in the tone of voice she habitually used when not demanding the impossible, "Honestly, Klaus, you don't have to do it *every* night." Well, really! I didn't do it *any* night! I didn't do it *at all*! It happened every night, admittedly, but through no fault of my own. Her imputation was a repeat of the one she'd leveled at my first hard-on. I had to do something about it.

I first considered sleeping in a diaper, but then I hit on the idea of stuffing a floor cloth down the front of my pajamas—a gray one, the best color for camouflaging stains. Being reluctant to share my bed with a semen-sodden floor cloth, I hung it up to dry on a bicycle wheel propped beside my bed for the purpose. The unwitting observer (I was thinking of my mother in particular) would conclude that the floor cloth was a cleaning rag. Yes, Mr. Kitzelstein, I know it sounds revolting, but what would *you* have done in my place? Besides, I always treated myself to a new cloth before the old one became too heavily starched. I wasn't a goddess of hygiene's son for nothing.

"Klaus," my mother said at table one day, "what's that thing doing beside your bed?"

"Beside my bed?"

"You know what I mean."

"No, I don't."

"Klaus, please! At the head of your bed."

"Oh, that. It's a cleaning rag."

"Don't be so silly, you know what I'm talking about."

How did one answer such a question? Where did mothers learn to conduct such inquisitions? Did I have to feel guilty *all* the time? Did she always have to wag her forefinger—whenever she wasn't pointing it at someone?

I preserved a sheepish silence. She'd seen through me yet again. What was I to do now, get myself castrated or resort to jerking off after all?

"Didn't we say you weren't to ride a bicycle?"

So that was it! The bicycle wheel! She hadn't been taking exception to my soggy floor cloth after all.

"I'm not planning to ride one."

"So what's that wheel doing in your room?"

"The wheel? Oh, it just happens to be there." Should I have told her that the wheel was merely an excuse for the floor cloth? That I regularly had wet dreams and that, rather than inflict their results on *her,* I stuffed a crackly floor cloth down the front of my pajamas every night?

"Klaus, I don't want you to build yourself a bicycle. Cyclists account for *so many* road deaths, and I know only too well how easy it is for them to end up under a truck."

"But I'm not building myself a bicycle."

"Get rid of that wheel, then."

Why get rid of it, if I wasn't building myself a bicycle? As long as it remained beside my bed, it couldn't convey me to my death beneath the wheels of a truck. Its absence, on the other hand, would be the signal for a nagging: *Where's that wheel? Are you building yourself a bicycle on the sly? Bring that wheel back at once, or I'll never sleep another wink!*

I was very attached to my bicycle wheel. A floor cloth without one would have looked suspicious. I held my mother at bay for a week or two by insisting that I was looking for someone who would buy the wheel for a fair price. Meantime, chance came to my aid.

A fabric designer who must have been well acquainted with my problem had created some bed linen in a camouflage pattern: white sheets liberally adorned with an irregular pattern of brownish blotches of the appropriate size—a design that cried out to be named "Garrison Brothel." It gave me an uneasy feeling, the prospect of getting in between blotchy sheets and laying my head on a blotchy pillowcase, but it would at least absolve me from having to stuff my pajama bottoms with a floor cloth as stiff as crackers.

I bought four sets at once. The woman behind the counter didn't even blink. What was her opinion of people who laid in a stock of such bed linen? Did she think I was a bed-besmircher—a pervert with a taste for filth? Had she taken my money gingerly and washed her hands as soon as I left the store? Had she tagged me as soon as I came in? *Ah, here comes another one* . . .

A sixteen-year-old with no private income, I had acquired four sets of bed linen for 260 marks (a sum for which I could have purchased eight hundred floor cloths). I naturally didn't want to admit having bought them—*What are you doing, buying yourself bed linen?* my inquisitive mother would ask, and what could I tell her?—so I announced at supper that I'd won them in a competition.

"What sort of competition?" demanded my father, every inch the man from the Stasi. He was probably an interrogator—the one who switches on the spotlight and shines it in your eyes, who roams the interview room in his shirtsleeves and expects you to earn your glass of water by confessing all.

"A chess competition," I said. "Checkmate in two moves."

"Which paper?"

"The *NBI*."

"And you entered it to win some *bed linen*?"

So *that* was the point of this grilling! He thought I must have answered an advertisement reading *Win Yourself Some Bed Linen!*—a subversive act, given that the most fiercely debated shortage in recent weeks had been a crisis in the East

German textile industry. "Bed linen" was a synonym for the incompetence of our economic planners, a key word fraught with symbolic significance. Any editor that printed it would have had the censor breathing down his neck. All his readers would get the message: "You know what I mean when I say 'bed linen,' don't you, my friends?"

"Bed linen is a serious matter because it isn't supposed to be a serious matter," he said doggedly. "I'll have to look into this."

Just what I was afraid of. He would call the editor, be informed that no bed linen had ever been awarded as a chess prize, and suspect that he was on the track of some monstrous conspiracy: *Nobody knows anything, they're all hiding something, they're all denying what I know for a fact* . . . He would alert his boss, the editorial offices would be raided, and he'd wind up with egg on his face.

"I bought them myself," I said.

"But why?" asked my mother. "Why buy yourself bed linen?" Didn't she ever give up? Wasn't there *anything* I could do without having to justify myself?

"Because I liked the pattern," I said. What would her next question be? What was it about the pattern that appealed to me? Didn't I realize what the pattern was reminiscent of? Hadn't we agreed that I would try to break the habit? She pulled a dubious face and said, "Well, I don't know. It might do for wallpaper . . ." Aha! What was that, a veiled hint that I ought to anoint the wall with my semen instead of voiding it on the sheets? *For wallpaper!* I would never fathom my mother, however long I lived.

"Or writing paper," I said brightly.

"Exactly," she said. "There's something very *discreet* about it."

Discreet! That, I swear, was how she saw the design I'd

christened "Garrison Brothel." Discreet! It was yet another nail in the coffin of my sexual stupefaction that I could never prove anything against my mother. How was I to put her on the spot if she never said what she meant? *We really must try to break the habit* was her reaction to the sight of a semen-stained sheet. How was I to know that she objected to whacking off? (Of course she objected to whacking off, but today she would claim in all innocence that I'd only imagined it, and that she'd always been honest and straightforward with me.) It was so frustrating, so futile! She always had the last word, which merely reinforced my complexes instead of resolving them. "But it *is* called masturbation!" Would I have reproached her for using the vernacular term? It wasn't her fault, after all, that *masturbation* sounds like Article 412 of the penal code, sandwiched between Articles 411 (*corruption*) and 413 (*collaboration*). The same goes for *onanism,* a word she also used a couple of times, but with a severity that suggested she'd taken elocution lessons from Ronald Freisler, the Nazis' hanging judge.

Well, the final revelation burst upon me at another mathematicians' summer camp, when I was sixteen or seventeen. My double-decker bunk mate was a youth from Erfurt who spent the day excelling at three-dimensional geometry and the nights sharing his privileged information about events inside the Politburo, a body to which he had family connections. One of his anecdotes concerned a Politburo member (he couldn't recall the name) who almost came to grief because photographs of him had appeared in several newspapers, and even on the cover of the *NBI,* in the company of a Young Pioneer at the Masters of Tomorrow Exhibition. A rival of his concocted some readers' letters that angrily demanded to know whether our Party leaders really needed to consult a *nine-year-old boy* on the subject of science and technology. These he had intended to circulate at a Politburo meeting— prior to bringing up the minister's other blunders and mis- demeanors—as evidence that he had damaged the hard-won basis of trust between Party and people—and that, in the rarefied air of the Party stratosphere, would have spelled his political demise . . .

So my cover picture was a fake! I owed the only thing in which I took any pride to a political intrigue. I was a Cover Picture only because consorting with me spelled disgrace! Had my father been behind it? Was I really such a miserable worm? Would the Politburo have been scandalized by the insensitivity of a comrade who had allowed himself to be photographed with *that* (i.e., me)? I felt so *debased*! Of course my father was behind it. His instructions had been to find the minister a pho- tographic companion sufficiently beneath contempt to shock the entire Politburo. And my father, intent on doing a good job, had picked the most contemptible of all failures, the Milk- sop of the Nation, the Last Dog-Paddler.

From then on, I was a person destitute of self-esteem— until the day when my father lowered his newspaper and said, "Well, how about coming to work for us?"

He was actually addressing me! If he thought me capable of doing the job he did himself, could it be that he believed in me after all? If so, did he consider me on a par with him- self? Me? Did he really mean *me*?

I had the most repulsive of all surnames, I was the most ill-informed person in the world, an inveterate toilet-blocker and loser of things, and the Last of the Dog-Paddlers. I couldn't even jerk off, and I'd only got onto a magazine cover for the wrong reasons.

Yes, that's how it was. That's how I came to join the Stasi.

■ ■ ■

To be frank, Mr. Kitzelstein, I'm quite surprised to have gotten thus far without giving you a detailed account of my political outlook at the time. To infer from this that politics played no part in my life would be untrue. I didn't have *one* political vision of the world. If you take the word "vision" literally, I had no less than *four* of them, dating from 1914, 1922, 1949, and 1975. Printed inside the cover of my school atlas were four maps illustrating "The Worldwide Advance of Socialism and the Collapse of the Imperialist Colonial Systems in Asia and Africa." "Socialist Countries" were naturally shown in red, that being the color of the workers' flag, the labor movement, and so forth. Green was reserved for "Young Nation States," a designation as optimistic as their color. Green was halfway to red, because tomatoes, for example, are the one before they become the other and attain the requisite degree of maturity. Besides, "Young Nation States" were reminiscent of Young Pioneers, who likewise endeavored to match the achievements of their grownup socialist comrades.

Now for the negative side of the spectrum. Dark blue denoted "Capitalist Countries," and anyone familiar with the chromatic spectrum (like me, the future Nobel laureate) knew that infrared and ultraviolet formed its opposite extremes. As in the spectrum, so on the map, the real battle raged between red and blue. "Colonies," on the other hand, were pale blue, which I interpreted as meaning that they were capitalist but had no real desire to be so. Their heart wasn't in it: they'd been bullied into capitalism and would happily exchange it for something else if only they were allowed to. Last of all, tinted ocher, came the "Dependent Countries." I thought it somehow disreputable to be *dependent*. These must be countries where corrupt monarchs still clung to their thrones, but they were threatened with extinction in any case.

The world of 1914, a vast wasteland extending from the Atlantic to the Pacific, was dark blue interspersed with large tracts of ocher. Africa was a pathetic, wishy-washy blue except for Liberia and Ethiopia, which were ocher, and the southernmost tip of the continent, which was dark blue. Asia, too, was sprinkled with colonies, and China was dependent. Disgraceful! So vast and yet dependent! The world of 1914 was in a lamentable state, one could tell that at a glance.

But then came 1922. Something had happened: the Soviet Union was now in existence. Some red at last—not just a timid little dab of it, but more than one could ever have hoped for! Socialism, it was clear, had come to stay. Lots of little dark blue countries jostled the Soviet Union's western borders, but they were grossly inferior from the visual aspect. It was only the Russians' paternal kindness, I felt, that had dissuaded them from gobbling up the nasty blue countries right away. But then, the Red World has always been noted for its good behavior. I'm sure you've heard of the *peace-loving countries of the Soviet Union?* Still, there it now was, the conflict between red and blue. In other respects the world map of 1922 remained the same, especially in Africa, where Liberia and Ethiopia retained their ocher hue.

By 1949 things were looking distinctly grim for blue. Red had put on weight in the West, and China, too, had made it at last. Yes, socialism was slowly but steadily making itself at home on the world map. Green was also in business, and in no small way: India, Pakistan, Indonesia. One had to hunt around to find some ocher. Liberia and Ethiopia were still the latter color, unfortunately, and Africa in general had preserved its deplorable 1914 condition.

That would soon change, however: by 1975 almost the

entire continent was green, Liberia and Ethiopia included! Even the New World had acquired its first dab of red: Cuba! It wouldn't be long before the blue side ran out of puff. Already on its last legs, it had to resort to the most underhanded tricks. Namibia, for example, bore diagonal stripes of ocher and dark blue, rather like a convict's uniform. Obviously, it was the only country reluctant to make the transition from colonial pale blue to independent green like all the rest. It wanted to turn dark blue but didn't have the guts.

So I wouldn't have bet on blue, Mr. Kitzelstein, and that was just the point: I was on the red side—the winning side. I held a status that others had yet to attain. Although I was the long-distance runner who always came in last (if I finished at all), and although I was the last of the dog-paddlers and usually wound up on the losing side at soccer, I often consoled myself with a glance at those four maps: I was one of the vanguard, I belonged to the Red World.

In first grade I joined the "Ernst Thälmann" Young Pioneer organization. That statement appears in almost all the CV's of my age group, because every member of my class became a Young Pioneer. Before the enrollment ceremony at which our Pioneer troop leader draped the Pioneer scarf around my neck and presented me with my Pioneer membership card—my first ever ID card apart from my vaccination certificate, but that didn't count because it bore no photograph—*before* the rites of admission, to repeat, our teacher told us all about Ernst Thälmann, the German Communist leader.

She began with the sentence: "Who was Ernst Thälmann?" Little of what she said has stuck in my mind. All I remember is the workers' nickname for him, which was Teddy, and a remark that must have been uttered when Teddy met his end in Buchenwald concentration camp and the other inmates spread the word: "The Fascists have murdered our Teddy." That sentence I do remember, as I say, and it moved me deeply. I was seven years old and devoted to my Teddy bear. So grownups, the mature adults who were allowed to do as they pleased and dictate what children did, had also had a Teddy, *our Teddy,* but the Fascists had murdered him.

I was anxious to learn all I could about their Teddy. As soon as I could read I borrowed books about him from the children's library with the librarian's assistance. I was in first grade and already borrowing books intended for children in fourth grade, a fact which I later construed as evidence of my intellectual precocity. A nice little point to bring out when interviewed after the Nobel Prize awards: "Even in first grade I used to go to the library and borrow books written for much older children."

But I was telling you about my interest in Teddy. One unforgettable story concerned the *Teddy in the prison yard* episode. Teddy spent years in solitary confinement at Moabit Prison, and the first time he was allowed to exercise in the prison yard—alone, of course, because the intention was to isolate him and break his spirit—all the other inmates noticed *who* was trudging around the yard. It was not only strictly forbidden for prisoners to communicate with one another but dangerous as well, because the Fascists tolerated no nonsense and shot people whenever it suited them. Despite this, one prisoner whispered, "Red Front, Teddy!" through the bars over his cell window. A smile flitted across Teddy's face. Surreptitiously clenching his fist, he whispered back, "Red Front, Comrade!" Then he heard "Red Front, Teddy!" issuing from another cell window and returned the greeting in a whisper, raising his clenched fist slightly at the wrist. During his final circuit of the yard, whispers of "Red Front, Teddy!" issued from every window that overlooked it, and he reciprocated with "Red Front, Comrades!" The Fascists couldn't break Teddy's spirit.

It was at summer camp, the year I was enlightened about the true dimensions of an adult dick, that I learned "The Ballad of the Little Trumpeter," a heart-rending ditty about a merry youth whose breast was pierced by an enemy bullet while he sat peacefully communing with his friends one night. To update this story and divest it of mawkish sentimentality, I should explain that the Little Trumpeter was a bodyguard of Ernst Thälmann's who threw himself in front of his boss when someone pulled a gun on him during a political brawl. The gun went off, the Little Trumpeter fell dead, and Thälmann escaped without a scratch. "The Ballad of the Little Trumpeter," which was written thereafter, described him as a "young blood" in the ranks of the Red Guard. The expression was unfamiliar to me, but I was young and had blood in my veins, so why shouldn't I have conceived of the Little Trumpeter as a boy like myself? I took to the song, especially when it was sung at an evening parade on August 16, the anniversary of Teddy's death. After the last verse a ten-year-old Pioneer played a reprise of the tune on his trumpet. Unlike most marching songs, it was a melody that sounded positively soulful as opposed to warlike. A summer night, the soft notes of the trumpet, quiet reflections on Teddy's fate, steel cables gently slapping flagpoles . . . God, how vividly it all comes back to me!

I'm talking about the totalitarian conception of humanity, Mr. Kitzelstein. At eight years of age, I considered it only right that someone should have flung himself in the path of a bullet fired at a superior being. The song we sang in his honor not only rendered him immortal but afforded him adequate compensation. Many people can cope with years of solitary confinement; they take it in their stride, trudge bravely around the prison yard, and acknowledge the salutations of their companions in misfortune. None of Teddy's brothers-in-arms ever cracked. I read of no instance where torture had induced them to betray their comrades—in fact, I seriously wondered why the Fascists bothered to go on torturing Communists if they all resisted so steadfastly. I skipped the torture scenes when I reached the speed-reading stage, not because I found them too gruesome, but because they always followed the same pattern, nor did I find it so extraordinary that Teddy's fellow prisoners should have risked their lives to cheer him up during his constitutionals.

What all these stories conveyed was not the value of solidarity but the relative lack of value attached to one human life. They taught me that some things mattered more than any individual, and that I and my fellows had, if need be, to sacrifice our lives for a higher purpose. Even now, when civilians are murdered or political prisoners tortured or killed somewhere in the world, I'm unable to share in the general sense of outrage. Brutality never shocked me. Shootings and the like were the order of the day—except in our own idyllic Republic. Many had been shot in the past, but they'd died for an exalted cause.

Then there was the story of Eisleben and the red flag— one to which I was, for some reason, peculiarly attached. The Communists of the town had kept a red flag hidden throughout the Nazi period by shuttling it—at the risk of their lives, naturally—from one comrade's house to the next. When Eisleben was liberated by the Red Army, they proudly hung it out. There can't have been any shortage of red flags in 1945 (plain red flags were just as easy to manufacture out of swastika banners as German flags out of East German flags in 1990); it was just a *symbol,* in other words, nothing that would have merited the sacrifice of a human life. This story was not supposed to imply that the Eisleben Communists were smart enough not to fly their flag from the highest building in town while the Nazis were in power, or that they valued their skins more highly than a courageous gesture; no, the point of it was that the comrades of Eisleben had told themselves that their flag, at least, must survive the downfall of Nazism.

The whole thing now seems so transparent, Mr. Kitzelstein, but in those days, when I was a youthful schoolboy, I read that story with shining eyes. It thrilled me with its talk of hiding places under floorboards, of danger and comradeship, of a secret kept from the evil by the good, and of how the weak emerged victorious in the end . . . And I yearned to be one of their number!

I'd like to have shown you the Lenin Monument, but I'm afraid they've pulled it down. It was at the foot of the Lenin Monument that I donned the red neckerchief as a boy of ten. Try to visualize the scene and you'll gain some inkling, even today, of what totalitarianism means: you're just a pygmy confronted by a giant who stands there gazing at some distant prospect visible only to him. How readily I accepted that difference in size, and how right it seemed that each of us insignificant manikins at the base of the plinth should sacrifice his insignificant life for *such* a man! I had to adjust my ideas accordingly: if not a Nobel laureate, a Little Trumpeter. At least I would have a nice, sad ballad dedicated to me.

I would remind you of one of the two promises I extracted from you at the start, Mr. Kitzelstein, namely, that you wouldn't groan if I mentioned my dick from time to time. Well, you've guessed it: here I go again. *Eh bien,* for my age I had the smallest dick imaginable. I'd never seen a smaller one than mine, and this, when I became acquainted with the theory of reincarnation, led me to conclude that I was the Little Trumpeter reborn. Little Trumpeters and little trumpets go together, and my little trumpet was the littlest of all. Although I felt uneasy and unhappy about it, there had always to be those who laid down their lives for the great (thereby making a major contribution to our great common cause). I looked at my dick, I looked at the Lenin Monument, and sensed that I was the Little Trumpeter reincarnate. More than that I didn't know.

Needless to say, my enthusiasm for these stories about Teddy in the prison yard and Eisleben's red flag did not endure forever. Within a couple of years I was preoccupied with theories to the effect that peace was so direly threatened because capitalism had lately become as vicious and aggressive as a wild beast at bay. Remembering the four world maps, I understood why. Of course! It was all on account of this cowboy of a U.S. President who planned to arms-race the Soviet Union to death, who had promulgated a law for the nuking of Russia when carrying out a voice test, and whose Secretary of State considered some things more important than peace.

Suddenly, everything revolved around peace and disarmament. Eager to live in peace, I signed petitions for it whenever invited to do so, demonstrated for it—with and without a torch—whenever a peace rally was organized, and belted out peace slogans until my throat was raw, often as leader of the chorus. In class we discussed the threat to peace and what must be and had already been done to preserve the same, and at 1:00 P.M. every Wednesday, when the air-raid sirens went off to satisfy us that they were in working order, our teacher remarked that this, too, was a contribution to the preservation of peace. When the winds of the Cold War howled about our ears, we had to draw closer together and cuddle up and put our faith in Lenin, who was greater than all of us and had seen so much further. We couldn't afford any individualistic self-indulgence or pluralistic blather, not in times like these.

We often discussed the progress of disarmament talks and the sly way in which the Blue World and its voice-test President were conducting negotiations, with their offers of *security in return for "human rights."* That the Blue World should insist on human rights in the Red World could only betoken something bad. Just as I regarded *love* as indecent, so human rights, too, struck me as somehow disreputable. *Their* claim that *we* possessed no human rights was merely an excuse to go on girding themselves for war. If human rights were something to be bartered for peace, they must be bad by definition. The whole thing was so absurd, so shoddy, we wanted no part of it.

It's easy today to claim that we never took the subject seriously, and even easier now that the Lenin Monument has gone. To say that our human rights were forever being "trampled underfoot" is, in my opinion, euphemistic. Shall I tell you the true position in regard to human rights? I didn't have the first idea what they were! I couldn't be deprived of what I'd never possessed, nor could something nonexistent be trampled underfoot. Never question an East German about infringements of human rights in the old days—we're sick of such insinuations. If you really want to peer into the abyss, ask us what human rights *are*. We know them as blind people know colors, by hearsay alone.

I believe it was also the talk of a *historic mission* that got to me. A mission—a *historic* mission, no less! To think that such a thing existed! The historic mission of the working class had been identified by Karl Marx (whose likeness appeared on the hundred-mark note) and Friedrich Engels (fifty-mark note). The historic mission was, in fact, the very *business* of the working class, but because workers found the production of material goods pretty arduous—you had only to look at their grimy, sweaty faces—they allied themselves with well-disposed members of other classes and social categories who assisted them with their historic mission.

How charitable of us not to leave the workers, groaning beneath the weight of their historic mission, to toil through world history on their own! Only the most noble souls—I always responded to appeals to my chivalry—championed the cause of progress. Anyone could believe in a cause, but how many were prepared to make sacrifices on its behalf? I, for example, who preened myself on my future Nobel Prize? Anyone could become a Nobel laureate as long as he possessed my intellectual brilliance, but only renunciation and self-denial were morally meritorious, especially when what was at stake was something great—nay, supreme: a historic mission. My Nobel Prize could wait. First I would dedicate my genius to the historic mission and help to turn the world red; I could always devote myself to other matters—cancer, nuclear fusion, and so forth—in due course.

Besides, there was something lone-wolfish and individualistic about Nobel laureates. They beavered away in solitude, and you could never tell what really made them tick. Not so the trailblazer of a historic mission, who, far from forging ahead on his own, was part of a mighty international movement represented in every part of the globe. Even when incarcerated and sentenced to solitary confinement, he was infused by the Teddy-in-the-prison-yard feeling with a warmth and solidarity denied to the individualistic Nobel laureate. Wherever I wound up, I would not be alone. There would be people who counted and relied on me—people to whom I meant something.

My commitment was not only intellectual but emotional. It would be easy for me to deny my intellectual commitment and ascribe it to ignorance, to medieval obnubilation, but emotions are harder to dismiss. I know, you see, that my emotions were those I'm loath to talk about: my angst, my shame, my desire for greatness, my ambition to be one of the winners of a long-distance race, my wish to do things "properly," and my fear of failure. If no East Germans are prepared to admit that today, it's a sense of shame that inhibits them from acknowledging disgrace and failure. Opposition, or what passed for it, they define as coinciding with the extent of their own sporadic intransigence. No one will admit to having conformed, everyone was in some way "anti," yet Herr Küfer, my physics teacher, was fired and the Wall continued to stand.

The system wasn't inhumane. Its nature wasn't such that it took no account of us. It was humane—it involved people like you and me in one way or another. And that's what we must talk about. About you and me. About us. About mutual affronts and humiliations. About ducking the issue. About human ignominy. I'm acquainted with everything human, human ignominy included. No, the system wasn't inhumane, but it was misanthropic. It didn't *disregard* human nature, it *contravened* it. It deformed people. It induced them to love what they should have hated, and to do so with an intensity they cannot bring themselves to acknowledge, even today. I've no need to tell them, "Remember!" I *know*, Mr. Kitzelstein, and in a few hours' time you will, too, that it wasn't anything any of them did that caused the system to collapse. Only one person was responsible, and that was yours truly. I'm one of their number, of course, but if I'm to do justice to their contribution to the end of the nightmare, I'd put it like this: some of them corrupted their fellow citizens, others abandoned them, and it wasn't until I became their most abject zombie that I finally went into action.

My first civics teacher (we were introduced to that subject in seventh grade) was the archetypal unpopular pedagogue. At the beginning of every class she would single someone out, make him stand up (a regular source of embarrassment because of my hard-ons), and question him on the content of the previous lesson. What are the objectives of the labor movement in Latin America? In what respect is capitalism fundamentally self-contradictory? She insisted on our reciting the answers she had dictated the last time, word for word. I found it easy to preserve my dislike of her and even developed the illusory belief that I was sufficiently different from *her*.

But later on, at my elite law school, I acquired a civics teacher whose very first step was to tell us that current events were far more complex than we had previously supposed. We must think and work things out for ourselves. After several years of stolid learning by rote, no injunction could have been more welcome. We all knew who the Beatles were, she said, and she herself enjoyed listening to them—indeed, John Lennon was active in the peace movement. The logical inference was that he must be on the side of progress—afflicted with bourgeois inhibitions, perhaps, but humane in outlook and opposed to capitalist aggression. But what, she asked, was the truth of the matter? Very few people knew that John Lennon had once written a song that embodied an advertising slogan from a firearms magazine: "Happiness Is a Warm Gun." The enemy often launched such insidious attacks on our young minds, so we must always be on our guard. Despite their hopeless historical situation—I thought of my four world maps and nodded earnestly—our enemies were incredibly shrewd. They were forever refining their manipulative, mind-bending techniques, whose effectiveness depended on their remaining undetected. We were at liberty to go on listening to the Beatles, naturally, but we must never forget that they meant us no good. Our new civics teacher concluded by asking us to spend the next hour writing an essay on some previously undetected mind-bending technique that had pierced our guard. *At what point has the enemy managed to infiltrate your mind? None of you will get a bad grade save those who refuse to acknowledge the possibility of enemy subversion.*

I already told you how I came to join the Stasi, but that wasn't the whole truth. I was more than the child of my parents; I was also the student of my teachers and the reader of my library books. I was "one of us."

SEX AND DRUGS AND ROCK 'N' ROLL

On my father's instructions I purported to be an officer cadet during my senior year and perfected my cover by attending the officer-cadet afternoon classes. When I was drafted, the members of the draft board conferred in portentous whispers. What was it about me that could have elicited portentous whispers? *Ah, so that's him . . . Yes, I've heard about him . . . That's right, he was scheduled to report today . . . Funny, I'd pictured him quite differently . . .* At length I was sent home: "We'll let you know."

A few months later I was back at Military District HQ for an interview with a State Security instructor. Unforgettable, the surroundings in which we met, we two secret servicemen: at a big *conference table*—you know, the kind of table at which historic decisions are arrived at or summit talks held. My instructor, by contrast, had little historic charisma; he looked more of a next-door neighbor type than a shaper of world events. I was particularly struck by his shoes, which were white and—well, *sporty,* with thin soles and neatly tied laces. He had somehow remained a little boy proud of being able to tie his own shoelaces—in fact, "shoe-

laces" may well have been his favorite word. His real name
didn't register with me, even though he flashed his ID when
introducing himself, so I christened him "Herr Shoelaces."

Seated alone at the conference table, he *smirked* at me
when I entered. I was subjected to that set, sustained, doggy
rictus hundreds of times in the Stasi, and I never really fath-
omed what it meant. "Well," Herr Shoelaces said at length,
doing his best to sound conspiratorial, "so you've absolutely no wish to become an officer in our National People's
Army—if our information is correct." Another smirk. "Not
that our information is ever *in*correct," he added proudly.

Really subtle, don't you think, the way Herr Shoelaces
worked on me by so clearly intimating that he was an expert
psychologist. You've no idea how superior I felt, Mr. Kitzelstein. So the Stasi put up dummy applicants for an officer's
commission—what a hoot! It was all deliberate, of course. If
a candidate's application failed, he would remember the Stasi
as an innocuous institution. I mean, if it was staffed by characters as quaint as Herr Shoelaces! Anyone who had dealings
with him would probably dismiss it as pure chance that he
had managed to efface all memory of his name in spite of
having introduced himself properly. It was too easy to underestimate those people, however, because he captured me
after all—took possession of my soul by transfixing my Achil-
les' heel with a *We need you; you're one of us* . . . "Today
we're giving you your first undercover assignment," he whispered, and I was a dead duck.

What! I? Today? An undercover assignment? My *first*?
From *them*? Was Herr Shoelaces a front man for more powerful operators who had great plans for me—who would entrust me with further undercover assignments at even bigger
conference tables? Was I already in the thick of a secret service operation? Would my life be in danger from now on? Did

the Superpowers have me in their sights? Should I don dark glasses right away?

Do you know what it was, my first undercover assignment? "Invent a cover for yourself." A *cover*! I wasn't in the Stasi yet, not properly, and already I needed a cover! The thing was, Mr. Kitzelstein, that ordinary cadets were drafted in mid-August every year and obliged to wear uniform from their very first day at officers' school. What if I bumped into an old acquaintance who thought I was there already? That's why I needed a cover story to explain why I hadn't been drafted at the same time as the others—one that would transform me into a different person! I would walk the streets and no one would know who I really was—fantastic! I, a Cover Picture engaged on a historic mission: a long-standing ambition of mine . . .

"This cover of mine, how long do I have to keep it up? I mean, when will you send for me again and—"

"Don't ask. You'll be told all you need to know. You know the kind of outfit you're in, after all."

Tough talk, just like something out of a movie. *I'll do the job, Herr Shoelaces. Tell your people I'm their man . . .* What now, though? Was I simply to construct my cover and await further instructions, or should I reconnoiter a dead-letter box or two? One never knew. Maybe everything would happen very fast. What did they have in mind for me? Who was I working for? Who was behind it? My father? The minister? And why me? Was Shoelaces merely the errand boy of some influential strategists who had singled me out? If so, someone must have taken charge of my destiny. I was part of a great process. I would be shielded, guided, directed. I wouldn't have to roam the bleak, cheerless world alone. Someone was protecting me. Whatever happened, I would be in good hands.

But my cover? With what cover story should I embark on

my double life? I pondered the problem for days, *weeks* on end. Was I recuperating from some "nasty stomach trouble"? Something to do with the pancreas, perhaps, or the gallbladder—something everyone had heard of but didn't know much about? Or how about I'm-not-really-supposed-to-talk-about-it-so-keep-it-under-your-hat and then spin some yarn about a fire that had destroyed a whole wing at officers' school? But then it occurred to me to play the innocent, a role that anyone would accept, coming from me, the most ill-informed person far and wide. The perfect cover: *No idea why, but they sent me home again. They called out eight names and promised to mail us some new induction papers in due course. I have no idea what the problem was.* That was it! I was universally known to be clueless. I would only arouse suspicion by being overly informative.

Not that I was ever questioned. I went around armed with a cover story of interest to no one. But what was the truth, if any? That I was starting work with the Stasi? No, Mr. Kitzelstein, I don't accept *that* imputation! No one had ever mentioned the Stasi. Herr Shoelaces spoke of "us," "our" information, and "You know the kind of outfit you're in." Not a mention of the *Stasi*. Did I really know what outfit I was in? My father had said he worked at the Ministry of Foreign Trade, and when I asked him, point-blank, where he *really* worked, all he said was "Well, so you've caught on at last." Did you hear the word "Stasi" mentioned? I didn't. Even when he casually suggested, "Well, how about coming to work for us?" there was still no reference to the Stasi. On his advice, I was to pass myself off as an officer cadet, and the Herr Shoelaces who interviewed me at Military District HQ never breathed a word about the Stasi either. If asked in the street whether the officer cadets' induction date hadn't expired, how could I have begun to blather about the Stasi?

The Stasi had never been mentioned. How could I be sure that I was working for the Stasi? In the circumstances, I couldn't possibly have told anyone I was working for the Stasi. Herr Shoelaces needn't have instructed me to devise a cover story; I would have adopted one of my own accord.

The situation remained obscure even when I eventually joined the organization I surmised to be the Stasi. The universal refrain was the one Herr Shoelaces had used—"You know the kind of outfit you're in"—and we novices had it flung at us continually. "You'll have to readjust your ideas completely. You know the kind of outfit you're in." "Never discuss, comment on, or allude to your activities in any way. You know the kind of outfit you're in." "The enemy will mercilessly exploit any weakness, however small. You know the kind of outfit you're in." I should have found it uncommonly reassuring to be told, if only once, that I was in the Stasi, just to be on the safe side. Although it wouldn't have been welcome news in view of my ineradicable hostility toward that organization, which continued to burn deep inside me, it wouldn't have found me unprepared. I could have lived with it. But as things were? Was I really in the Stasi, and, if so, was there an I? Was there life after a double life?

Don't dismiss all this as mere foolishness. How did the Stasi's "unofficial informants" fare when the Stasi no longer existed? Wasn't it touching, the way they defended themselves against the accusations leveled at them? They hoped against hope that they hadn't been in the Stasi, and when their hopes were dashed they felt the Stasi had duped and hoodwinked them. How else could they have lived with themselves?

"Good morning, Herr Schulze, I'm Herr Mielke from the Ministry of State Security, for which you, if I've correctly understood this signed declaration of yours, act as an unofficial informant. And, before I forget, allow me to preface our conversation by showing you my ID from the Ministry of State Security, which certifies that I'm a State Security Service employee, just to satisfy you, prior to your twenty-fifth State Security Service interview, that you're dealing with a State Security Service employee, and not, for example, with someone from the police, the municipal administration, or Social Security, to cite only the most common confusions that arise where meetings with State Security Service personnel are concerned." No, that wasn't how it went. Nobody wanted to be fully involved, but anyone unable to counter the Stasi's insidious approaches with a plain refusal could play down his collaboration inwardly. Try asking an unofficial informant. *I didn't harm anyone . . . I knew what I was telling them . . . I didn't tell them everything, of course . . . Anything I told them they knew already . . . Anything I told them they could easily have found out for themselves.*

There was never any mention of the Stasi, either in the induction papers I received in the mail, or at the military training camp at Freienbrink, where six hundred recruits scurried around in combat fatigues, drilled for hours on end, and held daily practice alerts. Was this the Stasi, the real, authentic, legendary Stasi? Would the Stasi have taught us what to do on the command "Take up an all-around defensive position"? No, the Stasi would have instructed us in how to encode secret messages, file duplicate keys, or wear a wire, not how to clean and assemble a gas mask. Whatever outfit I'd wound up in, it couldn't, I told myself, be the Stasi. How smart of them to hide me away in the ranks of an infantry platoon! I still hadn't solved the question of whether I was really in the Stasi three and a half weeks later, when I was sent home (believe it or not) with a dose of *clap*. I had, on the other hand, begun to grasp what went on inside my father's head. He'd had no choice but to spin me that yarn about the Ministry of Foreign Trade. He had concealed his occupation, day after day and year after year, behind a smoke screen of cover stories and prevarications. Should he have bared his soul to a naïve eight-year-old, just because the latter happened to be his son? Absurd!

Our quarters at Freienbrink were four-man tents containing double-decker bunks, and, sure enough, I was fated to have some more gaps in my education filled the very first night. "Know what the Yanks call the last post?" inquired Raymund from the bunk above me, when the bugle sounded for lights-out. " 'Taps.' And do you know why taps is called taps?" None of us did, so he answered the question himself. "Because that's when I turn on my tap." And he proceeded to generate a sound I'd heard once before—in a rowboat: *whack-whack-whack*. No doubt about it: he was jerking off immediately overhead.

A few nights later, Raymund managed to persuade our only married man, René, to describe how he did it with his wife. What an appalling state of affairs! Was nobody here acquainted with the *law* and aware of the *legal consequences*? Raymund had not only masturbated but induced René to *aid and abet an act of exhibitionism,* the very offense I myself had committed in the rowboat by wearing an ABBA T-shirt the wrong way around. Could *this* be the Stasi? Days spent trudging across plowed fields in a firing line, nights devoted to whacking off—in the *Stasi*?

It seemed doubtful. All else aside, my intake included half the members of the officer cadets' club at Heinrich Hertz College, and they were anything but budding secret servicemen (like me, for example). I could recall many of them proudly displaying their pocketknives with some such remark as "I bought it in Minsk" or "Mine can perform eighteen different functions." Others were gun freaks who saw every Soviet war film and pronounced it "totally unrealistic" when a scene ostensibly set in 1942 featured a machine pistol that hadn't been issued to Red Army NCOs until 1944, or hobbyists who always knew what model aircraft kits were currently available.

No, all my fellow cadets gave the impression of having been genuinely drafted. Every youngster at every school was subjected to *recruitment interviews,* stiff and disagreeable encounters that generally took place in the assistant principal's study, where one recruiting officer formed an impression of you by leafing through your personal file while another endeavored to create a relaxed atmosphere ("Well, do you have a girlfriend yet?"). Then it came: "How would it appeal to you, the idea of working with *people* later on? A simple question requiring a simple answer: yes or no?" *Every* youngster of sixteen to eighteen underwent these recruitment interviews at some stage, and who could say no when asked, pointblank, if he might someday like to work with *people*? (People, after all, were human-beings-how-proud-that-sounds.) Had you ever thought of becoming a political officer in the National People's Army and educating young people politically? Were you on the side of peace and socialism, and, if so, wouldn't you like to serve them in some capacity? "Your father," the file-perusing recruitment officer might chime in, "is an ordinary worker" (or, "Your mother is an ordinary housewife"). Weren't you grateful to the society that had enabled you to receive an excellent education at such an elite establishment? Did you wish to dissociate yourself from the great struggles of our age (in the presence of the note-taking assistant principal, no less)? "You've always wanted to be a forester? Perfect! As a tank commander carrying out frequent firing practices in prohibited areas you'll be able to enjoy the sight of unspoiled forest scenery all year round . . ."

The technique was as clumsy as that, Mr. Kitzelstein! And

I had spent one afternoon a month, during my elite secondary school career, with those who responded to it! Wherever they belonged, with their pocketknives from Minsk and their model aircraft, it certainly wasn't in the Stasi. The fact that I had been reunited with them at Freienbrink proved that I was exceptional, that I was the most undercover of undercover agents, because the fewer people saw me in the Stasi, the fewer could give me away when the day came for me, the executor of a historic mission, to receive my orders at vast conference tables. Incorrigible masturbators and other dregs of society couldn't possibly be in the Stasi, which wanted me, Klaus the Cover Picture, for one of its own. What did I have in common with the youths in my tent? Nothing! I was better, superior—more important by far . . .

No, Mr. Kitzelstein, shall I be honest? I was terribly envious of Raymund from the very first. "My name's Raymund. With a 'y.' " Raymund, a stylish, sophisticated young man, the ideal son-in-law: athletic, humorous, smart. And the "y" in his first name! Me, I was saddled with *Klaus* for the rest of my days . . . He once explained to us what "ray" meant in English, and since *Mund* meant "mouth" in German, Raymund was translatable as "radiant mouth." What a God-given name: Radiant Mouth with a "y"! And the way he talked about *position, career,* and *advancement*—quite irresistible! How fluently and naturally those words flowed from his radiant mouth! And his charm! My glasses regularly misted over in his presence, I was so envious of his charm. And the way he persuaded René to describe his marital performances as an aid to masturbation—you had to hand it to him! René bored us from dawn to dusk with his incessant my-wife-this, my-wife-that. She was five years older, it seemed, "but the marriage was approved right away." Eh? The marriage was *what*? "That's right, *approved*. You need a permit when you want to get married, but with my wife there were no problems." Whereupon Kai, the fourth occupant of the tent, growled, "We'd better not screw anything without a permit from now on." René told us, when introducing himself, that his name had "a line over the second 'e,'" at which Raymund amended, "Yes, an *accent aigu*" in flawless *parlez-vous-français* French. Not only was I surrounded by people blessed with "y"s and acute accents, but, just to compound my feelings of inferiority, I discovered in the communal showers that Kai had the biggest. I never whacked off and had the smallest, Raymund whacked off daily and didn't have the biggest. How, if at all, were those facts related? Questions, questions . . .

One night after lights-out but prior to his personal taps, Raymund said, "Hey, René, what's your wife like in bed? I mean, does she keep you properly supplied?" "What's it to you?" "Go on, tell us how she does it. You tell us a load of other stuff about her." "None of your goddamned business!" squawked René, who always squawked under pressure.

"Come on," said Raymund, "tell us how you fuck her, I want to beat my meat."

Beat my meat? I'd never heard the expression. Did it mean what I suspected?

"Well?" Raymund pursued. "Tell us how you take her. Or how you'd like to take her—your dream fuck—and we'll see who tosses himself off first, okay?" Tosses himself off?

After a while René said, in a tremulous voice, "Well, we'd lie down on the bed. Then we'd kiss and cuddle and undo each other's buttons." Raymund was away: *whack-whack-whack*. "Aren't you doing it?" he asked.

"No."

"How about you?" Raymund asked Kai and me.

"Count me out," I replied. "Me too," said Kai.

"Don't tell me I'm the only one here who enjoys jerking off," Raymund protested.

"All right," said Kai, "I'm on." Incredible!

"Where did I get to?" asked René.

"The buttons."

"We'd leave the light on the whole time, and I'd really, well, *handle* her. I'd give her breasts a real going-over." He giggled. Raymund was panting now. "Good," he said, "carry on."

"And then, with my right hand, I'd explore her vagina."

"Root around in her cunt, you mean."

"I'd tickle her clitoris and wind her pubic hair around my fingers. I might—" René broke off.

"Yes?" panted Raymund.

"I might even . . ."

"Yes? Go on!"

"I might even smell her vagina. Not just sniff it, I mean, but stick my hooter right up it." A deep breath. "Then I'd pry her legs apart . . ."

"Ah, her thighs!" said Raymund.

"Her thighs, if you like. And then I'd—"

"Fuck her!" said Raymund. "Shoot your wad in her!"

"Sleep with her," said René. "I'd try out a few different positions—"

"You mean you'd jack her up and take her from behind, right?"

René laughed. "Sure, jack her up and—"

"And you'd get her to suck you off, too?"

"I'd keep prying her legs apart so that—"

"So you could see her pale pink pussy flesh," Raymund supplemented.

"Yes, exactly," said René, with a mixture of fascination and frustration. He fell silent for a while, and all we could hear was *whack-whack-whack*. I wondered if there was something about me that always prompted other guys to masturbate in my presence. What was so special about me?

"And how do you really do it?" Raymund asked afterward in a soft, genuinely *humane* voice.

"We always put the light out so it's black as pitch. She doesn't even like me to watch her undress. We don't do it often. Pretty seldom, in fact." René was weeping.

"How often is seldom?" Raymund asked almost inaudibly.

"Seldom, seldom," said René. "Maybe six or seven times since we've known each other." And even that, one suspected, was an overstatement.

"And you've never really handled her boobs?"

"No."

"Nor sniffed her pussy?"

"No."

"Why not?"

"I don't know. I'm scared she wouldn't like it."

Raymund had a knack of worming things out of people—me, for instance, while I was brushing my teeth. Suddenly there he was, standing behind me. "Well, Klaus," he murmured, watching my face in the mirror, "so you haven't done it yet either . . ." Startled, I rinsed my mouth and haltingly replied in the negative. It was Raymund, too, who came up with the *moonlight cruise* idea. "Women have a weakness for romantic surroundings," he said, as worldly-wise as Casanova in person, and I turned green with envy. It was my fault for sneering when my thirteen-year-old companions stole off to the girls' hut after lights-out in summer camp. Raymund had surely been his hut mates' ringleader, whereas I, in all my well-bred refinement, remained in my double-decker bunk and demonstrated strength of character, to myself and the world at large, by stubbornly suppressing my carnal urges.

Raymund, quite the old hand, looked up the date of the next full moon on the calendar, applied for a group pass, and booked us on a cruise on the *Wilhelm Pieck*, the flagship of the so-called White Fleet. The September nights were mild, Raymund insisted. There would be a full moon, a deck overhung with Chinese lanterns, schmaltzy music, the murmur of the waves. "I've never tried to get laid on board ship," he said, "but it ought to be a cinch."

Why hadn't I hit on the idea myself? How did he think of these things? Why was he so flexible and I so rigid? Raymund jerked off whenever he felt like it and got other people to put him in the mood. How could he do that when I couldn't? He knew how to handle his dick—he knew what a treasure it was—whereas I was always running away from it. I stuffed a floor cloth down the front of my pajamas; Raymund simply came on his sheets. "You mean you sleep in it?" I asked him, aghast. (By "in it" I was doubtless questioning his ability to rest easy in a kind of piscine mortuary. I mean, could you sleep in a drained pond surrounded by fifty million gasping, flapping carp?) "What's a few little drops of come?" protested Raymund. "They've got to go *somewhere*." Brilliant!

Our group pass was approved. We traveled to Berlin under the supervision of a certain Major Schenk, who had leaped at the assignment because he was recently divorced and eager, as he put it, "to cast my nets again." We were scarcely aboard the *Wilhelm Pieck* when he proceeded to play the old salt, for instance by using phrases like "going aft" and "splicing the mainbrace." He also enhanced his rugged, manly *allure* by getting stinking drunk, and his last words before he finally slid beneath the table were "Permission to fuck granted."

She came staggering across our deck to buy some cigarettes at the bar. Raymund promptly dug me in the ribs. "What a figure!" he whispered. "I bet she's done some gymnastics in her time." Well, I thought, so women have *figures* one can discuss and entertain ideas about. "What do you think?" Raymund asked. What did I think? She was wearing a short, skin-tight, black knitted dress and bright red high heels that seemed to be giving her trouble. Although she kept looking at her feet, she stumbled at every other step. "She probably works in a factory and has to get up at five-fifteen every morning," I said, at a loss.

Her name, at least, would have lent dignity to any member of a large working-class family: Marina. She got her cigarettes and lit up at once, and because her roving eye came to rest on our table I felt called upon to take the ashtray from there to the bar, which lacked one. How helpful and attentive I was! She smiled at me. I deemed it appropriate to return her smile, and behold, she smiled again! I smiled again, too, and so on. She plucked at my sleeve and I followed her to her own deck, where she snapped her fingers at a waiter and called "Bubbly!" in a strident voice. The waiter brought the bottle, Marina took it from him and put it between her legs . . . No, Mr. Kitzelstein, I won't beat about the bush: *She gave it a hand job!* She actually *jerked it off*! Clamping the bottle between her thighs, she removed the wire and laughingly proceeded to massage the neck, hard and fast. Then she gave the cork a couple of flicks with her thumbnail *and it came.* Foam spurted from the bottle as she quickly conveyed it to her lips, but not without spilling some of the fizz on her dress. When the foam subsided she held the bottle aloft, still laughing, and kissed it exuberantly. Then she propped her head on her hands, regarded me with pride, puckered her lips, and crooned a little tune: "Toodle-oo-doo-doo." She knew the ropes all right!

I was reminded of how my parents handled bottles of fizz, and *when:* only on New Year's Eve, because alcohol was, generally speaking, to be eschewed. Only on exceptional occasions could one venture to imbibe something that *removed inhibitions* and, as countless experiments had proved, *induced aggression.* The sparkling wine (never referred to as "bubbly") was heavily chilled for safety's sake and opened in the kitchen on principle. My father, the only member of the family authorized to perform this operation, would place the bottle on the floor, clamp it between his feet, and—wait for it—envelop it in a tea towel. Having groped for the wire through the cloth and removed it, he slowly and carefully eased out the cork like a surgeon excising a foreign body. The cork never popped, and if a little foam escaped despite all his precautions, the tea towel absorbed it. If people in general fucked the way they open bottles of fizz—no, I refuse to pursue that idea! And the corks themselves! You won't believe this, Mr. Kitzelstein, but they were inscribed with the date and preserved alongside our family photographs as mementos of the passing years. That's what we were like at home, like shipwrecked sailors carving notches on a desert-island palm tree.

Eventually, after I'd returned Marina's smile about a dozen times, I summoned up the courage to smile at her first, and—surprise, surprise—she smiled back. Imagine that! Why hadn't anyone ever told me? Was there a catch somewhere, or was it as simple as it seemed? But there was more to come. When, after ten minutes' concentrated indecision, I inquired if she would care to dance, she jumped up and beamed as if she'd been waiting for me to ask all the time. We made our way to the upper deck and danced, and when she clasped me around the neck and plastered her warm, soft little body against mine, I was so overwhelmed my knees started knocking. The string of Chinese lanterns overhead swayed in a cool breeze as we danced without speaking, cheek to cheek. Unless I was much mistaken, there was a word for this: we were *canoodling*—a sensation so wonderful I doubted if I would survive. The band, four bleary-eyed Bulgarians in white tuxedos, played one schmaltzy number after another: "Yesterday," "Moonglow," "Strangers in the Night" . . . "My favorite song," Marina whispered rapturously, snuggling even closer. She had a *favorite song*! Me, I would never have admitted to anything less than a favorite *opera* (depending, of course, on the production). What other surprises did she have in store for me, this fragrant, pneumatic little creature? Did she have a favorite *color*? A favorite *meal*? A favorite *word*? Toodle-oo-doo-doo, for instance?

We took a cab to her place when the ship berthed. On the way there she rested her head on my shoulder and groped for my dick. Without asking—incredible! Not even I was entitled to touch my dick without a valid reason.

Once in her diminutive apartment she grabbed me by the waistband, gazed deep into my eyes, and drew me into the kitchen, where she perched on the kitchen table, sent her fingertips crawling over my chest, and unbuttoned my shirt. Rather than stand there idly, I set to work on her dress. That, however, was where gaps in my education manifested themselves. How to remove it? Peel it off over her head, pull it down over her hips, or unwrap her like a chocolate Easter egg? I dredged my memory. Had I, the possessor of four separate library cards, ever read anything about removing a girl's dress, and, if so, what? Of course: that there was always a jammed zipper to contend with, and that the man in such a situation, maddened by lust, had to tear the dress off her body. Before I could find a jammed fastener, however, Marina swiftly reached behind her and unzipped it.

Gingerly, I pulled the dress over her head, and, sure enough, two boobs came to light! I'd guessed as much: when unclothed, Marina displayed two genuine, miraculous boobs. What was more, they swung like bells when she shook her hair loose. It overwhelmed me to think that these legendary globes were so profanely subject to the force of gravity. Wonderful! Together, we pulled down the panties on which she sat, and while I was standing dazedly before her, still clad in my underpants, she performed a final, memorable little feat: drawing up her legs, she deftly hooked her big toes into the elasticized waistband and pulled the underpants down, massaging my loins with gentle, oscillatory movements of her dear little insteps. Almost simultaneously, she engulfed me as though threading a needle.

Where had she learned such a trick? Could every woman perform it? I was so fascinated I forgot my plan to locate the putative G spot—I who had so often, while daydreaming or consulting the anatomical sketches in our biology textbook (eighth grade), envisioned positions that would afford my pecker the requisite freedom of movement—both penetrative and rotary—for a systematic G-spot reconnaissance. How had I conceived of *sexual intercourse*? As an act requiring great care, rather like the removal of a midge from someone's eye, or as a wooden clamping-together of bodies, dancing class fashion, but never as something that inspired champagne-cork sensations. To think that one could happily leave matters to develop by themselves! After a while, a kind of explosion occurred down below. I'd actually made it at last! So that was the meaning of "Happiness Is a Warm Gun" . . .

Marina rose, donned a man's shirt, lit a cigarette, and put

a tape on. Settling herself on a kitchen chair, she held out the cigarette. I took a drag. Wow! We had fucked and were sharing the *postcoital cigarette*—to music, what was more. Sex and drugs and rock 'n' roll, what an adventure! My biographers would have to draw a veil over this episode: Klaus the Cover Picture's hippie period. I would preserve the epoch-marking cigarette butt for the Klaus Uhltzscht Museum to display after my death.

I still nursed the belief that a man must affirm his love before, during, and after copulation. Before and during were water under the bridge. What to do?

"I love you," I said experimentally.

"Hey, cool it," she said.

What, no love? Had it just been straight 6?

"It was a bit of fun, that's all," she added, expelling a lungful of smoke. Seated there on her folding chair, with her legs casually extended and only the bottom three or four buttons of her shirt done up, she had reduced me to the status of a 6 object. I lowered my eyes, thoroughly abashed, and what did I see? There was a *hamster cage* under the kitchen table! Quite apart from my abiding revulsion at the thought of having been observed in mid-fuck by a hamster, *hamster in the kitchen* was a phrase expressive of unimaginable squalor, a circumstance calculated to arouse my sympathy for the inhabitants of the Third World. In her *kitchen,* a room in which *food* was prepared for human consumption, Marina kept an animal covered with *fur* in which anything might be lurking. Hamsters, moreover, were *rodents*—like rats! Bacteria, parasites, infections—keeping a hamster in a kitchen was tantamount to courting death from bubonic plague!

Within a few days, any pleasure I took in what had now become my favorite bodily organ was blighted by a visit to the latrines. Repeated warnings against 6 had taught me what *a burning sensation when passing water* meant. I felt almost relieved: so divine retribution existed after all! I went to see the M.O., a general practitioner by the horrific name of Riechfinger (Stinkfinger to you, Mr. Kitzelstein)—a suitable introduction to the vocabulary that haunted me in the weeks that followed: swab . . . gonococci . . . gonorrhea . . . penicillin . . . mucous membrane . . .

Gonorrhea did not fall within the competence of a general practitioner. Dr. Riechfinger wrote out a referral note and sent me home with instructions to call at the Ministry's Polyclinic, which maintained a specialist in cutaneous and venereal diseases. My departure from the training camp was a moving experience. The first of six hundred recruits to catch the clap was always reputed to be a helluva fellow. Tributes poured in from all sides. Total strangers in combat fatigues slapped me on the back and hailed me as one of their own.

I surveyed myself in the mirror when I'd changed into civvies. Ghastly! What other people called their "gear" was referred to in my family as *garments,* and that's precisely what it looked like: sandy-colored windbreaker, black cords, pale green cotton-blend shirt, crepe-soled oxfords. I looked as if I had mumps, not the clap. In Berlin I bought some jeans in my size and put them on right away. I also acquired a flannel shirt whose reddish-violet checks reminded me of the one Marina had donned *afterward.* "Flannel" rhymed with "rebel," more or less, and jeans evoked a combination of "James" and "Dean." Was I still distinguishable from a terrorist? My mother had always laid out my *garments* in the past. No more! Never again! The sentence *Mama, no need to lay out my gear from now on* was already formulated and had only to be uttered. On the way home I thought up some more shocking remarks. It wasn't difficult: *Mama, just in case I'm out tomorrow, playing a few hands of poker, one of my new pals may drop by—a guy with a mermaid tattooed on his chest. Anyway, he'll be wanting a hundred for his Sex Pistols album—I was so drunk I left it behind in a bar when we were celebrating Union's road win. Don't be scared, he's on probation, so he knows he can't afford to try anything if he doesn't want to wind up inside again.*

I studied my reflection in store windows. Was that me? Until now I'd gone around looking like a Jehovah's Witness— I never even ventured to roll up my shirtsleeves. This semi-Elvis, was that *me*? Was it really me? Incredible how a fuck could change a person. I actually went so far as to invite bronchial pneumonia by leaving the top button of my flannel shirt open. Clicking my fingers, I sang softly to myself: *Doo-wop-a-loo-bop* . . .

When my mother opened the door I detected sheer horror in her eyes: *This isn't my son!* On being asked why I'd come home so soon, I casually replied, "Oh, no special reason." I sauntered through the apartment, lounged against the door-jamb, crossed my arms and yawned without putting a hand over my mouth, flopped down in a chair, even emitted a belch—all of them acts sufficient to get me disinherited. From now on, I wouldn't bend to pick up the vacuum cleaner cord when it caught on something. I would pee in a standing position, put my feet on the table, and greet everyone with "Hi!" I would leave doors open and disregard the time-honored arrangement of the sofa cushions—and all in jeans!

I punk-walked into the living room, where my father was reading the newspaper. I said "Hi" and slumped into an armchair. In my former life I would have sat down humbly beside him and waited for him to favor me with a glance or even listen as I told him of my doings, forever prompted by the illusory hope that he would finally take me to his heart and bring himself to treat me as flesh of his flesh . . . Enough of that! Never again! Let him sit there and rustle his immensely important newspaper. My mother, deeply concerned, prowled around me on the pretext of watering her houseplants. Ah, the way she irrigated her "little plants" with her miniature watering can! The innumerable sighs she heaved at having to traverse half the apartment to refill it! The sidelong looks she aimed at her open copy of *The A to Z of Houseplants* before carefully parting the stems! The way she picked off dead leaves! The devotion with which she sprinkled the last bit of foliage like a veritable Mother Teresa of living room flora!

Ten minutes later she experimented to see if I would still come running in response to her cry of "Strong man needed in the kitchen!"—and, sure enough, I came. How relieved she was. Jeans notwithstanding, I had answered her call! I was still the same dutiful son who always jumped up unasked to turn the Mahler record over. I was even amenable enough to sit down and "treat myself" to some of the cake she'd hurriedly gone out and bought "in honor of the occasion." Well, why not? She had no further hold over me. Never again would I submit to intimidation at table—or so I thought until she said, lips trembling, "Klaus, I came across something when I was putting your garments in the washing machine."

The referral note! She'd found my clap certificate—she knew *everything*!

"Good for you," I said unsteadily. My salivary glands packed it in, my mouthful of cake went lumpy.

"Who was it?" asked my mother. "Do we know her?"

"Her name's Marina," I croaked, scattering crumbs.

"Marina who?" said my father.

"Marina Kropf."

"And what can you tell us about this Fräulein Kropf?" asked my mother.

I shrugged. What *could* I tell my parents about Fräulein

Kropf? That I'd screwed her on a kitchen table? That Fräulein Kropf had shown me the 6ual ropes? That I'd nearly torn it out by the roots in ecstasy? That Fräulein Kropf had deftly hooked her big toes into my underpants? That she even knew how to satisfy a bottle of bubbly?

"How long have you known her?" my mother demanded.

"A couple of hours," I said. The words came out in a kind of death rattle, accompanied by more crumbs. I took my mother's initial silence to mean that she'd construed my reply as meaning "Let's talk about this in a couple of hours." Then my early training asserted itself. Hadn't she always enjoined me to complete a sentence? "I mean," I amended, "we'd only known each other a couple of hours."

"A couple of hours!" She wrung her hands. "And you went to bed with her just like that?"

If only she knew! I thought. We'd done it on a surface used for slicing onions and rolling pastry.

"Well," she exclaimed, "say something!"

"Perhaps we did jump the gun a little." I couldn't endure the lump of cake in my mouth any longer, so I spit it out on my plate. There was no outcry. The matter was evidently considered so serious that even spitting out cake had paled into insignificance.

"Jump the gun?" my mother wailed. "You can say that again! Do you know where she got it from? She may have picked it up from a long-distance truck driver. Or a foreigner."

"Exactly," my father put in.

"And if he'd infected her not just with . . . but with AIDS" —oh, Mama, must you!—"you'd now be as good as *dead*!"

"Yes," I whispered hoarsely, at the end of my tether. To this day I find it miraculous that I've fucked and lived to tell the tale. My mother's one desire was to preserve me from tempting providence a second time. She meant the best for me; she always did. Joking apart, Mr. Kitzelstein, let's get to the bottom of this. What was the nature of my parents' aura? Why did their presence paralyze me? How did they contrive to treat me like a child, despite my manifest sexual experience, and reduce me to impotent silence? When would they grasp (since I never would, that much was certain) that it was *my* dick and *my* business what I inserted it in and what adhered to it when I extracted it? Would I have to shoot them both before they left me in peace?

"I've got something to say." My father's turn. It was his conscience, you know; he could remain silent no longer. His words, though aimed at me, were as usual addressed to my mother. "Perhaps Fräulein Kropf wishes to quit our Democratic Republic. Perhaps she owes it no allegiance. It's always possible—the boy scarcely knows her, after all."

I didn't trouble to dispute this, so he went on to refer to *the nasty surprises that people can store up for themselves.* "Imagine what might happen"—he continued to address my mother—"if she emigrated to the West and mentioned, in the course of her obligatory interview with enemy intelligence officers, that she was intimately acquainted with Klaus Uhltzscht, a member of our own security service. They would naturally want to know all about their affair, and that would lay him open to *blackmail!*"

My father gave me a meaningful look. What did he mean? What could they blackmail me about—my little trumpet? "Uhltzscht, we happen to know you've got the world's smallest pecker. It'll be on page one of tomorrow's *Bild-Zeitung*— unless you tell us where your agents are located." Was that what my father meant to warn me about?

"Or there's another possibility," he went on.

"Eberhard, *please!*"

"No!" my father said stubbornly. "He's making a big mistake. He grossly underestimates the enemy threat! Grossly!" I sat defenseless on my chair, feeble and perspiring, while he enlightened my mother on my own potential threat to the State Security Service. "What if she gets pregnant? She could waltz up to him and say, So you don't want to be a father? Then tell me all about your work or I'll carry the child to term and you'll spend the next twenty years shelling out."

"She isn't like that," I whispered.

"Precisely!" my father cried in triumph. "That's just it! Now do you see what I mean about underestimating the enemy? They all say, 'She isn't like that,' but afterward there's hell to pay."

"Eberhard," my mother said soothingly, "he'll never do it again."

"Let's hope not," said my father.

Meaning what? What did he hope I'd never do again?

"Well," my mother pursued in a conciliatory tone, "we won't object if, next time, you introduce the girl who may be destined to become your life's companion. Will we, Eberhard?"

My father growled "Mm"; my mother beamed. What splendid parents I had—so sympathetic! *Hello, Mama, hello, Papa, next Sunday I'd like to introduce Fräulein Rossbaum, who may be destined to become my life's companion. I met her at the museum, where she immediately caught my eye because of her spotless handkerchief. We regularly attend piano recitals, and on rainy days we browse through the encyclopedia together, but last week, when we decided to buy a copy of* Mann und Frau Intim, *we felt it was time for the three of you to become acquainted.*

All anathemas notwithstanding, Mr. Kitzelstein, I had brought off the incredible feat of lodging my diffident pecker in a superlative pussy, so why didn't I feel *emancipated*? Why couldn't I even believe in a fuck which I myself had performed? Because *they* said it was potentially lethal? Because *they* said it might harm our great national cause? Because I invariably felt I'd done something wrong even when I hadn't?

If you imagine I took my dose of clap to the Ministry's Polyclinic, you're mistaken. I might have run into Minister Mielke himself, just as I was emerging from the door marked CUTANEOUS AND VENEREAL DISEASES. Minister Mielke would suspect the worst, and not without good reason: I, his most promising recruit, the former elite student and erstwhile Nobel laureate-to-be, had the *clap*!

So where else could I go for treatment? There was an outpatient clinic in Greifswalder Strasse. Greifswalder Strasse, right in the middle of the old quarter, with its decrepit, rat-infested buildings and outside toilets! My heart sank.

I rode past the place in a streetcar before I ventured near it on foot. The exterior made a wholly innocuous impression—indeed, contrary to my expectations, there were no tertiary-stage syphilitics encamped outside with hamsters swarming all over them. The passersby gave no sign of thinking it extraordinary that there should be a point of convergence for people who went around with infected sex organs. No big red neon sign flashed a warning to pedestrians to give the entrance a wide berth for fear of bumping into persons suffering from venereal diseases.

My mode of entry: I hugged the wall, intending simply to dart through the archway and disappear. My first attempt failed because a janitor was sweeping the entrance. I walked on, but I'd already swerved in the relevant direction. What a giveaway! Had someone walking behind me spotted my original intention? If so, had he pointed me out to others? Better beat it before a knot of jeering bystanders formed in my wake. I turned down the next street and circled the block. I passed a bar. Should I have a drink? *Alcohol removes inhibitions*—just what I needed to get me to a doctor who would prescribe me some penicillin. On the other hand, everyone knew that alcohol and antibiotics interacted in ways to which little research had been devoted. There was my unusual blood count, too! Who could tell what would happen if I received a shot of penicillin under the influence of alcohol? I might be paralyzed and have to spend the rest of my days in a wheelchair, unable to do more than babble and blink. I would be wheeled into schools and displayed to the senior classes with a placard around my neck: *He had his fun heedless of the consequences.*

I made one circuit of the block, taking fifteen minutes to do so, then scuttled through the gateway. The place was deserted. Did anyone actually live here, or was it thought unreasonable, even in this seedy neighborhood, to expect innocent citizens to dwell in the temple of the venereally infected? I had to cross a courtyard. If people did live here, they probably watched the comings and goings of the clap-afflicted with malicious glee from behind their curtains, and it would be just my luck if they threw open their windows at a given signal and laughed me to scorn through megaphones. Next—I might have known it—came a flight of stairs. One always passed people on stairs. What to do then? Turn tail? Put my jacket over my head? Leaving would be less of a problem—I could always jump out of a window.

The Treatment Center for Sexually Transmitted Diseases was on the second floor. The big door was not equipped with a buzzer or an intercom; infected persons were expected to open it themselves. But the *handle*! Would I have to touch a handle used by the venereally diseased? I? With my bare hands? I, who never touched my own dick without a valid reason—was I really expected to grasp a door handle on which millions of bacteria lurked in ambush? I enlisted the aid of an envelope I happened to have on me. There was a trash can just inside the door, so I was able to discard the contaminated envelope without delay.

I found myself in a passage with ten or twelve doors leading off it. As many treatment rooms as that? Was clap so labor-intensive—so economically prejudicial, even? Did irresponsible copulation tie up manpower badly needed elsewhere in the economy? Was gonorrhea considered a form of industrial sabotage? Would I be summoned before a Party tribunal? I tapped on the receptionist's window, presented my referral note, and was assigned a number. The waiting room was far from deserted, and I had so dearly hoped to be alone—to escape the gaze of others . . . (On my next visit, a morning appointment, I had the place to myself. This merely intensified my feelings of self-reproach: to think that I alone, with my screwing-induced bacilli, was taking up the time of the people behind all those doors!)

There were chairs in the waiting room. Was I expected to park my backside where . . . Was I to sit on *these* chairs? How many stray bacteria were swarming over them? Thousands? Millions? Fifty million? There they lurked, waiting to pounce on unsuspecting patients—how insidious!

And the waiting room itself . . . Everyone knew that everyone knew why we were here, but none of us knew anything definite about the others. *Don't stare at me like that!* I entreated inwardly. *I didn't pass it on, I only infected myself! I'm innocent, innocent, innocent!* I was marooned in the company of individuals with whom I wouldn't normally have shared a railroad compartment. It was another world, the world of the venereally infected. Two leather-clad bikers were discussing the procurement of hard-to-get spare parts in loud, raucous voices. My new friends: bikers with souped-up machines who broke the speed limit in urban areas! Worse still, they were tattooed. Tattooed, loud-mouthed, clap-ridden law-breakers! In one corner sat a diminutive bodybuilder who wolf-whistled at a peroxide blonde when she passed him on the way to the treatment room. He had clap, she had clap and was ugly, with ill-fitting slacks, yet he was still on the prowl. What went on inside such people? When a dark-suited man with a briefcase under his arm entered the waiting room the bodybuilder greeted him with "Hi, boss, back from another business trip?"

Anxious to find some way of distancing myself from these proceedings, I devoted my attention to the informative VD posters on the walls, drawings more detailed than anything in our biology textbook. "You should've checked those out first," the bodybuilder told me. I blushed crimson.

The bikers took leave of each other. "Stay cool," said one, and they shook hands in some esoteric manner. "See you around," said the other. Just a minute! They were clearly old friends, so how come they'd met up *here* of all places? Had they both got their gonococci from the same woman, or had one of them infected a woman who'd passed it on to the other? Where was I? Did everyone here fuck everyone else? Was it just the neighborhood? The human condition? Had it been all in vain? If Maxim Gorky were here, would he stand by his dictum: *A human being—how proud that sounds?*

My number was called at last. I was so eager to leave the waiting room I opened the door of the treatment room barehanded. Except that it wasn't the treatment room: inside, I was confronted by a species of female social worker. I had never dreamed that I would sink so low as to become the object of welfare work in a squalid neighborhood like Prenzlauer Berg. Social workers were on a par with probation officers and rehabilitation counselors. In other words, Mr. Kitzelstein, no sooner had I withdrawn my pecker from a pussy than I needed resocializing.

The woman inquired my "probable" source of infection. *Probable?* What an insinuation! Of course I knew who had infected me: Marina Kropf, No. 18, some street or other. It was typical of my cerebral processes to have noted the number although I'd forgotten the name of the street. It had stuck in my mind because, as a former elite student, erstwhile Nobel laureate-to-be, chess player, and number fetishist, I'd thought up a numerical mnemonic as soon as I entered No. 18. "Square what we're about to engage in," I'd told myself, "namely, 6, and divide the product by the number of participants, namely, 2. Six times 6 divided by 2 equals Marina's address." That's the sort of stuff that keeps running through my head, Mr. Kitzelstein. It's a constant, ongoing, uninterrupted process, and no one has ever managed to wean me from it.

"I'll bet it was 18 *Duncker*strasse," said my social worker. She was right, I could remember Marina telling the cabby. How humiliating! I knew I was the most ill-informed person imaginable, but that my social worker should actually know the address of the woman who had made a man of me . . . Why did other people always know things I didn't? I have never grasped the full extent of my ignorance, but at moments like that I at least gain some inkling of it.

I was sent next door to see a doctor, likewise female, who *took a swab*. I had to bare my little trumpet—a pecker crawling with vile bacteria—and a strange woman touched it with her own hands, her bare hands! How much did they pay her for such a job? Or was she compelled to do it? Had she lost a bet in her last year at university? Did her neighbors know how she spent her days?

I was given a jab and sent back to the social worker, who

promptly fixed me up with another three appointments. Three appointments! Was I going to have to sit in that waiting room *three* more times? I noticed her telephone while she was flicking through her desk diary: it was *red*! A red telephone on a desk in the *center*—could it be a direct line to the Central Committee? The Ministry? Were crisis meetings now being scheduled because of my incontinent way of life? Would my sponsors lose faith in me? Would it count for nothing that I'd already received my first assignment at a conference table? Would they dump me?

I took it all so personally. I was in the *Treatment Center for Sexually Transmitted Diseases*. The very name of the establishment was like a blow between the eyes, if not worse. I mean, let the words dissolve on your tongue: my *sexually transmitted disease* was to be *treated* by a *center*. What terrible thing had I done—I who had always aspired to be the most law-abiding of citizens? Observing the laws might almost have been a hobby of mine, and now this summons to the Treatment Center for Sexually Transmitted Diseases. It was all Marina's fault! I should have known better! How could I have done it on a surface regularly in contact with foodstuffs destined for human consumption!

During one of my sessions with the social worker she invited me to sit down at a small table in the corner of her office and offered me coffee. Did I know anything about radios? she asked. She planned to buy a radio-cassette player but was a total ignoramus. I didn't understand. She was asking *me*? Why did she think it appropriate to consult my clap-ridden self about a personal matter? Was it a ruse? Had she an ulterior motive? If so, what? Why wasn't I more perceptive? Had she been instructed via the red telephone to sound me out on the subject of radio technology? I had no choice but to answer her question quite normally, on the face of it, though I remained somewhat aloof. When I mentioned the word "Dolby," she broke in and asked what it had to do with recording equipment. "It's a device for the suppression of noise from recorded sound," I told her. "How funny," she said, "I always thought it was the name of one of those mass-produced dolls they're so crazy about in the West—you know, like Barbie." And she giggled.

Was she pulling my leg? And why was she giggling as if this weren't a place of shame? I ask you, *Barbie*! When I'd finished my impromptu lecture and was at a loss to know what to say next, she glanced at her desk diary. "We can keep chatting for a while," she said. "My next appointment isn't for another half hour."

An invitation to *chat*? How exciting! I'd heard of that activity but had never known exactly what it entailed. Could one really engage in it just like that? Unbelievable! And to do so here, where . . .

No, Mr. Kitzelstein, I gave her no opportunity to chat with me. If I'd thawed out I might even have confided some of my childish misapprehensions—for instance, that a premier was a government minister who had to attend first nights, or that I'd confused foreign traders with street traders and imagined the world market to be the biggest vegetable market in the world. It might have been quite pleasant, but how *could* it have been, when I was sitting there rigid with embarrassment, not even venturing to touch her coffee?

And when I thought things had to be that way?

FEM. PERS. EMRGD. ST. 0834

Before I left Freienbrink Camp the Training Company commander summoned me to his hut, leafed through a folder, and, with the words "Your marching orders," handed me an envelope containing instructions to report to the Berlin District Headquarters of the State Security Service in a few days' time. When I did so, a "cadre officer" issued me with my ID and further instructions. "You're to go to No. 75 Rigaer Strasse, Berlin 1035, and report to the Accounts Department of the Periodicals Postal Subscription Service."

"What do I do there?"

"Not ask so many questions, for a start. You know the kind of outfit you're in."

That sounded promising, but what would I do in the Periodicals Postal Subscription Service? Wait for my special assignment? Go underground until X-Day? Lead a normal life, do the shopping, etc., until I was sent for, physically transformed by plastic surgery, and dropped on the Blue World by parachute?

According to the notice on the door, the ground floor of No. 75 Rigaer Strasse really did house the offices of the Periodicals Postal Subscription Service. I rang the bell. It was answered by a man in his mid-thirties.

"Good morning," I said. "I was told to report here."

"By whom?" the man demanded.

"I can't say." I had a problem: I didn't know who I was dealing with, the Stasi or the Periodicals Postal Subscription Service.

"Well," the man said impatiently, "what's it about?"

"I assume I'm supposed to start work here."

"Work here? With us? Are you sure?"

An older man came out into the passage. "It's all right, Martin," he called. "Let him in."

The door closed behind me, the older man simply said, "Wunderlich," and shook hands. I gather you know no German despite your name, Mr. Kitzelstein, so I'll translate: for your information, *wunderlich* means "odd" or "eccentric." I was understandably disconcerted. Had he been commenting on my appearance? Who were these men? Why didn't anyone ever tell me anything? Why was I, the Nobel laureate *manqué*, always—but *always*—left in the dark? Still holding my hand, the older man amplified his original remark: "Wunderlich, Harald, Major."

The man who had opened the door to me introduced himself. "Eulert, Martin, Lieutenant." We shook hands.

A third man had joined us in the passage. "Grabs," he said, "Gerd, Captain." We shook hands likewise.

I now felt sufficiently versed in the local conventions to say, "Uhltzscht, Klaus, Officer Cadet."

"Good," said Major Wunderlich, "but from now on you're plain Klaus. We're on a first-name basis here." Beckoning me to follow, he set off on a tour of the offices.

"You'll have noticed that it says 'Accounts Department, Periodicals Postal Subscription Service' on the door. We have to put something or people might smell a rat. We're not in the phone book, but members of the local population sometimes turn up and (a) ask us to cancel their subscriptions or (b) complain that we've invoiced them incorrectly. If they do, we redirect them to the right address. Anyone who wants to take out a subscription is given an application form and told where to hand it in."

"It has to look convincing," said Lieutenant Eulert.

"Precisely," said Major Wunderlich, handing me three transparent report covers in quick succession. "That's why I want you to commit the following to memory by tomorrow morning: (a) where the relevant post offices are situated; (b) the advance notice to be given when taking out subscriptions or canceling them; and (c) how subscribers can participate in a bank-account direct-debit arrangement." He patted a cardboard box. "In here are the forms we distribute as window dressing. Everything has to seem one hundred percent authentic."

"It's the negation of negation," said Lieutenant Eulert. "Our setup looks quite genuine but isn't. The negation of negation." He laughed. Then, in an undertone, as he was leaving the room: "Philosophy is a hobby of mine."

My new associates welcomed me into their midst. They had, for example, deferred their daily conference so as to include me, the newcomer, in their deliberations. Major Wunderlich assumed the semi-official role of my "comrade sponsor," a species of mentor or Zen master. "But we'll all look after you," he told me. Captain Grabs nodded, and Lieutenant Eulert generously cried, "Of course we will!"

The daily conference took place around a small, rickety table in a small, cramped room. Having received my initial assignment at a regular conference table, I found this somewhat demeaning.

"In the first place," said Major Wunderlich, depositing a paper bag of miniature pretzels on the table, "we always have pretzels here. It's (a) everyone's responsibility to (b) ensure that we never run out of pretzels."

"Pretzels," I repeated.

"Precisely."

There followed a lengthy dissertation in the course of which Major Wunderlich referred to (a) professional commitment, (b) unswerving loyalty, and (c) obedience to orders. If I understood him aright, he was telling me what I ought to know about the Stasi. So I really was in the Stasi—I should have known!

"Oh yes, before I forget," said Wunderlich as I was leaving the office at the end of the day, laden with periodical subscription literature, "tomorrow is our exercise day. We run a couple of laps of the stadium once a week. Be sure to bring (a) sports gear and (b) soap and towel."

Whaaat! Athletics? Here? I thought this was the Stasi—I thought I was on a historic mission! Why should I run? Hadn't I done enough running in my time? I'd spent longer running than anyone else because I always came in last and was consequently longer en route. Couldn't they take that into account and exempt me? Would it never end? *A couple* of laps? What did that mean? One lap more or less might seal my fate. What if I didn't manage to complete my laps? Where would that leave my career?

Exercise day was a dread occasion, if only because it took place in the World Youth Stadium, a vast arena. I pictured myself being laughed to scorn by tens of thousands of spectators and headlined in the *Bild-Zeitung*—EAST BERLIN MOCKS STASI'S SLOWEST SLOWPOKE—complete with photograph. The very prospect of running in such a stadium made me break out in a sweat, I felt so hemmed in and constricted by the towering stands. "Pretend the place is packed," Wunderlich told me with a sweeping gesture. "Every seat a potential spectator . . ." I sometimes spend hours picturing my prestigious appearances before cheering crowds, Mr. Kitzelstein, but never in an *athletic* context. I took up my position on the starting line, inside lane, with the laughter of sixty-five thousand nonexistent spectators ringing in my ears. Why couldn't I make a fool of myself on an ordinary track? "Do we run in a group?" I asked Major Wunderlich. His reply made my blood run cold. "Each of us runs at his own pace," he said. "Don't let us oldsters cramp your style."

By "a couple" of laps Major Wunderlich meant five. After one and a half I could feel every aching muscle, after two and a half I'd lost my will to live, and on the fourth Wunderlich overtook me. He even had enough breath to spare, as he pounded past, to coach me in bursts: "Your arms . . . too high, lad . . . They should be . . . (a) . . . lower and (b) . . . parallel to . . . the ground . . . like this!" Major Wunderlich, the oldest member of the Accounts Department, Periodicals Postal Subscription Service, was also the fleetest of foot, and he reveled in the sensation of driving himself to the limit. Stoically following far in his wake came Captain Grabs, lips compressed with the tenacity of an American Indian, eyes grimly focused on the cinder track. I did at least keep up with Lieutenant Eulert for two laps before letting him—perforce—draw ahead. "You can do it!" he exhorted me cheerfully. The frustration of it! *I* was gasping for breath, but *they* had the puff to lecture me before leaving me in their dust. I cursed my existence, my fate, and the day I was born. My one unavailing desire was not to come in last. Why did I have to humiliate myself in front of sixty-five thousand imaginary spectators?

"Excellent exercise, running," Major Wunderlich rhapsodized under the shower. Running *excellent*? The showers were filled with the sound of splashing water and echoing voices. Could I have misheard? Shampooing his balls, which were—needless to say—bigger than mine, Wunderlich went on, "And you know why? Because physical exertion causes the human body to secrete endorphins, and those create a sense of well-being. It's a scientifically proven fact."

"Keep on running," said Captain Grabs, "that's the only thing to do when exhaustion sets in. Keep on and on and on."

"Precisely," said Wunderlich. "The endorphins are a reward."

"It's the negation of negation," said Lieutenant Eulert. "You torture yourself until the feel-good factor asserts itself."

And the following week we would run another "couple" of laps. And the week after that, and so on ad infinitum.

Was I really in the genuine, legendary Stasi, or in an outfit that only called itself by that name the better to disguise the *genuine* Stasi, which would one day send for me? The genuine Stasi wouldn't expect me to memorize periodical subscription regulations or run a disastrous *couple of laps*. Whatever I was in, it couldn't be the Stasi, which was omniscient, omnideceptive, and referred to only in whispers. My colleagues were simply men who munched pretzels and exercised once a week.

On one occasion, when Major Wunderlich was reading the paper, he handed me the sports page, which bore a chronological list of the names and performances of East German record holders at 800 meters. "I know 'em all by heart," he announced proudly. "Like to test me?" When Wunderlich reeled off the East German 800-meter record holders' names and times or performed similar absurd feats, I always expected such statistics to embody some lesson for a secret-service greenhorn like me, for example that the numerical sequence of records between 1950 and 1972 formed the key to some complex cryptographic system employed by the major when transmitting clandestine radio messages from the cellars of NATO Headquarters in 1978. But Wunderlich merely recited statistics, period, and expected to be admired for his fabulous powers of recall.

"Why am I here?" I kept asking myself. I wanted to make a name for myself, I wanted to help turn the world map red, I was awaiting my first major assignment—the abduction of NATO's chief planning officer, for instance—so why on earth did I have to listen to my boss rattling off sports statistics as proudly as a six-year-old reciting the alphabet?

Gerd Grabs tended to go around with his teeth clenched. He was married to a schoolteacher and had two children, and it was his ambition that all his offspring should have monosyllabic names beginning with the letter "G." (Know what my mother said when I told her this—naming no names, of course? "All those identical initials! How do they tell their handkerchiefs apart?") Anyway, his son was called Götz Grabs and his daughter Grit Grabs. If my name were Grabs, Mr. Kitzelstein, it would be better than Uhltzscht but bad enough, and I should welcome any first name that distracted attention from what followed it. Grit Grabs . . . Sounds like a one-two punch, doesn't it? "What's your wife's name?" I once asked him. "Julia," Grabs replied sheepishly. It embarrassed the poor man that she didn't conform to his system.

Not knowing any monosyllabic first names beginning with "G" apart from Gerd, Götz, and Grit, Grabs would become more and more antsy as the birth of his third child drew near. Three weeks before it was due, while we were burglarizing an apartment in search of subversive literature, I came across a book entitled *The World According to Garp*. It was our practice when searching premises to unnerve their absent owners by effecting subtle changes in the decor. We would smash a vase, or draw the curtains, or upend a chair. Grabs was thus able, pursuant to Stasi practice, to make off with *The World According to Garp* as evidence that Garp was a legitimate first name. He failed to convince the registrar of births but was saved at the last minute by a stint as moderator of a debate at the House of German-Soviet Friendship. When one of the platform speakers—the Soviet cultural attaché, to be precise—happened to mention the name Gleb Panfilov, Grabs became very excited. Quite out of character, he seized the microphone. "*What* did you say it was, the name of that Soviet film director?" he demanded. "Gleb Panfilov, you mean?" queried the cultural attaché. Grabs's eyes shone. "Gleb?" he repeated. "With a 'G'?"

Then there was Martin Eulert, whom we called "Eule," or "Owl" ("All my friends call me Owl"). Whenever I had dealings with him, I *knew* I couldn't be in the genuine Stasi; Owl and the genuine Stasi were mutually exclusive and incompatible. Where should I begin? With his linguistic bloopers, his politicostrategic misconceptions, his pseudophilosophical interpolations, his utterly inept analogies, which he liked to introduce by remarking that one must always have an apt analogy ready to hand? On one occasion, while he and I and Raymund were conducting a surveillance operation from a car parked outside a house in Wilhelm Pieck Strasse, I asked him whom we were observing and why.

"You'll find out soon enough," Owl replied. "Observation is an end in itself. The criminal always feels an urge to revisit the scene of his crime, it's a scientifically proven fact. Besides, it's the negation of negation."

"But what *is* the negation of negation?" I said. "I've been meaning to ask you for ages."

"The negation of negation? That's easy. I'm sure you're familiar with *The Smile of the Sistine Madonna* by Leonardo. Think about it while I go off for a pee."

Where did the negation of negation come in? *The Smile of the Sistine Madonna* by Leonardo . . . I was bewildered. Did he mean the smile of the *Mona Lisa* by Leonardo or the *Sistine Madonna* (which, being my mother's son and the holder of four library cards, I knew to be by Raphael)? Had Owl confused the *Sistine Madonna* with the *Mona Lisa,* or had he saddled the *Sistine Madonna* with a smile and then confused Leonardo with Raphael? Or did he mean the Sistine *Chapel*? That would bring Michelangelo into the equation. The smile would be wrong in both cases, and Owl would have not only confused the Madonna with the chapel but mistaken Michelangelo for Leonardo *as well*.

Or was it all a deliberate, subtly constructed paradox designed to illustrate the negation of negation? (If so, Owl had confused himself with Umberto Eco.)

Pretty good, don't you agree, that piece of logical analysis (conducted during my surveillance instructor's pee break)?

I repeated my question when Owl returned. "Well," he drawled, "surely you know Leonardo's *Smile of the Sistine Madonna*? It stands in Dresden."

Was it the negation of negation to atone for one blunder by committing another? *It stands in Dresden* . . . If anything Sistine *stood,* it was the Sistine *Chapel* in *Rome.* The *Sistine Madonna* was in *Dresden,* but it *hung* in the Old Masters' Gallery and was as devoid of a smile as the Sistine Chapel in Rome. Renaissance art, freely interpreted by Martin Eulert:

The Smile of the Twelve Apostles by Pontius Pilate. Spend a few weeks sitting in a car with Owl and you would know what he meant: he had confused *The Twelve Apostles* with *The Last Supper* and Pontius Pilate with Leonardo da Vinci. As for *The Smile*, he was under the impression that all Renaissance works of art were entitled *The Smile of* . . .

I was disconcerted. "But the *Sistine Madonna* is by Raphael," I said.

"Who cares?" Owl retorted. "I can never tell those guys apart."

And now, Mr. Kitzelstein, the negation of negation as defined by Lieutenant Martin Eulert: "The painter who produced that work of art," he said with great deliberation, "was profoundly religious. Our people aren't religious anymore, but they admire the picture and delight in its beauty." He gave me a look of triumph. "That's the negation of negation."

"I see," I said dispiritedly.

"And if you want any further tips on philosophy, don't hesitate to ask me."

What more need I say, Mr. Kitzelstein, to convince you that Owl was just a sham secret serviceman, and that I was bound to believe that whatever outfit he was in, it wasn't the Stasi, or certainly not the *genuine* Stasi?

Owl couldn't bear to sit in the car for long. He often got out to stretch his legs on some pretext or other. Brimming with a self-confidence born of his philosophical erudition and the knowledge that he was "one of us," he would pace up and down in the shoes that his sense of practicalities prompted him to wear: flat shoes with non-slip soles, these being an undeniable advantage when in flight, in pursuit, or stalking a quarry. Picture a man striding proudly along in heelless shoes with non-slip soles, and there you have it: the legendary, springy, *Stasi walk.*

Owl's diction and pronunciation left much to be desired. Raymund and I took weeks to figure out what he meant by *phamphertahl,* a word he used whenever we sighted a woman taking her dog for its walk. (Owl had uttered it twenty or thirty times before we caught on.) Finally it dawned on us that *phamphertahl* was Owl's version of *femme fatale.* He must have picked it up when a genuine *femme fatale* happened to be walking her dog, and this had led him to believe that it was a term for any female dog-walker.

On some boozy occasion—a New Year's Eve party, I seem to recall—Major Wunderlich slumped drunkenly into a chair beside me, put his hand on my shoulder, and proceeded to tell me the story of Lieutenant Open-Brackets-Illegible-Close-Brackets. It meant nothing to me at first, but Wunderlich was my *comrade sponsor* and, even when tipsy, merited a hearing. So what was he blathering about? Was he broaching a forbidden subject, a secret mission that should not have been assigned me for several weeks, and then at a massive oak conference table?

"Did you know," he said thickly, "that you spend every day sitting in a car with Lieutenant Open-Brackets-Illegible-Close-Brackets?" How was I supposed to react? Take him seriously? Listen in silence? Say yes? Say no?

Wunderlich went on to relate how, ten years earlier, Owl had lost the notes he'd been keeping on a weeks-long surveillance operation. To make matters worse, he'd dropped them outside the house of the person under surveillance, a writer, who had promptly found them. Wunderlich looked at me expectantly.

"Embarrassing," I said for something to say, though I felt sure the story was fictional. Owl was stupid, but not *that* stupid.

"Jussaminute, let me finish." With one arm draped around my shoulders and his beery breath fanning my cheek, Wunderlich picked his way through the convolutions of a tale I expected to end with him dead drunk and slobbering on the tablecloth. The writer had forwarded Owl's notes to a West German magazine, which published them verbatim—except for Owl's squiggly signature, which was reproduced for all time as "[illegible]." The magazine in question, *Der Spiegel,* had splashed the story and advertised it on the cover. My heart sank, because I knew it must be true. It aroused my primal fears: *An inveterate loser of things on the cover of a Western tabloid* . . . I, too, was threatened with that humiliating fate!

On one of his next break-ins, Owl was so flustered (or so emotionally disturbed, perhaps, by justified hatred of *Der Spiegel*) that his camera slipped through his fingers and smashed a *Spiegel* (which, Mr. Kitzelstein, means "mirror" in German). To crown it all, this incident occurred in the apartment of a writer, a female one this time, and past experience boded no good: publication, scandal, humiliation . . .

"Know what we did then?" Wunderlich inquired, slurring his words. I stared at him helplessly. "We had to do *something,* after all, the woman was a writer, could've made trouble for us. A nearthquake."

A nearthquake? How did you "do" an earthquake? "I don't understand," I said.

"*You* know, a nearthquake. Mirrors can get broken when there's a nearthquake, so we decided to arrange one ourselves. Know how you arrange a nearthquake? No idea? You put a teensy-weensy little notice in the paper saying a nearthquake did a teensy-weensy bit of damage the day before.

When Madame kicks up a stink and complains the Stasi smashed her mirror, we say, Jussaminute, madame, don't you read the newspapers? Didn't it occur to Madame that a nearthquake mussa knocked her mirror off the wall? Tut-tut, we thought Madame was smart, being a writer. Didn't she realize mirrors get broken in a nearthquake?"

Major Wunderlich, an earthquake-maker? Could this burbling, inebriated, incapacitated believer in the scientifically proven sense of well-being induced by physical exhaustion, this memorizer of sports statistics and expounder of (a), (b), and (c), be the lord of the earthquake? Could he contrive solar eclipses or the resurrection of the dead? If Wunderlich could initiate newspaper reports at will, had my father really done the same for the cover of the *NBI*? Was the whole of my existence a theater set—were the Stasi the sceneshifters?

One of my first daily conferences concerned leaflets.

"Here," said Major Wunderlich, passing around the leaflet in question. "I found it in our mailbox."

It read: GLASNOST.

"The enemy are becoming more and more audacious in their hostility," said Grabs. The week before it had been "The enemy are becoming more and more hostile in their audacity."

"That proves we mustn't bury the gauntlet," said Owl. "It must have been AE Individualist again."

Turning to me, he murmured, " 'Individualist' is a code name. The 'AE' stands for Arch-Enemy."

"Agitator Extraordinary," Grabs amended.

"Antisocial Element," said Wunderlich. "Any of you know how widely this leaflet has been distributed?"

"No," said Grabs, "but we can find out."

"How do you propose to do that?" asked Wunderlich.

"Question the local inhabitants," said Owl. Like my father, he probably concentrated on the door of a streetcar when running to catch it, not on the driver.

"Very well," said Wunderlich, "let's question some of the citizens in the neighborhood: (a) policemen, (b) schoolteachers, (c) veterans of the labor movement, trustworthy comrades, and our UI's."

"Unofficial Informants," Owl enlightened me in a whisper. "They have code names, too."

"Usually connected with their occupation or something similar," Grabs amplified.

"UI's are allowed to choose their own code names," said Wunderlich.

"For identification purposes," said Owl.

"We welcome anyone who's keen to lead a double life," Wunderlich said with a Stasi smirk. "And, just so all UI's get the feeling their double lives are their own, we let them begin by choosing their own code names."

"All we do is make suggestions," said Owl, "and explain them with reference to their occupations. I always do that by means of an analogy, because I once attended a course in conversational psychology—or was it psychological conversation? Anyway, we were taught to explain everything by means of analogies. For instance," Owl went on, turning to me, "we've recruited a UI code-named UI Lens. He's a press photographer."

"That's a good code name," Grabs put in. "Why? Because every press photographer has a lens, get it?"

"Absolutely," I said. "Like, if you recruited a cook, you could call her UI Rolling Pin."

"Because there's a rolling pin in every kitchen."

"We even have a composer on our books who calls himself UI Mozart."

"Because there's a Mozart in every composer," I said lightly.

"Is there a God?" Grabs asked suddenly.

"From an objective point of view, no," said Owl. "You should have read your Lenin." He turned to me and lowered his voice. "Philosophy's a hobby of mine, did I tell you?"

"I mean, is there a UI God?" said Grabs. "I've been trying to recruit a theology student for the past few weeks. He's shaping quite well, but he still doesn't have a code name."

"UI God would make an excellent code name for a religious prig," said Wunderlich.

"Sure," said Owl. "After all, there's a God in every religious prig, even though, objectively speaking, he doesn't exist." To me, in an undertone: "That's the negation of negation."

"Think of it," Wunderlich said jocularly. "You'd be able to rendezvous with God as often as you liked."

"And he would speak unto thee," I put in as I went off to fetch some more pretzels. In the kitchen I could hear Owl vituperating against pamphleteers and their Western accomplices.

Wunderlich was holding up the leaflet when I returned. "So what about this thing?" he said. "Are we going to do something about it?"

"That depends," Grabs said after a while. "If AE Individualist is responsible, let's allow him to carry out another couple of similar operations. What we've got on him at the moment might be good for one-eight—"

"One year eight months," Owl explained in a whisper.

"—but if we give him a little more rope we can put him away for three-six."

"Hm," Wunderlich said thoughtfully.

Owl explained to me later that the longer a political

prisoner had to serve, the more it cost the West German government to purchase his freedom. The whole thing was a question of money, of *foreign exchange,* but every detainee had to spend at least a year inside—"otherwise," as Owl put it, "justice would be blind in both eyes, not just one."

"And if it wasn't Individualist?" said Wunderlich.

"If it wasn't," said Grabs, "we ought to do something about it."

"Like what?" said Wunderlich. Then an idea struck him. "Let's ask our young comrade here."

That was me. Was *I* expected to tell them how to prevent the distribution of subversive leaflets?

"Well," I said after a while, "I'd make it more difficult to reproduce such things."

"Very good," said Wunderlich. "Meaning what, in concrete terms?"

"No photocopiers or printers to be sold to private individuals."

"That's the present position."

"Slap an import ban on duplicating equipment."

"Already in place and strictly enforced."

"Access to printers in offices, etc., to be limited to a very small number of personnel."

"That's current practice."

"Seek prior approval for any large print runs and keep a record of them."

"We do that in any case."

Although I'd run out of ideas, this was the moment when I came of age in the Stasi. I simply *had* to think of something: novel forms of suspicion, hitherto unexplored areas of mistrust, measures of unprecedented severity. My historic mission was at stake!

"In spite of the import ban," I said, "can we exclude the possibility that there are printers in private hands?"

"No," Wunderlich said at length, "we can't."

"Then we mustn't sell any paper! Why should reams of duplicating paper be dished out over the counter, just like that? Who needs it in such quantities? Only a pamphleteer, not an innocent citizen!"

"I hadn't looked at it that way . . ." Wunderlich said slowly.

"But of course!" I exclaimed breathlessly. "Every blank sheet is a potential leaflet! To believe otherwise is to underestimate the enemy!"

Wunderlich turned to the others. "Did you hear that? 'Every blank sheet is a potential leaflet!' A lot of people take twenty years to learn to think like that." He made a note.

"Why do we need paper *at all*?" I cried. "For schoolchildren? The teachers can hand out sheets one by one. It's not too much to ask of them—they're public servants, after all—and if they have to sign for every ream they're issued they won't be able to salt away sheets without attracting attention."

"Printers are the weapons, but paper is the ammunition," said Grabs, who liked to formulate problems in military language. "Ergo, we must cut the enemy's supply lines."

"Exactly!" I broke in, fearful lest Grabs come up with some better idea than mine. "What do people buy paper for? Letters? Sell nothing but expensive notepaper. Give every pamphleteer a financial headache! Make twenty sheets of notepaper cost as much as a ream of duplicating paper, and we're that much nearer our objective. Of course," I said wearily, "we'll never be able to solve the problem altogether, but—"

"But we can keep on our toes and the enemy's heels," said Owl. "That's the negation of negation."

That afternoon I saw Major Wunderlich on the telephone, standing at attention, a sure sign that he was addressing his superior at the Ministry. "If we ban all duplicating paper . . . the innocent citizen . . ." I heard him say, and, "Every blank sheet is a potential leaflet. To believe otherwise is to underestimate the enemy!"

That was *my* idea! My idea had taken wing! It was being disseminated, communicated to higher authority—even, perhaps, to Minister Mielke himself! If he acted upon it, if he implemented it with vigor, *everyone* would experience its effects. I would be important at last, I would go down in history (with photograph) as the man who put an end to the leaflet scourge! Perhaps this was just the start, perhaps this would qualify me for greater tasks, perhaps my presence would henceforth grace the biggest conference tables in the country, perhaps Minister Mielke would marvel and raise his eyebrows when my proposal landed on his desk, perhaps he would inquire the source of this exceptionally novel and stimulating suggestion: Is there an ambitious, highly talented newcomer in the Stasi's ranks? *This is the idea I've been waiting for ever since I took office,* he would exclaim (no small compliment, considering that he'd been in office for more than thirty years). *Who thought of it? Send for him and be quick about it, I want to meet him at once!* And if, as custom demanded, I were granted three wishes, I would request (a) that I be sent on a secret mission to the Blue World under my new name; (b) that every page one and magazine cover celebrate my faithful return; and (c) that I at last be informed of the exact nature of my father's job.

Minister Mielke failed to send for me, but he may have had his reasons. Was it that he didn't want anyone to know that he knew me, even though I was already considered his secret weapon in the Communist-capitalist conflict? If I could eliminate the leaflet problem after only a few weeks' professional experience, almost in the twinkling of an eye, might I not hope for assignments of greater, if not supreme, importance?

I can tell you how I saw my situation. I was destined for great things, so there was, of course, a deeper meaning to all that I did. Although that meaning still eluded me, the day would come when it revealed itself. Someone had deliberately banished me to an insignificant outpost and assigned me tasks unworthy of a master spy. Someone endowed with great influence and perspicacity, someone whose desk bore a battery of telephones, someone whose hands held all the reins of power—someone who would make himself known to me when he deemed the time ripe. My part in this game was to stick it out, to fulfill my allotted role and never let on that I was a top-flight secret agent. The master of my fate was simply assuring himself of my patience and commitment, and the harsher and more humiliating the ordeals to which I was subjected, the more important my future mission. Why ask questions? Being the most ill-informed person imaginable, I was used to living in a state of nebulous uncertainty. It was enough that I and *he* (whoever he might be—Minister Mielke himself?) knew of my special status and realized that all my current experiences were merely a prelude. Someone had *plans* for me, and all the things that were happening to me now were pieces of a mosaic that would combine to form a picture and convey a meaning. I felt certain that I only had to do as I was told, and that anything more was beyond my present scope. I was waiting, and nothing I did at this time was the product of deliberate intent on my part. It wasn't *I* that burglarized, abducted, hunted, harassed, and intimidated. *I* merely waited.

At seven one November morning my doorbell rang and Owl excitedly informed me over the intercom that I had been given a new assignment and must come with him at once. That was how I had always pictured my X-Day: a routine, unheralded operation on a gray, rainy morning. Owl hustled me into his car and drove to the center of the city. We didn't speak on the way, but anyone familiar with novels and films of espionage knows that little or nothing is ever said on such occasions. Owl made for the Spittelmarkt and pulled up outside the offices of USIMEX, an export-import agency.

After a minute Raymund emerged and joined us in the car. Yes, Radiant Mouth with a "y," the devil-may-care onanist and organizer of moonlight cruises. What was up? What was his game? Why had he got in with us? Was I at liberty to disclose to Owl that we knew each other? Was this a test of my sangfroid? *(How did our most promising recruit react when confronted by an old acquaintance in the presence of a third party?)* At first I merely looked out of the window, feverishly analyzing the situation. I: outwardly calm and casual, inwardly alert and focused. A person of my caliber was simply *bound* to make it someday!

Owl drove off and turned into Leipziger Strasse. We were nearing Checkpoint Charlie. I might have guessed: they would hand me a manila envelope and allow me half an hour in which to memorize its contents. Then I would be given a false passport in a new name and some last-minute verbal instructions. Before passing the barrier I would turn for a moment, see my colleagues bidding me a clenched-fist farewell from a safe distance, and, like Teddy in the prison yard, surreptitiously return the salute. If not, it could be inserted in the film version.

Instead of bearing left for Checkpoint Charlie, however, the car turned right into Friedrichstrasse. I guessed I was being taken to Friedrichstrasse Station, where the East and West Berlin S-Bahn tracks ran parallel to each other. There was rumored to be an agents' "rathole" somewhere in the vicinity, with an insignificant-looking little door, unguarded but firmly locked, beyond which lay a dusty underground passage that led straight from an S-Bahn station to the street. So it was true, I thought: they were going to "insert" me by way of that passage. Owl must have the key to the sinister door in his glove compartment, and I would soon be boarding one of the U-Bahn or S-Bahn trains that ran beneath the city and the border guards' killing ground at ten-minute intervals. I would be lying if I said the prospect didn't excite me.

While we're on the subject of Friedrichstrasse, Mr. Kitzelstein, I shall finally reveal how, as an eighteen-year-old youth in sexual torment, I strove to get as close as possible to the forbidden West—how I tried to smell, hear, and touch it. I didn't station myself at the Brandenburg Gate, where the West was still a hundred and twenty meters away—no, I crouched over a subway ventilation shaft, so whenever a train passed beneath it, the West was only four meters from me! I spent *hours* on those subway grates, sexually tormented by my first sight of a Quelle mail order catalogue. A fellow student of mine had thrown a big party to celebrate his eighteenth birthday, and there it was, lying around in his apartment: eight hundred pages of four-color printing on glossy paper. Was *that* the West? Did the West look like a Quelle catalogue, or was there a difference between the two? The stereos! The bicycles! The cameras! I formed an entirely new picture of the West. They could do anything over there!

That socialism was historically superior to the West went without saying, but bicycles with twenty-one gears existed only in the Quelle catalogue!

From then on, I held the West in awe and spoke its name in a whisper; from then on, I was convinced that only *Western* power stations supplied a stable alternating current of precisely 50 Hz; from then on, I failed to see the joke about the man who takes half a roast chicken to the vet and asks if he can save it. Having studied the Quelle catalogue, I felt convinced of a Western vet's ability to restore half a roast chicken to health sufficiently for it to resume clucking and lay lots more Western eggs.

But the bicycles and cameras were nothing, absolutely nothing, compared to what I saw on the lingerie pages. Did Western women really look like that? Were such creatures an everyday sight in the West? Incredible! Those laughing faces, that long, wavy hair, those figures, that skin, those alluring eyes! And the eyelashes! Captivating! Breathtaking! Downright *besotting*! I positively melted. I was infatuated with them, those stupefyingly beautiful Western women. I couldn't tear myself away from the lingerie section throughout the birthday party—in fact I ended by surreptitiously ripping out four double-page spreads (an early indication of my criminosexual proclivities).

But that wasn't enough for me. I wanted to be so *near* those women I could inhale their perfume and hear them nibble on chips. But where in the East was the nearest I could possibly get to women of the West? Where save above a U-Bahn shaft in Friedrichstrasse, at a distance of only four meters! I couldn't see them, admittedly, but I did have my four double-page spreads (carefully preserved in four transparent sheet protectors). I spent hours on those grates, and every time I heard the rumble of a U-Bahn I would cast a languishing glance at the Quelle women on my four ripped-out double-page spreads and know that the train just below me was full of such creatures. I strained my nose and ears. Perhaps the train's slipstream would waft a minuscule whiff of eau de toilette in my direction. Perhaps one of the little transom windows would be open, enabling the scent of a Western woman's skin to penetrate my nostrils or a Western woman's giggle to be heard above the noise of the train. It wasn't just that they resembled the women in my transparent sheet protectors; they probably possessed those legendary G spots as well! Had I already been ruled by the perverted urges that took possession of me only a few years later, I would have raped the grates. At eighteen, however, I still had scruples.

So Owl drove Raymund and me from Leipziger Strasse into Friedrichstrasse and headed in the direction of the S-Bahn station. I felt a trifle sentimental as we passed the places where I'd wallowed in youthful fancies, the mute witnesses of my burgeoning sexuality, but I permitted myself that luxury. I was expecting to be sent through that fateful little door and into the West. Another few minutes, and I would be surrounded by Quelle catalogue beauties, by women who possessed G spots and suffered themselves to be photographed with dicks in their mouths—a poetic prospect indeed!

But we drove straight past Friedrichstrasse Station. What, no spy thriller, no Quelle women? Could we be making for another crossing point? There were two more possibilities, one in Invalidenstrasse and the other in Chausseestrasse, the continuation of Friedrichstrasse.

But no, we turned right into Wilhelm-Pieck-Strasse and my hopes of an assignment in the Blue World evaporated. After two hundred meters, Owl turned, pulled in to the curb, and switched the ignition off. Having given us each a clip-board, pencil, and paper, he lit a cigarette.

"All right," he said, expelling a plume of smoke, "keep your eyes open, both of you."

Huh? Was something about to happen? What was there to see? What did he mean?

"It all looks pretty normal to me," I said, at a loss.

"Keep your eyes open just the same," he said. "And write everything down."

We sat there for hours, saying nothing and making notes of all that happened. Nothing did happen, most of the time, but that wasn't the point. I knew it was part of my probation to endure boredom. I'd already renounced a Nobel Prize in order to pursue a career as a historic missionary; now I must show that I could possess my soul in patience, stoically and without complaint. There had to be some reason why we should sit outside this building for weeks on end, an activ-ity—no, *in*activity—that would have tried the patience of a Buddhist monk. Raymund often complained of its tedium and futility, but that I took to be a ploy designed to erode my own perseverance. Being just as smart as "them," I re-fused to be provoked and conscientiously maintained my sur-veillance while Raymund and Owl got in each other's hair.

"What are we sitting here for? Why does it take three of us to—"

"Observation is important, Raymund. There's a basic rule of detection: the criminal always feels an urge to revisit the scene of his crime."

"So what?"

"It's a scientifically proven fact. That's why observation is so important."

"Fair enough, but who's committed a crime and where?"

"Well, imagine if, one day, you had a chance to get at the

NATO Secretary-General's microfish." Owl broke off. "No, that's a stupid analogy," he amended swiftly, and produced another, but it was too late: Owl had let the cat out of the bag.

I pricked up my ears. Had he inadvertently divulged some aspect of my *real* assignment? But what did he mean? What were *microfish*? Why didn't I know the word? Was it yet another of the gaps in my knowledge? Were microfish very small fish? So small that one could see them only under a microscope? The microfish of the *NATO Secretary-General* . . . Great heavens! Had *I* been assigned to get hold of them one day? How did "they" envisage the operation? How was I to purloin a phial of the NATO Secretary-General's microfish, and what did our people want with them? Were microfish replete with DNA, genetic material from which they proposed to clone a second NATO Secretary-General? A doppelgänger to be dispatched to Brussels, where, armed with the authority of his office, he would order NATO's surrender? What a coup! Almost the whole of Europe would turn red overnight, with North America thrown in, and all without bloodshed! Was that why I had to steal the microfish, because no perfect double could be fabricated without them? Was it scientifically feasible? Could I believe it?

Of course I believed that artificial people could be fabricated, Mr. Kitzelstein; what do you expect? After all, I lived in a city traversed by a killing ground—the "death strip," as we called it—that ran right across its densely inhabited heart, not even along a river. Would I have believed *that* if I hadn't seen it with my own eyes? Beneath that death strip, day after day, U-Bahn and S-Bahn trains ran strictly according to schedule. Would I have believed *that* if I hadn't heard them myself (and inhaled the breeze of their passing)? How sinister must imaginings become before they cease to be fanciful?

Fabricating a human being was a mere bagatelle to *them*. Anyone who could drive a hermetically sealed frontier through the middle of a normally functioning city could do absolutely anything. Fabricating one measly human being would be child's play—provided *I* came up with the requisite microfish. A team of geneticists must even now be waiting for the phial in a secret underground laboratory. The rest was just a matter of days. Not a life would be lost, and I would take the salute at the victory parade up Broadway. Streets would bear my name, newspapers and magazines my likeness . . .

After work, as part of our observers' training, we compared notes. Our target, whom I judged to be in his early forties, was short and wiry and intellectual-looking. We were not told his name, just his code name, which Owl said was AE Harpoon. Why such a grisly code name? Were we keeping watch on a terrorist who wrought havoc with a harpoon? If so, would the Little Trumpeter's modern successor, when laying down his insignificant life, have to let himself be skewered by a *harpoon*? Wasn't that expecting a bit too much? I had no wish to shirk my responsibilities, but I was rather squeamish, and the thought of having my chest transfixed by a weapon that protruded from my back put a damper on my spirit of self-sacrifice. My absolute commitment was not as absolute as it had been. Or was Harpoon a metaphorical code name? Did it have something to do with "sharpness": for instance, with the official belief that the class struggle was growing steadily more *acute*? Was Harpoon someone who represented a *thorn in the flesh* of the socialist political and social system?

I didn't ask, knowing the kind of outfit I was in, but all became clear the day we were instructed to raid Harpoon's mailbox. Owl still refused to tell us his real name. All he said,

between chuckles, was "See if you can figure it out by yourselves. Our brand of humor is an acquired taste." Raymund
and I ran our eyes over the mailboxes and came across a Fred
Armbruster. *Armbruster* equals "crossbowman" in German,
so Fred Armbruster had to be Harpoon. I stood guard while
Raymund extracted the mail from the box.

"Well?" said Owl, when we were back in the car.

"Nothing much," Raymund replied. "Just a couple of
Christmas cards and a letter."

"A letter? Anything in it?"

Owl tore open the envelope. After half a minute he cast
his eyes up to heaven and passed the letter to me. "Can you
read that writing?"

"Well?" Owl asked impatiently. "Anything in it?"

"Like what?"

"Like something interesting—like where to apply for tickets for concerts and things."

"No, nothing of that kind."

"I got into a Mary and Gordy concert once," Owl said
proudly.

"No, there's nothing about tickets."

"Photograph it all the same. That goes for the postcards,
too, back and front." Owl handed me a camera and I did my
duty. "You've got to try your hand at everything once." He
stuffed the letter back in its torn envelope and told Raymund
to return it to the mailbox. A few days later we evaluated the
quality of the photographs, discussed their shortcomings, and
photographed another batch of mail addressed to Fred Armbruster. Owl timed us with his stopwatch—we were inside
the time limit—and the photographs proved satisfactory. We
never had to "collect the mail" again, as Owl put it.

After two weeks' surveillance, Raymund demanded to
know why we were watching Harpoon at all.

Owl sighed. "Look to your right," he said. "Where are we?"

"In Wilhelm-Pieck-Strasse."

"Correct. And what can you see, right on the corner?"

"A children's library."

"Correct. Now look straight ahead. What do you see about a hundred meters away on the left-hand side of the street?"

"The West German Diplomatic Mission."

"Wrong. That's two hundred and fifty meters away. What do you see at a hundred meters?"

"The youth club?"

"Correct. And what runs the full length of the left-hand side of the street?"

Silence.

"Well?"

"Apartment houses?"

"Of course! And how long do you think those buildings have been there?"

"They're new. Three or four years at most."

Then it came. Owl was Eulert, Martin, Lieutenant, once more: "Although we've done our utmost for our fellow citizens—they've got a children's library, a youth club, brand-new housing—there are, I regret to say, one or two elements in our midst who oppose our system and disrupt our communal life. They're the ones we deal with."

Owl sounded like the supervisor of a model playground: *We've got such lovely swings and such a lovely jungle gym. All the children play nicely together except Karl, who's naughty sometimes and pushes the others into the sand-box.*

Owl once more, surveying the new apartment houses: "I can't think why these scum are allowed to live in such nice apartments. They don't know how lucky they are." The very thought of them put Owl in a really bad mood. Not even the negation of negation could console him. Life was unfair.

"What has Harpoon done?" asked Raymund. "Or *possibly* done?"

"Not a clue," said Owl. "How should I know? It's immaterial, anyway. This is all about you two, not him. You've got to learn to write a surveillance report, and write it—so to speak—in a *new* language. You'll sit here until you've done it."

I stared at him. "You mean this is all to do with *language?*"

"Of course," said Owl. "What else?"

It had happened on our very first day's surveillance, ten minutes after Owl told us to keep our eyes open: *A woman came out of the building.* My palms began to sweat. What should I put down? What terminology should I use? Woman? Female person? Member of the female sex? She? How did you write down *A woman came out of the building* if you worked for the Stasi? Had she come out of a building or a five-story edifice? Had she emerged from an apartment house or the object under surveillance? Had she come out into Wilhelm-Pieck-Strasse or simply the street? And the time—was that important? How precise should I be? Would "approx. half-past eight" be good enough, or must I be accurate to the nearest minute? Or less than a minute? Or not at all? Did I have to describe the woman? Detail her appearance, her clothes? Whether she looked as if she'd had a good night's sleep? Whether she could be an ovo-lacto-vegetarian? Or ignore her altogether?

Eventually I wrote down *fem. pers. emrgd. st. 0834.*

When I had stolen the microfish—when the world was as red as I was famous—this entry in my log would be displayed in a showcase at the Museum of German History (or the Klaus Uhltzscht Museum), and tour guides would jocularly point out that everyone has to begin somewhere. All the same, Mr. Kitzelstein, don't you feel that *fem. pers. emrgd. st. 0834* betrayed a certain promise?

Every day's surveillance ended with a comparison of our notes.

"All right, Raymund," said Owl, "read yours aloud."

"Seven-fifteen: Took up position level with No. 204 Wilhelm-Pieck-Strasse."

"Klaus?"

"Seven-fifteen: Commenced surveillance of Harpoon. Location: parked outside No. 204 Wilhelm-Pieck-Strasse."

"Very good! 'Commenced surveillance of Harpoon'— very precisely worded. Raymund, yours means nothing. 'Took up position'? What were you watching, the sunrise?"

"Harpoon."

"Make a note of it, Raymund, make a note of it! Go on."

"Ten-forty: Harpoon left building accompanied by woman, thirty-fivish, flat-chested . . ." Raymund dissolved into laughter. His first log entry after three and a half hours' surveillance. He'd been waiting all day to get his little joke out. And the amateurish wording! This wasn't the Stasi, or not the genuine one.

"Stop that coarse laughter and get on with it!"

". . . flat-chested, blue jeans—"

"Why this obsession with her flat chest? We're not judging a beauty contest. If you think it's so vital to inform higher authority that the person was flat-chested, give her a code name like Salt Flats or Flat Battery. For the last time, Raymund, stop that coarse laughter, this isn't a burlesque show! Unless, of course, you'd like to make an inventory of the contents of Harpoon's garbage can? We'll see who laughs then. You wouldn't be the first cadet I've seen knee-deep in garbage."

Raymund drew a deep breath. "All right, woman, mid-thirties, Levi's, umber jacket—"

"We don't say Levi's—this isn't America. We say blue denim trousers. And your colors! They're an absolute disaster! Her jacket wasn't umber, it was ocher."

"It was umber."

"This isn't an art college! For service use we have a color guide containing thirty-nine standard shades. *Umber* doesn't exist! The color in question is *ocher*! What you call it for your personal amusement is your affair." Owl lit a cigarette. "Confront our comrades with wholly utopian colors, to coin a phrase, and the result would be chaos. Let me illustrate what I mean with an analogy. On that course I attended—conversational psychology, or was it psychological conversation?—we were always taught to illustrate our points with an analogy, so here goes: Imagine you've got to describe the appearance of a football team, Bayern Munich, for example, because they're playing an East German team in the European Cup. We'd need some soccer strips in our opponents' colors, but that would be impossible unless you'd defined them in advance, exactly according to the color guide. If everyone employed his own definition, our comrades would only get confused."

"Why would we need some Bayern Munich strips?" asked Raymund.

"Well . . . For substitutes, for example."

"Substitutes?"

"Yes, substitutes. Send one of our boys onto the field in a Bayern Munich strip and Bayern wouldn't know him from their own." Owl broke off, floored by his own cock-eyed reasoning. "Well, maybe that wasn't a good analogy," he conceded, "but you know what I'm getting at."

"Besides," said Raymund, "you wouldn't have to keep Bayern under surveillance, you'd only have to watch them on TV."

"I wouldn't advise it," I said, seeing a chance to score some more points. "Everyone knows our adversaries use the electronic media for disinformation purposes."

"Surely not where soccer strips are concerned?" Raymund protested.

"We must be careful not to underestimate the enemy," I retorted, giving Owl a look that invited him to arbitrate.

"I already said it wasn't a particularly good analogy," said Owl, disheartened. Owl wasn't Wunderlich, but if the major got to hear of my remark he would sing my praises again. *A lot of people take twenty years to learn to think like that . . .*

Besides, someone obviously had plans for me. Our present activities couldn't be as pointless as they seemed. Color guides! Soccer strips! Substitutes! Such an absurdity was inconceivable. There had to be some plan behind it all.

Owl would read out his own surveillance log at the end of every day and gaze at us triumphantly when he was through.

"I'll never get the hang of it," said Raymund.

"Don't worry," said Owl, "you will sooner or later." One could almost see the burden of responsibility weighing him down. "I mean, that's why you're sitting here."

It must also have been the burden of responsibility that prompted him to share the fruits of his experience with us. Our return journey in the evenings was almost always held up by the traffic lights near the Friedrichstadtpalast. Owl gestured at the surrounding area. "I once did a long-term surveillance job here," he said with a sigh. "It was hard to leave the place: a shit house nearby, a hot dog stand just across the street, and a big parking lot where the pedestrians-only mall is now. We could position the car so we didn't have to crane our necks. You'll appreciate the value of a spot like this once you've done a couple of weeks' surveillance."

"We have already," I said.

"A couple of months, then," said Owl, yawning. "Or years."

I never prostrated myself in Friedrichstrasse and raped a ventilation shaft. No, but I did spend many a cold winter night in Chausseestrasse, the continuation of Friedrichstrasse, on the lookout for a fuck. Raymund had told me to station myself there, and Raymund knew what was what. Besides, he cited reasons that were as plausible as the reasons for his moonlight cruise idea: cabbies did it, and if anyone knew his way around, it was a cabby. What exactly did the cabbies do? They lurked outside dance halls like the Altberliner Ballhaus or Klärchens Ballhaus, and when the chairs were stacked and a lone woman hailed a cab you could generally assume she was lamenting her solitary state and the fact that her charms were waning and that life bore no resemblance to a romance novel. What she needed then was a comforter, a fast worker, a torero. It seemed so obvious, I couldn't imagine why I hadn't thought of it myself.

I settled on the Altberliner Ballhaus, an establishment at the back of a courtyard in Chausseestrasse, and waited outside for nights on end, shivering as I listened to the thump of the band and titillated myself with the thought that the place was jam-packed with women in heat while U-Bahn trainloads of Western females ran past four meters beneath my feet. Where was there another such place in the whole of the Eastern Bloc? I was at its raunchiest, most infamous point, the *sexual epicenter* of the Warsaw Pact! Only nineteen, and already so far gone in depravity!

My chilly vigil lasted, as I have said, for nights on end. I never had more than a few seconds in which to make up my mind. The clock started ticking as soon as the door to the courtyard opened, and my chance was gone once the potential fuckee got in a cab. I was simultaneously assailed during those thirty seconds by all the reasons why I shouldn't do it: *How low you've sunk—you, the glorious Cover Picture! Imagine lurking in a backyard for the sole purpose of picking up and screwing some female regardless of her age and fighting weight! It'll be goodbye to your career, goodbye to your secret mission. Look at that one, notice how scrawny she is, she's bound to have AIDS. Besides, she looks so nervous she'll scream blue murder if you accost her and they'll arrest you. Think where your last fuck landed you—think what your parents would say if they knew their son was so recklessly ignoring their advice! Another thing: how do you know this really is a dance hall and not a Stasi front like USIMEX or the Accounts Department of the Periodicals Postal Subscription Service?*

And when the cabby drove off with his prey, I would castigate myself in a different vein: *Idiot, why stand here twiddling your thumbs all night? You didn't come here to watch cabs drive off, so be a man—do what you came for and never mind about AIDS, you've got your three-pack. Forget about the VD clinic, your social worker was very nice—another dose of clap will mean a pleasant reunion with her—and don't worry about blighting your career, earn yourself a reputation as a stud and the Minister will find it all the easier to decide to unleash you on the enemy's secretary-*

receptionists. To hell with your inhibitions: the only cure for fear of flying is flying, so what are you waiting for? You're standing, on Raymund's recommendation, at the Red World's sexual epicenter . . .

It would simply have to be the first woman who emerged—provided she emerged on her own; that was the sole criterion. But if a woman couldn't pick up a man, argued the skeptic in me . . . On the other hand, it was now or never. Unless they left the dance hall in squealing, yacking groups, most of the women were escorted by men who cracked such lousy jokes that it made even an outsider (me, for instance) want to throw up. So I awaited my opportunity like a chronicler of human inadequacy.

I'm not making any excuses: *the full moon was shining brightly when it happened.* She came stumbling doggedly across the courtyard, as short and plump as an assortment of charcuterie—hence the name she bears in my memory: the Sausage Woman. I wouldn't care to guess her age. I was nineteen, and she . . . No! No, I'd sooner not speculate, but it's still my fervent hope that her fortieth birthday wasn't too many years in the past.

I went up to her. "Well, well, all on your lonesome?" I inquired, though I already knew the answer: *Yes, because I'm a frustrated mouse of a stenographer who spends her nights watching TV till it goes off the air and who eats too much candy.* She looked up at me with an artless expression, too tipsy to reply. I put my arm around her cellulite. "In that case . . ." I said, looking down at her. It was her last chance to shout "Help!" or the like, but she gazed at me longingly and fluttered her nonexistent eyelashes. Before we could engage in kissing or some other distasteful activity, I proceeded to bear her off: that's to say, I maneuvered her out of the courtyard. Draping her sausagelike arms around my neck, she tottered along beside me with a look of gratitude, as if I'd just rescued her from a fire. It was like a scene from a disaster movie.

We traveled to our love nest by streetcar. While waiting at the stop I had to whisper sweet nothings and permit myself to be smothered with kisses. Could she hear wedding bells, I wondered.

Well, I told myself, if I could do it with her I could do it with anyone. Screwing Marina had been an unadulterated pleasure, but how was I to convince my superiors that I could make it with *any* of the enemy's secretary-receptionists? I would cross the nausea barrier with the Sausage Woman; to do anything else would be to underestimate the enemy.

After twenty minutes in the streetcar, we got out at Bornholmer Strasse. Clasping me in her arms once more, she steered us in the requisite direction by throwing her weight from side to side like a loose barrel rolling around on deck.

She lived on the second floor. The sight of the fretwork sign on her door—WIPE YOUR TOOTSIES—suddenly brought home the full enormity of what I had in mind. Was I really going to fuck a woman who nailed WIPE YOUR TOOTSIES to her door? Would I really let my Red Soap region be engulfed by the pussy of a total stranger, an inebriated dance-hall habituée more than twice my age? There were also the verbal connotations that inevitably occurred to the holder of four library cards: "wipe" recalled "swab," and "feet" was a euphemism for "genitals," so "wipe your tootsies" could be interpreted as "swab your dick." Who else had crossed this threshold after wiping his tootsies, and how could I be sure that his occasion for doing so was other than mine? Again, why should she take the trouble to nail WIPE YOUR TOOTSIES to her door if she didn't receive a whole host of visitors?

Be that as it may, a few minutes later I was installed on

her couch with my face buried in her shoulder, where I could feel safe from her kisses. Simultaneously, my roaming hands summoned up visions of every kind of sausage. I untied the bow on her blouse. She unzipped my fly and burst out laughing.

"My," she said, still laughing, "what a shrimp." Embarrassing, really embarrassing.

"Do something," I panted lecherously. "It'll soon get bigger."

She continued to stare at it and laugh.

"Well, carry on, do something," I moaned in her ear, nuzzling her in the hope of coming across an erogenous zone, but she merely giggled. I unhooked her brassiere, fumbled with her breasts—the word "pudding" flashed through my mind—and waited for an erection to manifest itself. Nothing happened. My intimate physical reflex was not what it had been. "Go on," I panted, still at pains to summon up a ruttish tone of voice. "Go on, grab hold!"

She sat there, allowing me to palpate her breasts a moment longer, then said, "Oh, leave me alone."

"What do you mean?" I said. "Go on, do something!"

Her only response was a sulky "No!" She proceeded to do up her blouse. Did that mean that all the kisses I'd endured were to no avail—that I'd allowed myself to be sexually abused without being able to indulge in some sexual abuse myself? It wasn't fair! Besides, she was drunk, and alcohol removed inhibitions, *dozens* of scientific experiments had proved it. As for me, had I shivered through countless winter nights in vain? She was a *wallflower*! No one had picked her up and borne her off, only me. I'd whispered sweet nothings—I'd even murmured an amatory poem in her ear (claiming that I'd composed it for her personally). The romantic requirements had been fulfilled, so why couldn't she bring herself to fuck (any more than I could)? Panic overcame me. "Besides, there's a full moon tonight!" I exclaimed. "It's . . . it's a scientifically proven fact . . ." I was horrified. What was the matter with me, blurting out meaningless phrases? It had never happened to me before. Could I be in love?

She continued to get dressed. That was when I pounced on her.

"Gedoff me," she snarled. "Leave me alone!"

We went rolling across the floor. I don't know why—perhaps because I'd always thought of sex in terms of a wrestling match or some such strenuous activity as loading sides of beef—but I suddenly developed an erection.

"Well?" I said, standing up to display my hard-on. "Okay now?"

"Get lost!" she snapped.

What! Did this aging, sausagelike, wipe-your-tootsies woman, who had left the Altberliner Ballhaus alone and was in an alcoholically disinhibited condition, propose to spurn me, a young and lustful Nobel laureate *manqué*, a Cover Picture with hard-on ready for action?

"Hey!" I said. "We can do it now."

She looked at my tumid dick and laughed derisively. I swooped on her again, but she kicked and struggled. This made me even wilder, and I only hoped that she wouldn't have a renewed urge to bury her tongue in my mouth.

"No!" she gasped. "Don't want to! Gedoff me!"

I had hauled her brassiere off and was wrestling with her skirt. The way she was struggling, it would take me quite a while. Then would come her panties. It was while I was working out my *modus operandi* that a sudden thought struck me: What were we doing? What was *I* doing? I was in the act of forcing a woman to have sexual intercourse against her will! She had said *No!* She had said *Don't want to!* What would the state prosecutor call that? *Rape!* I was in the act of raping a woman! I a rapist! My composite picture would be in all the papers, and at the lineup at police headquarters she would level her finger at me and cry, "That's him!" Every policeman in the building would find some pretext to pass my cell and sneak a look at the nineteen-year-old violator of a forty-something human sausage. Psychologists would compete to obtain their doctorates with dissertations on my case. And my parents! What would they think of me?

It was the thought of my parents that prompted me to stop short. What a dutiful son I was! *Mama, Papa, I was in the middle of raping a woman last week when I remembered how much you disapprove of such activities, so I stopped raping her at once.* What parents wouldn't be proud of a son like me?

I snatched up my clothes, fled barefoot, and got dressed outside the door. Although I wasn't acquainted with the legal niceties, I guessed that the worst offense I could be charged with was *attempted* rape. I hadn't parted with a single one of my fifty million microfish. Would my parents forgive me? Would they at least send me an occasional package in prison? Would they read my despairing letters? *Mama, as long as AIDS can't be transmitted by kissing, your son is definitely in the clear. Papa, your son won't have to face a paternity suit.*

So there I stood in the hallway, Mr. Kitzelstein, trying to get dressed but afflicted with a recalcitrant hard-on that itched for action after so many weeks of waiting on cold winter nights. And somehow I sympathized with it—a stiff prick is only human, after all. Thanks to my four library cards, I tended at such moments to be suddenly reminded of the great poetic works of mankind, for instance, the *Odyssey,* in which our hero could not afford to consort with the Sirens because they would have spelled his doom. His only recourse, as you're doubtless aware, was to grind the mast he was lashed to. Grind the mast . . . I ran up the stairs, right to the very top. The door to the roof was locked, so I took up my position on the topmost step and—*whack-whack-whack*—whacked off. *Mama, Papa, please! Before you scold me, remember I was only masturbating as an antidote to rape!*

The viscous droplets—the first microfish I had ever deliberately summoned forth—flew down the stairwell and landed with a soft, spattering sound that lingers in my memory to this day. Instantly, my conscience pricked me again: had it been worth risking all for the sake of those few little droplets? I would be done for if the Sausage Woman had called the police and said *I've just been indecently assaulted by a man in my own apartment, come quick, he's still on the premises.* The police would arrest me for exhibitionism and attempted rape—they would read me my rights and lock me up in a cell full of tattooed miscreants. My double life would come to light: by day a respectable citizen and loyal member of the Stasi; by night an outlaw, a violator of women and besmircher of stairways. Scene-of-crime officers would scrape millions of telltale clues off the stairs, and when the forensic scientist looked up from his microscope, thoroughly dismayed, he would utter the dreadful sentence *This could have been a human being.* My selfish emission could have been *a human being—how proud that sounds*—"our own little darling," a winsome toddler who delighted in blowing dandelion puffs and did all kinds of cute things and was always being photographed for the family album. But no, *my* genes were courtroom material.

The criminal always feels an urge to revisit the scene of his crime . . . Back home I plumbed the depths of my psyche:

Did *I* feel such an urge? Yes, I did! The top step was the scene of *my* crime, and once back there—what can I say?— I pulled it out again! Why? What would I tell the court-appointed psychologist? What would I tell the judge, my mother, the Minister? Those, Mr. Kitzelstein, were the very specific questions that ran through my mind whenever I returned to the Sausage Woman's building—not once but innumerable times—and polished my trumpet. And my *trepidation*! The Sausage Woman might have preferred charges against a person unknown! I might be a would-be rapist sought by the police, a dangerous sex offender whom no one—least of all myself, being the most ill-informed person imaginable—knew what to expect of next! Perhaps my description was posted in every police station, perhaps the house had been under surveillance for weeks, perhaps it was already surrounded!

Don't ask me why I returned to the scene of my crime— how should I know? For one thing, it was a scientifically proven tendency; for another, I was on the way to becoming a sex offender, and a sex offender's actions are unpredictable by definition. But I was afraid nonetheless—afraid of discovery—and my fear distracted me. A vicious circle: fear prolonged the masturbatory process, which increased the likelihood of discovery, which intensified my fear, which spoiled my concentration, which prolonged the masturbatory process . . . It was a miracle I ever made it at all, but I swear that I always ended by shooting my wad down the stairs. Any other masturbator would have given up long ago; me, I continued to beat my little drum without flagging. In my fear of being discovered and arrested, I worked on the speech that would justify my actions to the Minister when he summoned me to his office, showed me the headlines in the Western tabloids, and hauled me over the coals.

Comrade Minister—whack-whack-whack—*permit me to point out*—whack-whack-whack—*that it was, so to speak, my proletarian duty*—whack-whack-whack—*because my superiors had hinted*—whack-whack-whack—*that I might be assigned*—whack-whack-whack—*to steal the NATO Secretary-General's microfish*—whack-whack-whack—*and to gain some idea of how long it would take*—whack-whack-whack—*given that I might have to drug him first*—whack-whack-whack—*you'll understand, Comrade Minister*—whack-whack-whack—*that I decided to time the operation in advance*—whack-whack-whack—*by producing some microfish of my own.* —whack-whack-whack—*Why did I do this in a stairwell, of all places?*—whack-whack-whack—*Because, Comrade Minister, I did it there for the first time*—whack-whack-whack—*when I'd very nearly committed rape.* —whack-whack-whack—*I stopped when I became aware of the consequences.* —whack-whack-whack—*I was not only leaving myself open to blackmail*—whack-whack-whack—*but underestimating the enemy*—whack-whack-whack—*and risking a paternity suit*—whack-whack-whack—*which would have harmed our common cause*—whack-whack-whack—*and had to be avoided at all costs.* —whack-whack-whack—*To repeat: no rape occurred*—whack-whack-whack—*so the public prosecutor can only charge me with attempted rape.* —whack-whack-whack—*That being a crime in itself, however*—whack-whack-whack—*a basic criminological principle entailed*—whack-whack-whack—*that I felt an urge to revisit the scene of my crime.* —whack-whack-whack—*What else could I do?*—whack-whack-whack—*Had I not returned to jerk off there*—whack-whack-whack—*I would have invalidated my training.* —whack-whack-whack—*The nonsense my instructors have taught me*—whack-whack-whack—*which thousands of my colleagues have also learned over the years*—whack-whack-whack—*would have been rendered null and void.* —whack-whack-whack—*I couldn't impair the quality of our training* —whack-whack-whack—*that's why I continually returned to the scene of my crime.* —whack-whack-whack—*The criminological principle remains valid.* —whack-whack-whack—*My ejaculations are legitimate*—whack-whack-whack—*and underscore the validity of our faith in Marxism-Leninism.* —whack-whack-whack—*So you see, Comrade Minister*—whack-whack-whack—*that far from being a dirty pig*—whack-whack-whack—*I'm jerking off*—whack-whack-whack—*for socialism*—whack-whack-whack—*and the humanist tradition.* —whack-whack-whack—*You need only think of Odysseus.* —whack-whack-whack—*I'm jerking off to equip myself to steal the microfish*—whack-whack-whack—*and uphold the validity of a criminological principle.* —whack-whack-whack—*My masturbation has been purely patriotic.* —whack-whack-whack—*I've never jerked off for personal pleasure.* —whack-whack-whack— *What's more, I do it in my spare time*—whack-whack-whack —*without payment.* —whack-whack-whack—*So permit me, Comrade Minister, to . . .*

And then I finally came.

I was prepared for anything—discovery, arrest, conviction, derision, dismissal, castration, page one publicity, disinheritance, or all at once—but not for broken bones. One night the timed-switch light on the stairs went out just as my wad shot over the banisters and landed lower down. Well, it was my custom to dab my overheated piston with a towelette, thereby imbuing it with the scent of a meadow in springtime. Bereft of the light I required for that procedure, I groped my way downstairs, slipped on a millionfold blob of microfish, and fell, fracturing my left thumb and right wrist. My pants were down, my pecker was exposed, my scented towelette still nestled in its sealed envelope—and both my hands were out of commission! Any man worthy of the name would have committed suicide by holding his breath, but I, my mother's pampered son, was incapable of such fortitude. I writhed and rolled around on the stairs for all of ten minutes, but not in pain alone—I mean, *you* try hoisting your pants the vital few centimeters without the aid of your hands! And my fly? What was I to do about my open fly? Waltz into a hospital emergency room with my pants gaping? Ask some respectable male citizen to zip me up? I might pick on an inveterate homophobe, a brutal type who had always sworn to pulverize the first person to proposition him in such a way, and I couldn't defend myself, not with *those* hands. Or should I go back upstairs and make myself known to one of the Sausage Woman's neighbors? It was ten o'clock on a dark night. How would a woman react at this hour and on these premises, so recently the scene of an attempted rape, if asked to manipulate a panting stranger's zipper? She might instantly call for help (the most sensible course of action in the case of an unpredictable sex offender like me) and bring a lynch mob down on me. What if I made my exit and rang the first doorbell I came to? Better not: it would be bound to be answered by a woman, and with similar results. Or how about simply requesting the help of a group of people waiting at a streetcar stop? There would be *spectators,* though! How could I, who valued my privacy too much even to use a public urinal, bring myself to have my fly zipped up in public? Everyone would *stare,* wondering what my "game" was, and even if someone believed and took pity on me, I would spend the rest of my life avoiding *witnesses.* I would have to emigrate to Australia or Togo or, best of all, to some unknown country founded for my exile's sake alone. If not, someone might at any moment cross my path and destroy my career by saying, *Excuse me, haven't I seen you before somewhere? Ah yes, you're the man who walks around town with his fly open and asks strangers to zip it up for him . . .*

In the emergency room I posed as the victim of an icy sidewalk, a cunning lie but one I hoped would pass muster because I doubted the existence of an injury pattern typical of falls on semen-coated stairs. Although I couldn't incorporate my open fly in this fiction, it was my incredible good fortune that no one in the emergency room gave it a second thought. I left the hospital incapacitated by plaster casts on both arms. On taking my temporary disability certificate to the Accounts Department of the Periodicals Postal Subscription Service, I was asked by Major Wunderlich what had happened. "Slipped and fell," I mumbled, which wasn't even a lie. Wunderlich was enchanted: "That gives me a brilliantly simple idea!" he exclaimed. Injured hands were more effective than handcuffs, he went on. If only our dissidents could have their bones neatly broken in some way . . . People with both hands out of action couldn't print leaflets or accompany subversive songs on the guitar, piano, or accordion—they couldn't even pick up a phone.

If I'd told Major Wunderlich the truth about my accident, would he have assigned me to bespatter the staircases of all our civil rights activists? I would have done so gladly. It had always been my ambition to jerk off legitimately, in the interests of historical progress, and my fifty million microfish wouldn't be simply discarded and forgotten—no, their death would acquire some *meaning*! They would be dying for our cause, like the Little Trumpeter!

But the biggest miracle occurred when I got home: my

parents refrained from asking how I'd smashed up my hands—that's to say, they did ask *once*, but I discreetly dodged the question. "I'd rather not talk about it," I said, and they nodded understandingly. Oh, Mr. Kitzelstein, wasn't it wonderful, being in the Stasi? In a home where my first self-induced orgasm was regarded as attempted suicide coupled with high treason and grounds for a brainwashing session, it was suddenly sufficient to murmur such meaningful remarks as "Surely you can figure it out for yourselves" or "You know where I work" or "I can't tell you *everything* these days, please understand." No outraged exclamations rent the air. No cry of *Our son has abnormal tendencies!* ever traveled from kitchen to living room. I was spared such reproaches as *How could you do this to us!* or *Words fail me!*; nor was I reminded that I had committed a penal offense and laid myself open to blackmail—no, I was a front-line soldier on convalescent leave.

Mama baked me the most delicious cakes and took time off to look after her "child," forever stressing that I was her child and would always be so, even as a sixty-year-old. In fact, *child* was putting it mildly. I was helpless as a *baby*. I couldn't even manage by myself on the john. How could I, without *her* assistance? How old had I been, the last time I sang out, "Mama, I'm finished!" Four? Five? I was nineteen now, but when Mama responded to my call she didn't pull my pants up right away, oh no! Armed with a container of the baby powder that was as ubiquitous in our apartment as ashtrays elsewhere, she hurried to the scene and inspected my dick, turning it this way and that with her fingertips. What was she looking for? The signs of chafing that would brand me a habitual masturbator? Why did she powder me—can you think of a reason, Mr. Kitzelstein?

"Mama, why—"

"It can't do any harm." What sort of answer was that? Did she powder me because baby powder belonged, as a matter of principle, on a baby dick like mine? At least she refrained from fetching the encyclopedia from the bookcase and looking up → TALCUM, the main ingredient of baby powder.

Then as now, I simply didn't understand her. She painted the lethal dangers of copulation in the most glaring colors—fair enough; but why, on the other hand, did she prompt me to examine my innermost self by asking, in a hopeful tone of voice, if I found Katarina Witt 6y? Would fucking Kati have been considered innocuous? Don't dwell on this or look for any deeper meaning, Mr. Kitzelstein, but why did I get up at half-past two in the morning to watch female skaters going through their Olympic paces? Because, ever since Marina, I'd taken a secret interest in athletically gifted girls. Did they, too, do it on the kitchen table? Could they, too, without looking, pull down underpants with their big toes?

Well, the night took a surprising turn. When, after Kati's free-style program and before the marks were announced, we were shown a close-up of her coach, Jutta Müller, my mother began to rhapsodize: "What a fascinating woman! I don't know how she does it, but she really gets her students to perform!" Well, really! I dreaded to think exactly what that fascinating woman did to make her students "perform." To crown it all, my mother prefaced every artistic impression mark with a cry of "6! 6! Come on, 6!"—and this in front of a TV screen normally frequented by Dagmar Frederic! That did it: I couldn't restrain myself any longer. Three minutes after she'd asked me if I found Katarina Witt 6y and a few seconds after she'd pointed out that Jutta Müller got everyone to perform, she cried, "6! 6! Go on, 6!" Well, Mr. Kitzelstein, you can inform Jutta Müller that in 1988, at a range of over ten thousand kilometers, she made a nineteen-year-old youth "perform." Now you know it all. It wasn't Dagmar Frederic, or the Sausage Woman, but Jutta Müller who was the doyenne of my sexual interest. Any older than that, and women left me cold.

The removal of the plaster casts meant that I at last had both hands free to lose things with. A mere twenty minutes after my release I left my wallet in a phone booth and headed in blissful ignorance for home, where my mother, solicitous as ever, fussed over me.

"Klaus, where's your disability certificate? I want to see it. They certified you unfit for work for longer than six weeks. That puts you in an entirely different legal category. A defective disability certificate is no laughing matter, it could have serious repercussions. You're still a trainee, you wouldn't notice them till later on, but by then it would be too late, you'd have no proof. Better let me make sure it's all filled out correctly. Come on, show me your disability certificate, there's still time. After all, I know what a disability certificate should look like."

"It was the Charité, Mama! They must know how to make out a disability certificate!"

"Don't give me the Charité, I know what I'm talking about. That hospital's so vast they can't keep track of things—they could easily have forgotten to add a signature. I'm not insinuating anything or accusing anyone, but you never know, so show me your certificate."

"Mama . . ."

"Why are you making such a big deal about it? And why don't you take this seriously? I just don't understand you sometimes. You're only storing up unnecessary problems for yourself. Think of all the running around you'll have to do to get your pension rate worked out."

There we have it, Mr. Kitzelstein. Without that piece of paper I could kiss my pension goodbye. I would have to await my demise in an unheated apartment wearing Social Security dentures of the very poorest quality. Faced with that prospect, I decided to show her my disability certificate after all— if I could find it.

"Mama," I said, "I think I've lost it."

"Whaaat! *Lost* it?"

"I think I put it in my wallet. And my wallet . . ."

My father came storming into the room. "What is it now?" he demanded.

"Klaus has lost his disability certificate and everything," she groaned.

"Your ID as well?" asked my father, looking at me sternly.

"No, I've got that," I said, feeling like a little boy again. The loss of my wallet had instantly immersed me in a caldron of seething passions: murder and revenge, guilt and atonement, crucifixion and resurrection. As for the deep-seated fears latent in that ambiguous "Klaus has lost his disability certificate *and everything* . . ." I stood there naked, bereft of my disability certificate, my transit pass, my library cards. If they fell into the wrong hands, the liability for any books withdrawn would be mine! I'd signed the conditions of membership; if I couldn't pay, my salary would be docked. I would have to bite the bullet for decades, getting nowhere fast, until I finally retired on the *minimum pension rate*—and all because I'd lost my disability certificate in March 1988 . . . I'd mislaid my wallet and my life was in ruins. How could I behave so casually when I'd lost *everything*!

Everything except my Stasi ID.

"Where is it?" asked my father.

"In my coat."

"Let's see it!"

"But it's there. I always keep it in my coat—on its little cord, the way it says in regulations."

"Let's see it all the same."

I showed it to him.

"Were there any checks in your wallet?" my mother asked.

"No."

"What about your civilian identity card?"

"Yes, that was there."

"With your checks and your identity card someone could clean out your bank account!"

"But there weren't any checks, Mama."

"You never know," said my father.

"You must call the bank at once and cancel them!" said my mother, darting to the phone.

"But—"

"It can't do any harm." The argument she'd used a few days ago, when dusting my dick with talcum powder! She proceeded to look up the number of the bank in the phone book, wasting precious minutes in which whole shelves could have been emptied on the strength of my library cards.

"Was there anything in your wallet to indicate, well, you know . . ."

What? That I was in the Stasi?

"No."

"Are you sure?"

Another question that always annihilated me, whatever the context in which it was uttered. How could I ever feel sure of *anything* in the presence of those two? I couldn't even be sure of being Klaus Uhltzscht, the son of Lucie and Eberhard, while I remained uncertain whether they had ever had it off together. If I didn't know for sure I was me, how could I know for sure what was in my wallet? *Are you sure?* What a question! As long as my existence was only hypothetical, all else was pure conjecture.

I said nothing.

"Well, what *was* in there?" my mother insisted, still feverishly leafing through the telephone directory.

"Some money, eighty marks or so. My identity card, my transit pass, my library cards . . ."

"*Then call the libraries,* for heaven's sake!" wailed my mother, and handed me the receiver.

"Which should I call first, the libraries or the bank?"

"Both! What else did you have in there?"

"Two appointment cards." One from the dentist, the other from the VD clinic. "A shoe repair ticket . . ."

"Then call the shoemaker, too."

"Really, Mama, that's going a bit far."

"These appointment cards," my father put in, "is there anything . . ." He left the sentence unfinished. What was he getting at, the VD clinic? How did he know—had he checked the contents of my wallet? My mother retrieved the telephone and discreetly turned away. Oh yes, she certainly knew how to humiliate me with one of her *considerate gestures.*

"What do you mean?" I asked my father in a pallid voice.

"Is there a stamp on the appointment cards that indicates . . ." What? That I'd caught a dose of clap? Oh, Mr. Kitzelstein, there it was again, that atmosphere: Klaus the Clod was desperately trying to understand his parents. What was my father getting at? What did he mean, and why should I think myself cloddish for failing to interpret his nebulous allusions? Why didn't I punish him with a long, mute stare instead of trying to read something in his eyes that might help

me decipher them? I was probably looking so dumb and confused that he couldn't but tell himself, yet again, what a miserable failure I was.

"Did the appointment cards have anything to do with the
Ministry's Polyclinic?" my father demanded irritably. So that
was it! Being as considerate as he was, he only wanted to
remind me, not too urgently, that I was in the Stasi.

I summoned up my last reserves of energy. "No," I said.

My mother beckoned me with the receiver and put her
hand over the mouthpiece. "The bank," she murmured. I instructed the bank to cancel the checks I hadn't yet lost, then
dialed the first of my four libraries. The line remained engaged for a solid twenty minutes, time enough for me to tell
myself that the librarian must have taken her receiver off the
hook for convenience' sake while processing a mountainous
stack of books requested by the tattooed ruffian who had
found my wallet . . .

I also called the shoemaker. We experienced communi-
cation problems.

"Of course," he assured me, "you'll get your shoes back
even if you can't produce a ticket."

"No," I said, "what I mean is, if somebody presents my
ticket and asks for my shoes . . ."

"Klaus," hissed my mother, "say *customer receipt*!"

"It's better to have a ticket, naturally, because of the number on it," the shoemaker said. "It means we can find your
shoes straight away. We've got a system, you see."

"That's what I meant," I said. "I want to be sure you
don't hand over my shoes in return for a receipt."

"No?"

"No."

"If you don't want a receipt we won't give you one.
What's the problem?"

"The thing is, I've lost my repair ticket . . ."

"Customer receipt!" amended my mother.

". . . and if someone finds it . . ."

"What was that about a receipt?" asked the shoemaker.

"I mean, if someone comes in with my ticket and collects my shoes . . ."

"I shouldn't give him a receipt?"

"No, you shouldn't give him my shoes."

"Why would we, if they're yours?"

"Because he'd have my ticket."

A brief silence. Then the shoemaker said, "Let me get this straight. You've lost your repair ticket, right?"

"Right."

"And now you're afraid someone else will find it and collect your shoes?"

"Yes."

"It's never happened yet."

"There's always a first time."

"And you're calling me to make sure I give the shoes to you and no one else?"

"That's it!" I said, greatly relieved.

"No problem. Just give me the number."

"What number?"

"The one on your ticket."

Spots swam before my eyes.

"But I've *lost* my ticket!"

"So how am I to know I'm giving your shoes to the wrong person if he produces it?"

All I had to do now was persuade the shoemaker to identify my number by consulting the duplicate book in which he noted down customers' names against their ticket numbers. On the other hand, my name was unpronounceable. He was bound to have misspelled it, and that would make it almost

impossible to locate. Given the ineffectual nature of our conversation to date, I thought this might be too bold an under-
taking, so I capitulated.

"Yes, well, thanks a lot," I said dejectedly, and hung up.

The phone rang at once. Rather than admit to my mother
how embarrassingly unproductive my exchanges with the
shoemaker had been, I snatched up the receiver.

"Hello?"

"Hello." A bright young female voice. "Is that Herr—
heavens!—Herr Uhl . . . Utsch . . . Utschl . . ."

"Uhltzscht."

"Klaus Uhl . . . *How* do you pronounce it?"

"Klaus Uhltzscht. Yes, speaking."

"Oh, good. Have you lost something?"

It flashed through my mind that we ought to have one of
those phones that record callers' numbers. She might be a
blackmailer.

"Yes, my wallet. Have you got it?"

"Uh-huh, and I've been trying to get through for the last
hour. Are you a phone freak or something?"

That was Yvonne for you: nothing if not spontaneous. *I*
had feverishly phoned around to close a totally unendangered
bank account and check on the safety of shoes whose ownership no one would ever contest; *I* had obediently showed
my father my ID; *I* had feared for my pension rights and
imagined whole stacks of books being stolen with the aid of
my library cards; *I* had responded to the finder's call with
Stasiesque suspicion and lusted after a caller ID facility while
my parents played a scene out of a film that might have been
entitled *Panic at Headquarters* (my mother mouthed unintel-
ligible instructions with exaggerated lip movements and
meaningfully dilated eyes; my father strode up and down,
gesticulating fiercely in his eagerness to speak with the

"blackmailer" himself). Not so Yvonne: *she* had let it all hang out. The poise, the composure! *Are you a phone freak or something?*

We arranged to meet the following day, which didn't please my father at all. As usual, he addressed himself to my mother, not to me. I was back in an American courtroom: he, the D.A., harangued the jury (my mother) on the subject of the accused (me): "Have you any idea what someone can do with an identity card in twenty-four hours? His most important document, but *he* doesn't care. In the hands of a stranger! He'll regret it, you mark my words!"

My mother raised another subject for discussion: "Klaus, have you thought about the finder's reward?"

"I'll give her twenty marks. Fifty, maybe."

"*What* did you say?" Oh, God, how was I to interpret that?

"Or should I give her all the notes that were in my wallet?"

"*Money,* you mean? It wouldn't look right."

"Look right!" sneered my father. "Him and look right!"

"Eberhard, please!" my mother said soothingly, and went on to specify flowers.

"Flowers as a finder's reward?" I protested.

"Of course. Women always like flowers."

"If you say so," I said feebly.

"You must buy them from one of the stands at the railroad station. Be there at 7 a.m.; then you can pick out the nicest ones."

"At *seven?*"

"Of course, that's when they open."

"You expect me to get up at six on a Saturday morning, just to buy some flowers?"

"But Klaus, she found your i-den-ti-ty card!"

"He should really go there at once," my father put in.

"Where could he buy flowers at this hour?" said my mother, and that was that.

I should mention that the flower sellers at Frankfurter Allee station became a favorite topic of my father's. He would calculate aloud, for anyone who cared to listen, how much money they earned "on the side," meaning tax-free. This he arrived at by multiplying some figure by 365. "Why do we bother to work?" he philosophized. "If I were to stand in the street with a few flowers, I could earn three times my salary in no time." Resignedly, he added, "And *we* help to line their pockets."

For the eight marks with which I helped to line a flower seller's pockets I got a bunch of long-stemmed roses, which I chose because they were the most expensive. I hoped I'd done the right thing, but as I trudged through Fredersdorf with my bouquet—that's where Yvonne lived, in Fredersdorf, a Berlin suburb whose upscale houses stood in gardens ablaze with flowers—I wondered why I'd let my mother talk me into it. Why flowers, of all things, and what would be the most appropriate way of presenting them to her? (A disastrous phrase, "the most appropriate way," but that's how my mind works . . .) What if I committed a social gaffe? Unimaginable! She might be a diplomat's daughter with a thing about etiquette. How best to present a bunch of flowers to a protocol-loving diplomat's daughter from Fredersdorf?

I'll tell you this much in advance, Mr. Kitzelstein: Yvonne and I hit it off right away, and her story is my life's only love story—a tale so ineffably sad that I wouldn't recount it if I didn't have to.

Look, this postcard was from her. Just look at it! I'm talking about the handwriting, Mr. Kitzelstein. My God, what handwriting; I'd never seen its like before. Butterfly writing, as if she were drawing an endless succession of butterflies (whereas my own wretched, angular scrawl betrays Bauhaus, Neorealist, and Minimalist influences). Ask a graphologist: Isn't this the handwriting of a fairy princess? Look at that letter—yes, believe it or not, it's a letter: the letter "K" for Klaus. Those curlicues! What opulence, what extravagance! And this word here—no, it's not a sketch of two butterflies mating on a chrysanthemum, it's my hideous surname: Uhltzscht. And all of it spontaneous, all without the least attempt to parade her possession of the biggest, most beautiful, memorable, butterflyish handwriting ever. An intrinsic and unquenchable attribute, it came quite naturally to her. She went through the motions of writing, but in reality she was laughing softly to herself and drawing butterflies. Yvonne, the butterfly artist.

First things first, though. I stood outside her house, convinced that she was a diplomat's daughter with a thing about etiquette. Should I wait at the garden gate after ringing the bell? Wouldn't it be a nuisance for her to come out or call to me? But if I rang and went straight up to the house, wouldn't that be presumptuous? I *did* ring, but without any perceptible response. How long should I wait before trying again? The last thing I wanted was to seem importunate. Although I was the best-brought-up child in the neighborhood, nobody had ever taught me the rules of behavior to be observed when calling at an upscale residence standing in its own garden.

The front door having finally opened to reveal Yvonne, I called, "May I?" and gestured at the house. "May I?" I called again as I reached for the handle. I even asked, "May I?" before I depressed it. But shouldn't I have called "Good morning!" first of all? Surely that was what one always said first? By way of compromise, I uttered my first "Good morning!" as I approached the steps leading up to the veranda and another "May I?" before I began to ascend them. Once at the top I said a renewed "Good morning!" and shook hands. "Hi there," she responded with a smile. And do you know what she said next, after I had said "May I?" four times and "Good morning!" twice? She smiled again and said, "You look nicer than your photo."

"What photo?"

"The one on your identity card."

To illustrate the vast extent of my social savoir-faire, my response to that compliment was "Should I take my shoes off?"

"Suit yourself," she said.

Suit yourself. When was the last time anyone had said that to me? What did "Suit yourself" imply? Did it mean that, whatever I did with my shoes and whether or not I removed them, she would have no objection? Was that the deeper meaning of *Suit yourself*? Fantastic! I resolved to make a note of the phrase. It might come in useful sometime.

I held out the bunch of roses. "For *me*?" She beamed and went inside to fetch a vase. I stood transfixed, watching her go. She was wearing jeans and a fluffy red sweater. In the doorway she turned and beckoned me with the flowers. I shut my eyes and saw her waving the same flowers outside the registry office, and me beside her. I wanted to marry her.

Later we went up to her room, a small attic room with a map of Amsterdam on the wall. She didn't know that I made a point of studying *any* map. "Hey," she said eagerly, "are you interested in Holland?" How could I have denied it? She was kind enough to treat me to a two-hour dissertation on the Netherlands. She could imitate a Dutch accent, she spoke of houseboats with tulips growing on deck, of an armed forces trade union and an *alternative secret service,* of bicycles and soccer players. Yessir, she was a fan of the Dutch soccer team—of eleven grown men with nothing better to do than run around after a ball, in shorts! "Do *you* play soccer?" she asked exuberantly. How dearly I longed at that moment to be able to answer in the affirmative, and how embarrassed I suddenly felt by my arrogant disdain of the game. "No, only chess," I replied apologetically. "Chess? *Jan Timman!*" she exclaimed.

Why this boundless enthusiasm for the Netherlands? Didn't she realize that it lay within the Blue World? What did I know about the country? That its official designation was the Kingdom of the Netherlands, its largest city Amsterdam, its administrative capital The Hague. Fifteen million inhabitants, forty-eight cruise missiles. That was just it: Holland didn't make *me* think of tulips, cheese, windmills, bicycles, soccer players, or Jan Timman, still less sunflowers and houseboats; it put me in mind of forty-eight cruise missiles!

We listened to a record by Herman van Veen, a songwriter whose work I had hitherto classed as *apolitical romanticism,* a term of which I was singularly proud; I, the universal genius, formulator of an ultimate definition of Herman van Veen based on new conceptual dimensions of aesthetic classification . . . Here, by contrast, was Yvonne on Herman van Veen: "This record makes me feel so *happy*. I only have to hear the crackle and I could *weep* for joy." Mr. Kitzelstein, how can I convey to you what a *boon* it was to know Yvonne and sit beside her listening to a record by Herman van Veen?

She still hadn't returned my wallet, though, and I suspected that this whole performance—listening to records, admiring my flowers, inviting me to tea in her little attic room— was just a way of making the hand-over ritual slightly less embarrassing. Being my father's son (if I really was such), I naturally had a precise idea of the unavoidable reprimand to which the loser of an identity card should be subjected by the finder: *You realize that your identity card is your most important document, and that you're under a legal obligation to safeguard it against loss? I should really have handed it in to the People's Police.* You see? I credited even my father with a capacity for bending the law on occasion, though he couldn't have resisted wagging his finger: *But if I hadn't been the one to find it!* (An allusion to check and passport forgers, defectors, confidence tricksters, etc.) And the concluding piece of friendly, conciliatory advice: *So take better care of it in the future!*

That's the way he was, Mr. Kitzelstein, and those were the words I expected to pass between the finder and loser of an identity card. But Yvonne? Between two Herman van Veen songs: "By the way, here's your wallet." Was that how they did things in Holland, or was it a trap? No rebuke, reprimand, or admonition, no moral drawn from history, no recriminations? *Could I be wrong about everything?* (Forgive me, I was only nineteen.) Homeward-bound on the S-Bahn, I pictured what it would be like to be married to Yvonne in Holland. We would live on a houseboat and grow tulips on the deck, and the houseboat would double as a lost property office, and all the Dutch who had lost things would drop in for a chat about the national soccer team, and before leaving they would casually retrieve their umbrellas or bunches of keys, though I myself wouldn't see too much of them because I had to bike off every morning to my job in the alternative secret service, which was combating the black market in tickets for Herman van Veen concerts . . .

▪ ▪ ▪

One Monday morning, with a Stasi smirk, Major Wunderlich handed me a housing allocation form. Why assign me a Berlin apartment in May when I was due to embark on four years' study at Potsdam in September? What lay behind it? What did they have in mind for me? Were the plans of my unknown spy masters assuming definite shape?

The "apartment" consisted of one and a half ground-floor rooms in the Hellersdorf district. The windows looked out both ways, onto the street as well as the inner courtyard. No doubt about it: someone had procured me a pad with two escape routes. Did I need protecting, and if so, from whom? Why now, of all times? Or was this only the beginning? Was I now a member of the *inner circle*? Was I about to start work for the *genuine* Stasi, or for a counter-Stasi within the Stasi? Why didn't anyone tell me anything? What was the significance of Major Wunderlich's smirk? Was I in mortal danger? Alternatively, was I on the way to becoming his right-hand man? Or the right-hand man of another important man—even, perhaps, of the right-hand man of an extremely important man?

My apartment was equipped with a telephone. I had no immediate neighbors, and the elevator was located right outside my front door. None of this was fortuitous, but what did it portend?

I felt sure the apartment was bugged, and that every visit from my parents might terminate my career. Could the Stasi really afford to employ a top agent who had to endure such admonitions from his mother as never, ever, to let an opened can of sardines stand for a day, "not even in the refrigerator, not even covered, because the metal oxidizes and forms toxic compounds. Never, Klaus! Promise me!" My interior monologue during these lectures: "Walls have ears, Mama! Someone will be drawing conclusions about me! Please try, just for once, to sound like the mother of a master spy!" But no: "Klaus, how are your bowels? You've used hardly any toilet paper since I was here the last time!" "But Mama, that was only *two days* ago." "Aren't you *going* regularly anymore?" "Yes, but . . ."

If they heard that, they'd never infiltrate me into NATO Headquarters.

"Poststructuralists," Wunderlich said one morning, at our daily conference. "What do you know about them?"

Owl and Grabs haltingly assisted each other.

"They're a group of . . ."

"One can't call them artists . . ."

"Elements . . ."

"A group of elements who, in the guise of artists, transmit . . ."

". . . encoded messages . . ."

". . . encode encoded messages . . ."

"Yes, they use signs . . ."

". . . signs and symbols."

"Get to the point," said Wunderlich. "All these subversive elements employ symbols, but they make no secret of their object, which is (a) to investigate the structure of our postal and telephone service so as (b) to undermine the efficiency of our communications network in the event of an international crisis."

"Shall I cite you an analogy?" asked Owl. "I once attended a course—"

"We know," said Wunderlich. "For example . . ." No example occurred to him.

"For example," said Owl, "they could compile a nationwide list of mailboxes and collection times. If the situation became acute . . . No, perhaps that's a false analogy, but—"

"For example," said Grabs, "they could find out the location of telephone junction boxes so as to sabotage the entire network if a crisis arose."

"And that's poststructuralism?" I asked.

"Only a part of it," said Wunderlich. "*We* pose as a branch of the Periodicals *Postal* Subscription Service. Anyone who conducts a detailed reconnaissance of the country's postal structure endangers our cover."

"But we'll thwart their plans," said Owl. "The traitors will get their just deserts."

"One moment," said Wunderlich. "Poststructuralism has recently assumed a more acute form. The subversive elements in question have been engaging, quite blatantly, in post-poststructuralism."

Puzzled silence.

"Sounds like an anti-missile missile," Grabs said at length.

"Or the negation of negation."

"It's given me food for thought, too," said Wunderlich. "In my opinion, they're no longer (a) investigating the structure of the postal and telephone service but (b) exploring the structure of the decision-making processes affecting it."

"Can you give us an example?"

"Certainly," said Wunderlich. "Hitherto, in the event of a crisis, they would knock out a major telephone junction box, but the damage would be repaired as soon as it became apparent. So much for the normal poststructuralist situation. In the case of *post*-poststructuralism, however, the enemy knows precisely (a) which telephone engineer to call and (b) who to pose as in order to get him to disconnect the junction box in question. All concerned could thus be convinced, by means of deliberate disinformation, that the situation was above-board."

"And the damage would never be repaired," I said.

"Not only that," said Wunderlich. "It would be possible for the enemy to fabricate official instructions of the most devastating nature. I don't have to tell you what that would mean."

"Mailboxes would remain unemptied and overflow."

"Post office opening times would be changed."

"Money orders would be redeemed at ten times their face value."

"Thereby bankrupting the national treasury."

"You're forgetting something," said Wunderlich. "The postal service is also responsible for the *time signal*. The enemy could manipulate the time!"

"Trains and airplanes would collide."

"Clocks would run backward."

"And we'd all go crazy."

"What's more," said Wunderlich, "the enemy pays our subversives well—very well. According to our information, the post-poststructuralists brazenly celebrate the New Year by playing Monopoly. They're already rehearsing what to do with their ill-gotten gains."

"Harald," I said, "is there a chance that you've misunderstood the term 'post-poststructuralism'? The thing you mean should surely be called poststructural structuralism."

"Really? And if you're wrong? Perhaps they want us to think as you do—perhaps they've deliberately chosen a term calculated to put us off our guard."

"To believe otherwise would be to underestimate the enemy," said Owl.

"So what do you suggest?" asked Wunderlich.

"I think we should deal with AE Individualist first," said Grabs. "Then we can concentrate on the post-whatsits."

"What's the present status quo of the situation where Individualist is concerned?" Owl inquired pleonastically.

"I have to conduct one more search of his apartment," said Grabs. "Then we can arrest him. If the interrogation sessions go well, he won't get off with less than three years."

"Let's do it, then," said Wunderlich. "But thoroughly."

And that's how I became a burglar. A *burglar*! I tiptoed through Individualist's apartment with imaginary police sirens wailing in my head, so scared that I almost soiled my pants—not that I ventured to use Individualist's bathroom (my toilet seat complex, remember?). Grabs toured the apartment photographing letters and other documents while I merely got in his way, cheeks ashen with fear and forehead beaded with cold sweat. Who could tell how it would end? Any child knew that breaking and entering was prohibited, and in films burglars usually got caught in the act and had to eliminate the witnesses of their crime. What had I gotten myself into? I was halfway to becoming a murderer—one who, according to the autopsy report, had killed his victim with *a blunt instrument, probably a monkey wrench* . . . I would get life—I would stew in my cell like the Count of Monte Cristo and, while apathetically rotting away, tattoo mermaids on my arms. Then there were the headlines in the Western tabloids: MONKEY WRENCH SLAYER GETS LIFE!

I wanted to flee Individualist's apartment before it became the scene of my crime, but any moviegoer knows that a fleeing intruder always encounters a startled neighbor on the stairs, the outcome being a scuffle and a fall which, according to the autopsy report, results in *fracture of the second cervical vertebra* or a *cerebral hemorrhage*. All would be well if *I* broke my neck, but if I inadvertently killed a neighbor, an *innocent citizen* . . . The relatives clustering around the open grave! The handcuffs! The widow sobbing into her handkerchief and her tear-choked words in the lobby of the courthouse after the verdict was announced: *Nothing can ever bring my husband back to life.* The safest thing would be to call the police from Individualist's apartment itself, ask to be arrested on the spot, and so obviate the risk of having to murder any unexpected witnesses. I, the rapist and burglar, was on the verge of committing my first *murder* (discounting my numerous acts of genocide on the Sausage Woman's stairs). I wasn't armed with a monkey wrench, admittedly, but in thrillers there was always some murder weapon within easy reach.

For safety's sake I snatched up the first object that came to hand, one that couldn't possibly prove lethal if I lost control of myself—court reports often documented the results of blind panic—and brought it down on some innocent person's head. The first object that came to hand was a paperback with a picture of a baby on the cover. As long as my hands were clasping a child-care manual, they couldn't reach for a monkey wrench.

When Grabs caught sight of me with the book he looked dumbfounded. "Well," he said, "you don't miss much, do you!" The putative child-care manual turned out to be the book I mentioned before, *The World According to Garp*, and Grabs thought I meant to give it to him because I was aware of his obsession with monosyllabic first names beginning with "G." He bore it off, as I have said, to demonstrate to the registrar of births that Garp was a legitimate name. He also, at our next daily conference, praised my sangfroid and circumspection. I modestly minimized the importance of the operation and my part in it.

Wunderlich: "You consider Individualist small fry, eh?"

"Well, not exactly," I prevaricated.

"We sometimes have to deal with even smaller fry," Wunderlich said, smirking. "It's all in a day's work to us."

Even smaller fry—an allusion to *microfish*! So it was true, they were going to send me after the NATO Secretary-General's microfish. Sheer excitement spoiled my concentration, and I'd lost the thread of the daily conference by the time I tuned in again.

". . . as a Quelle catalogue is indispensable to us," Grabs was saying. Two words were enough to recapture my full attention: "catalogue" and "Quelle," of which the latter, Mr. Kitzelstein, means "source" in German. The Quelle catalogue! "Hm," said Wunderlich. He turned to me. "What do you think?"

"What . . . what was that about a Quelle catalogue?" I asked bemusedly.

" 'Catalogue' is just the code name for our source," said Wunderlich.

"She's code-named UI Catalogue because she works in a library," Grabs explained.

I almost swooned. *She?* Had he said *she?* A woman—a real, live woman? I became breathless with lust. Worse still, I pretended to myself—and refused to abandon the illusion—that we were talking about one of my beloved Quelle women. Reason told me that it was folly, but my imagination willed it so.

It appeared that the librarian, an acquaintance of AE Individualist's, was refusing to cooperate. To complete his case against Individualist, Wunderlich had envisaged rewording a few items of information about him into incriminating evidence. He was adept at doing this. He had only to be told that a suspect played Monopoly on New Year's Eve, and it became *The enemy pays our subversives well—very well. Ac-*

cording to our information, the post-poststructuralists bra-
zenly celebrate the New Year by playing Monopoly. They're
already rehearsing what to do with their ill-gotten gains!

Wunderlich suggested kidnapping UI Catalogue's child for
an afternoon. "We need to throw another scare into her,
that's all." He offered me the job and I accepted, still under
the impact of his allusion to the *small and even smaller fry*
that were all in a day's work to us. It seemed logical that I
should start by kidnapping children and gradually perfect my
technique until the day came when I would carry off fifty
million NATO Secretaries-General at a stroke.

The child I kidnapped was an eight-year-old girl named
Sara. I waited outside her school and identified her with the aid
of a photograph that Wunderlich had procured from a UI who
now—you can stake your life on it—claims that he "never
harmed anyone" and "only gave the Stasi a few harmless vacation snapshots." I told Sara her mommy had sent me, and
we were going to spend the afternoon together. She held my
hand on the way to the car. We drove to a Stasi safe house,
where I asked if she'd like to call Mommy. Sara opened her
"Mommy book," the first page of which bore her home telephone number. Having dialed it, she announced that she was
at "an uncle's" apartment. Then she held out the receiver and
said, "Now you." I heard a faint, faltering "Hello?" and hung
up. A Quelle woman had said "Hello?" to me—a promising
start! I would soon be off to the land where the Quelle women
bloomed, to return with fifty million microfish!

Sara and I spent the afternoon playing old maid and concentration. I cheated sufficiently to prevent her from winning
even once. The more games she lost, crying bitterly, the better
I felt. At seven that evening I drove her to Alexanderplatz
and dropped her at a spot where she was bound to bump
into a policeman.

What a day! First the commendation for my sangfroid during the break-in, then Wunderlich's veiled confirmation that I was to steal some microfish, and finally my telephone contact with a Quelle woman. And the successful kidnapping! Anyone would have thought I'd been doing it all my life!

Having heard the Quelle woman's voice, I wanted to see her in the flesh—a notion so absurdly reckless that Minister Mielke would, if he'd known, have fired me on the spot. If Sara visited her mommy's place of work she would recognize me as her abductor. Led into court in handcuffs, I would be tried and convicted to the accompaniment of banner headlines in the Western tabloids: STASI KIDNAPPER JAILED FOR LIFE! It would make the Minister look a fool and furnish my father with proof positive that I was a failure. But none of this deterred me from visiting the library that employed UI Catalogue. You know me, Mr. Kitzelstein: where Quelle women are concerned I cast caution to the winds.

UI Catalogue worked at a library for which I didn't yet possess a membership card. I got a colleague of hers to make one out while I watched her sorting through a card index. On one occasion the telephone rang—someone was requesting a due-date extension—and she said, "Simone de Beauvoir, very well, till the seventeenth." Then she caught my eye. Did she suspect me of being her daughter's kidnapper? I felt scared. Why linger?

For authenticity's sake I borrowed the first book that came to hand, *The Diary of Anne Frank*. I'd never read *The Diary of Anne Frank* despite my four—now five—library memberships, and my only purpose in reading it now was to dispel suspicion when I returned it. If UI Catalogue asked me how I'd enjoyed the book and I couldn't think of anything relevant to say, she would inevitably conclude that I hadn't read it and wonder why I'd taken it out in the first place: *Odd of him to join the library for the sole purpose of borrowing a book he hasn't read. SUSPICIOUS, no?* So you see, Mr. Kitzelstein, I knew exactly what might arouse suspicion and was determined not to be thwarted by something as trivial as the abduction of a child on the verge of my departure for NATO Headquarters in quest of fifty million microfish. That, and that alone, was my motive for reading *The Diary of Anne Frank*. Thereafter I was in a position, for the very first time, to view my own existence with a certain degree of horror.

Anne: *What's the matter with you, Klaus Uhltzscht? You aren't in hiding, your life isn't in jeopardy. Whither are you sailing, captain of your fate?*

I: I've kidnapped a child, nosed around in other people's letters, stared at a stranger for weeks on end, subjected people to intimidation and derision. I'm making the world a worse place than it is already. I've enjoyed making an eight-year-old girl cry . . .

Anne: *Why?*

I vegetated in my ground-floor, one-and-a-half-room apartment, thinking myself the scum of the earth and watching TV, and when Holland won a European Cup match I recalled my visit to Yvonne and my daydream on the S-Bahn on the way home: what life with her would be like. A sunflower existence. A life innocent of burglaries and kidnappings. A life filled with delicious trivialities. I felt an urge to write to her—a love letter, of course—but I didn't know how.

I: Anne, I can't even write a love letter.

Anne: *Anyone can. We're all brimming with love and*

hungry for it—you too, Klaus Uhltzscht, so try! If I were still alive, writing love letters would be my favorite secret occupation . . .

That finally swayed me.

Dear Yvonne,

Although, when I said goodbye to you after that nice afternoon we spent together, I thought it was a pity we wouldn't meet again, I couldn't bring myself to tell you so.

As the weeks went by, it struck me that I was taking an inordinate interest in newspaper articles about the Netherlands. I eventually went so far as to comb the newspaper for reports on Holland before I devoted myself to other items. Lately, I've even started to buy magazines I never read as a rule, just because there's something about Holland in them. I find it easier to remember you that way, and that, I think, is the whole point of the exercise. I actually watched the European Cup Final—not my style at all—and pretended to myself that you were doing the commentary.

Dear Yvonne, people can go on telling themselves things like "Think before you speak!" or "You don't believe that yourself!" or "Forget it!" But they can also say, "Oh, what lovely flowers!" or "Are you a phone freak or something?" or "Suit yourself," or "This record makes me feel so happy!" Wonderful! Words are delightful little gifts we exchange like the Easter eggs we paint and hide for others to find and enjoy. I'd forgotten that, but you reminded me of it.

I'd like to see you again.

Yours,
Klaus

She didn't reply, needless to say, with the result that I heaped innumerable reproaches on my head. Had I choked her off with my emotions? Did I see her as the kind of person she wasn't and had no wish to be? Did she feel overwhelmed by my expectations? I mean, this was *love*!

She did reply in the end. She'd been away on vacation, and my letter had languished in her mailbox for a month. She wrote that it would have absolutely *made* her vacation if she'd received it, and that I was to visit her next Sunday. And all in her sensational butterfly writing (to which this was my first introduction).

It was the last Sunday in August. Her parents, whom I'd never met, were away for the weekend, and we sat in deck chairs on the lawn behind her house and talked of this and that. Yvonne had bought herself a kaleidoscope, an acquisition of which she was very proud. She often picked it up and put it to her eye, and if she saw an especially beautiful pattern she would smile and hand it to me, very carefully, so that I could see it, too. I would look into it and feel called upon to present her with an especially beautiful pattern in return. The kaleidoscope shuttled back and forth the whole afternoon, and her patterns—this I would swear—were always more beautiful than mine.

If there's anything noteworthy to be said about Klaus the Cover Picture and kaleidoscope, it's this: that at the age of eight, when I'd already spurned things of beauty and developed a positively Faustian thirst for knowledge, I dismembered one of those miraculous contraptions to see how it worked. What I brought to light—three little mirrors and a handful of beads—was far too banal to sustain my interest.

On an August Sunday twelve years later I sat beside a butterfly sorceress and repented. I was ready to give up everything in return for an ability to appreciate the full beauty of a kaleidoscope. It hadn't fallen from the sky, either, that kaleidoscope; Yvonne had actually bought it. She must some time have gone into a toy store and said to the assistant, "I'd like a kaleidoscope, please." Could *you* do that? Could *you* walk into a toy store and spend good money on a cardboard tube containing three little mirrors and a handful of beads? What was she, a weirdo or a fairy-tale princess?

Which reminds me: did I already mention that the ceiling of her little attic was draped with orange and violet shawls, like the princess's bedchamber in a fairy-tale castle, and that the main source of illumination was a kerosene lamp! *Like the inside of a house of horrors,* I could hear my mother saying, and my father would have delivered a scathing lecture on the fire hazard: *All those drapes above a naked flame? They'd burn like tinder—the roof would go up in no time . . .* To illustrate the difference between Yvonne and me, I can't help pointing out that, in addition to patronizing a toy store, she must also have gone into a—what kind of shop sells kerosene lamps, Mr. Kitzelstein? A lamp shop, a kerosene shop? Where? In Minsk?—anyway, she must also have gone in there and asked for a *kerosene lamp.* Had it really mattered to her how her room was illuminated? Had she devoted some thought to it? Had she taken the trouble to acquire precisely the kind of light she wanted? Did this imply that, to her, "light" meant more than a thing you switched on and off? Did she appreciate its special qualities? How strange! And *I* had always been given to believe that artificial lighting existed solely to prevent you from "ruining your eyes."

We gazed lovingly at each other for half the afternoon and *chatted,* another novel and relaxing experience from my point of view. In the evening, when it became cooler, we went indoors, touching and kissing in the process. We retired to her room, and pinned to her corkboard of *favorite things—*

together with a view of Amsterdam, a pen drawing of the Marienkirche (was she religious?), a photo of Herman van Veen, a handwritten list of phone numbers and addresses of jazz clubs, and an old black-and-white photo of a hot-air balloon—pinned to it, as I say, was my letter. I, here? Was it possible? Had I, the Stasi guy, the human scum and tormentor of children, succeeded in writing a letter that meant something to a butterfly princess—a letter she numbered among her sacred relics? Should I tell her who I really was? If I did, would she take my letter down?

She lit some candles and settled herself in my lap, and we kissed. I found myself in a genuine ethicomoral predicament. Why? Because it became clear to me that I wanted—let's not beat about the bush—to *fuck* her. Could my conscience permit me to fuck an *angel*? An angel, what was more, whom I *loved*? Could I really want that? Did it have to be Yvonne whom I abused for such a piggish purpose? That I (I!) should want (want!) to fuck (fuck!) her was reprehensible enough, but why *her* of all people? Weren't there umpteen thousands of pussies I could have penetrated?

And the consequences! One could never tell who lived in these elegant houses on the outskirts of Berlin. What if her father were an artist critical of the regime—possibly even one with an international reputation? The West German tabloids always pounced on such stories: STASI THUG VIOLATES DISSIDENT'S DAUGHTER. Castigated for *unauthorized contact with the enemy* by Major Wunderlich, my father, and Minister Mielke, I would never be privileged to smuggle any microfish out of NATO Headquarters. As for Yvonne, when she learned the truth about my profession she would hang herself because she was so *ashamed* of having betrayed her father's ideals. I would have Yvonne on my conscience. I dreaded to think how that would affect the ideological class struggle:

STASI VICTIM'S SUICIDE NOTE: "I FEEL TOO SOILED TO GO ON LIVING."

Nonsense, I told myself, perhaps her artist father wasn't classified in our files as "critical" of the regime but only "skeptical" or "not entirely reliable." Perhaps he was just— to cite the official term—an "internal émigré." Such was the twaddle that ran through my mind as I engaged in what is commonly known as *foreplay,* and my sense of political responsibility finally took possession of me to such an extent that my pecker subsided. To gain time, I devoted myself to Yvonne's anatomy, a procedure that fairly soon ended with me nose-deep in her pussy. I started to caress her flanks, whereupon she stretched and tensed and grasped my hands and drew me upward. I willingly complied, the more so because I hadn't really known what to do with my nose where it was.

And then she said something she shouldn't have said: two fateful words. "Hurt me!" she whispered. That did it. Please try to understand: I'd mentally reconciled myself to the idea of fucking an angel, but that I should be expected to *hurt* her when I ought in theory to demonstrate my love for her—no, that was really over the top. I sat on the edge of the bed and tried to figure it out. *Hurt me. Hurt me. Hurt me . . .* I groped for her hand beneath the covers and squeezed it, but she didn't respond in any way, just lay there with her eyes shut. I couldn't think what to do next. What did it mean, *Hurt me?* At that moment, Mr. Kitzelstein, my world disintegrated. Was I supposed to scratch her? Draw blood? Hit her? Bite her? Dislocate her arms and legs? I didn't feel equal to anything of the kind.

I rose, got dressed, and left.

Half-past four under a paling sky, and I knew that my life was in ruins. Gravel crunched beneath my feet, a dull day was breaking, the garden gate didn't squeak, I didn't look back. The world was filled with poetry, with things that cried out for my attention. All that was happening was doing so for my benefit, but I was blind, blind, blind. I had no eyes for the morning star, for the lichen on garden fences, for tree stumps' annual rings. As for sunrises, I preferred to see them on TV. The taste of the air and the shape of a puddle were no concern of mine. The sky that morning was a certain color (pastel, was it, or gray, or pale pink? It wasn't blue, of that I'm sure—I'd have remembered a *blue* sky). The sky was a certain color, yes, but it was the same color *every* day, there was nothing *special* about it. There were people who wondered what animal they'd been in a former life or what flower they'd like to become. There were people who imagined they could see faces or mythical beasts in clouds and wasted time thinking up stories about them. Lying sprawled beside the bus stop was a dead cat with wet, matted fur and a gaping mouth—it had been run over—and all that occurred to me was that you mustn't touch dead animals for fear of disease. People who shed tears of joy were alien to me. There was a proper time and place for everything. Why had she whispered "Hurt me!"? I didn't understand it, not any of it. Half-past four under a paling sky, and I knew that my life was in ruins. If the world had been able to call after me, it would, from that day forward, have accompanied my every step with a cry of *Waste! Waste! Waste!*

TRUMPETER, TRUMPETER

Wunderlich often exhorted us to "(a) put ourselves in the enemy's place so as to (b) render his actions predictable." I once found, on Grabs's desk, the transcript of a bugged telephone conversation in which AE Individualist was referred to as "Chicken-fucker." I was intrigued despite myself. *Chicken-fucker?* What did it mean? Was it to be taken literally or metaphorically? How had Individualist earned such an appellation? Would it be easier for me to put myself in the enemy's place and render his actions predictable if I myself became a chicken-fucker?

With this in mind, I bought a whole broiler after work, took it home, and, without consulting higher authority, sexually abused it. It did not occur to me until later that Wunderlich had also warned us that putting ourselves in the enemy's place was "(a) not always easy and calls for (b) great strength of character and (c) a firm class-conscious stance that renders us proof against (d) certain emotive words and (e) a certain logical consistency inherent in the enemy's arguments."

Had I gone too far? Were strength of character and a

class-conscious stance diametrically opposed to the violation of foodstuffs? What did Siegfried Schnabl have to say on the subject? Did his book *Mann und Frau Intim* also deal with questions relating to the subject of "intimacy between man and broiler"? Chapter 9 ("Sexual Aberrations") of Part III ("Sexual Variants and Deviations") contained a brief reference to *zoophilia*, a form of *deviant sexual behavior* into which Schnabl did not delve too closely, for fear, he said, of boring the reader. *Deformity fetishists* and their *irrational passion for mutilated limbs* were likewise dismissed in half a sentence. *Pedophilia,* on the other hand, was exhaustively addressed, whereas *necrophilia* did not appear at all (even though the "Sadism" section did not balk at mentioning the *perverted sex murder,* or *murder for sexual gratification*). Space was also devoted to *frotteurs, voyeurs,* and *exhibitionists* . . . There was no doubt in my mind, Mr. Kitzelstein: *sex with a broiler* far exceeded the scope of Chapter 9. I had done it with an *animal*! A *dead* animal! A dead *young* animal! A headless, i.e., *mutilated,* dead young animal! I had simultaneously indulged in *four* perversions, three of which were so bizarre and loathsome that Siegfried Schnabl's standard work on sex said little or nothing about them.

"Does 'top landing' mean anything to you?" When Wunderlich asked me that question the day before Individualist's arrest, I saw myself being summoned to the Minister's office. I might have guessed: without letting on, they had known about my masturbatory excesses all the time, but how? Had I been watched for weeks as I slunk back to the scene of my crime, the Sausage Woman's apartment house? Were there witnesses who had seen me roaming the streets, fly open, on the night of the accident? Ever since falling downstairs I had regarded masturbation as a dangerous sexual practice—a potential neck-breaker—and had never again projected millions of innocent young lives down the dark stairwell (or down anything else, for that matter). Would that count as an extenuating circumstance?

Owl: "Have you ever done a 'top landing'?"

I: "Mnhmnh . . ."

Grabs: "You'd know it if you had."

Wunderlich: "Then you'll do it tomorrow. Top landing, right?"

I didn't see how I could give myself a hand job and arrest Individualist at the same time.

Wunderlich: "Escape prevention procedure."

Was he a mind reader? What form was this escape prevention procedure to take? Was Individualist to slip on my microfish? Was there a connection between Wunderlich's jerk-off order and the rumor that many detainees who had been beaten up were expected to sign a declaration that their injuries had been sustained "while falling down the stairs"? Were the stairs they fell down specially treated in advance? Was I expected to prepare the stairs for Individualist? Why was I in the dark yet again? Why, why? But perhaps Wunderlich had no idea that I usually stationed myself at the top of the stairs before shooting my wad onto the floor below? If Individualist fled *up* the stairs he would be startled by the sight of a Stasi employee in mid-wank and, on his release, unburden himself to the West German press: DISSIDENT HOUNDED BY MASTURBATING STASI EXHIBITIONIST! What would my Minister say with a headline like that in his briefcase? I might impair the attractions of socialism and cause an outcry among the human rights experts, weaken our negotiating position, and prevent the signing of a disarmament agreement. I might set off World War III!

Oh, Mr. Kitzelstein, why do I always dwell on the potential consequences of my actions? Why do I think of nothing else? I'm adept at formulating grammatical constructions that begin in the subjunctive and end in the indicative. If only I formulated them and left it at that, but I *think* in just the same way!

The day of Individualist's arrest finally dawned. "You want me to, er . . . lubricate the stairs?" I asked Wunderlich in the car.

"No need," he replied. Less than ten minutes later, he and Grabs emerged from the apartment house with Individualist between them. Individualist didn't look particularly individualistic. He was no Jimi Hendrix or Karl Lagerfeld—indeed, his was such an ordinary, unremarkable face that I couldn't have compiled a composite picture of him and wouldn't recognize him if I saw him in the street today. "Clever camouflage," Owl gritted between his teeth.

Going home after work, I sat in the S-Bahn with a foil-wrapped broiler in my lap and took stock of my historic missionary work in the Stasi: AE Individualist had been arrested and would sometime (though not before a year was up) be ransomed and released, thereby swelling our foreign exchange reserves. That was something at least. What else? Had we intimidated a few people, Wunderlich, Grabs, Owl, and I? Yes, we had, but only those who courted intimidation. To say that we *instilled fear* would be an overstatement. Peace and good order reigned in our Republic. Yes indeed, we kept order and they kept the peace. Innocent citizens were on the increase—alarmingly so. If more and more people allowed themselves to be intimidated by ever-milder methods of intimidation, how would we find enough dissidents to sell to the West for hard currency? Wouldn't it be disastrous if people became so afraid of us that none of them could be detained and ransomed?

"That *is* a problem, to be sure," said Wunderlich when I

questioned him on the subject. "However, lack of foreign exchange harms our economy. The more our economic position deteriorates, the more exit visas are applied for, and applying for a exit visa is an offense under Article 213 of the Penal Code: 'Interference with Government Activity.' The applicants' offense being punishable by imprisonment, they become salable detainees and everything evens out again." "Another example of the negation of negation," said Owl. "And the best part is," said Wunderlich, "that our future detainees naturally have to enter their names and addresses on their application forms. Processing these can take years, which means we're able to detain them systematically."

It was true: Article 213 was absolutely brilliant—in fact, an erstwhile future Nobel physics laureate could not have failed to note its resemblance to a perpetual motion machine. Was my seemingly pointless year with the Stasi, during which I had helped to arrest only one ransomable detainee, a discreet introduction to the foreign exchange problem? Was it the Minister's way of intimating that he expected me to produce some brilliant ideas for improving our balance of trade?

Having once grasped his intention, Mr. Kitzelstein, I racked my brains incessantly for unexploited sources of foreign exchange—a tough nut to crack, even for a genius of my caliber, seeing that we had already converted donated blood, imported garbage, political prisoners, and alimony claims into D-marks. But then, one night, I (illegally) watched a West German TV show entitled *Wetten, dass . . .* , or, freely translated, *Bet you can't . . .* , in which people were challenged, for instance, to produce fifty firemen on tricycles, each with a parrot perched on the handlebars singing the national anthem. That was when it came to me: *Bet you can't produce anyone in the transmission area who has invented a quadruple perversion.*

What an idea: the invention and exportation, in exchange for foreign currency, of patented perversions! Who, if not I myself, was better qualified to become a pervert? If I fucked away blithely I caught gonorrhea (what would it be the next time, AIDS?); if I fell genuinely in love I couldn't get it up (a phenomenon defined by experts as profoundly humiliating); if I jerked off I wound up in plaster casts (what would it be the next time, my neck?); and rape, regrettably, was a criminal offense. My urges were threatening to bring me before the courts, quite apart from the other legal hazards that I— I especially, given my glowing prospects—could not afford to ignore: paternity suits! I might be hauled before a judge who would castigate me while pointing to a tearful woman with a bawling bundle lovingly clasped in her arms.

No, Mr. Kitzelstein, *fucking* was for ordinary folk. *I* aspired to be a disciple of Part III, Chapter 9—to plumb the cavernous depths of *Sexual Aberrations* and illuminate them with the torch of scientific research. I knew what it meant to have a vocation. I would be a historic missionary instead of a Nobel laureate, become a Great Pervert instead of persisting in my potentially lethal, physically injurious, legally hazardous sex life. I was already on Chapter 9, after all—the penultimate chapter, Mr. Kitzelstein. That was how far I had got in my unremitting quest for higher things. Barely twenty years old, and already at home in Siegfried Schnabl's penultimate chapter! That left only *Homosexuality,* the theme of Chapter 10.

Schnabl's preamble to Chapter 9 read: "The phenomena with which we shall concern ourselves in this chapter were until recently—and to some extent still are—defined as 'perverted.' " He made much use of the milder term "deviant." It may be that some functionary at the Sixth, Seventh, or Eighth Party Congress had proclaimed that socialism had deprived perversions of their basis in society—I don't know, but these deviations were too bourgeois for an extremist like me (only twenty and already in the penultimate stage, as I have said). They weren't shocking or exorbitant enough. Even my very first perversion had been too strong a meat for Chapter 9! Siegfried Schnabl would have to write a Chapter 11 whose opening sentence would read: "The phenomena with which we shall concern ourselves in this chapter must once more—now that we have entered the Klaus Uhltzscht era—be defined as 'perverted.'" Yes indeed, I and my perversions would go down in history.

You doubt the existence of a market for perversions? Don't you ever watch talk shows? How much more market research do you want? Quelle catalogues titillate you with their immaculately smiling Western women, but any desire to have sex with them is knocked on the head by talk shows. I await the day when TV producers will tackle the ultimate taboo: *Sexual harassment on the wedding night.* They're forever stimulating the libido, but they turn up their noses at sexual tourism. Such was the dilemma that beset me at home—until I discovered perversion. My own creations—my trend-setting, internationally marketable perversions—would be free from this fusty image. I was determined to invent something fresh and peppy. Perversions for all! Perversions could become a theme for parties or relax the atmosphere during job interviews, and I wouldn't consider the market saturated until there were as many avowed perverts as credit card carriers.

I think it important, Mr. Kitzelstein, to stress that I became a pervert in order to promote the triumph of socialism. My field of research was a tricky one, given that the relationship between socialism and perversion had never been clarified. *Socialism needs perversion; perversion needs social-*

ism—how does that dialectical entity appeal to you? Heartwarming, isn't it? I know how to concoct a great slogan, you see—one to be pondered for a moment and then accepted with an acquiescent nod, like *My workplace is my battlefield for peace,* or *Our reach exceeds our grasp,* or *Socialism is only as good as we make it every day.* It was never my intention to abandon the fundamentals of socialism, so I confined myself to perversions that had no need to rue their socialist origins. I resolved to be as consistent as a television programmer and as demure as a sports commentator. No little girls were to be lured into cellars with candies.

One exemplary item of my research equipment was the Index of New Perversions in which I entered my findings diary fashion. Although it would be a long time before I became the most perverted of perverts, I considered it advisable, given the importance of my task (you need only think of the potential market), to begin by pursuing my studies and developing my perversions in patient solitude. Later on, when my research had progressed to a stage where no one could dispute my preeminent status, I would publish my findings and initiate their exploitation on an industrial scale. I was as mindful of Henry Ford and his vision of "cars for the masses" as of Steven Jobs and his vision of "computers for the masses." I, too, had a vision: perversions for the masses!

I proposed to quit the seclusion of my study and unveil my findings to the world in 2005, the hundredth anniversary of the publication of three important works: Einstein's *Special Theory of Relativity*; Freud's *Three Essays on the Theory of Sexuality,* one section of which is devoted to perversions, which Freud likewise calls "deviations"; and Lenin's *Two Tactics of Social-Democracy in the Democratic Revolution,* a treatise on revolutionary theory so often quoted that bibliographies abbreviate its title to *Two Tactics* . . . The publication of my labors in the field of perversion was to be a tribute to all three authors: it would combine Einsteinian genius with Freud's object of research and Lenin's political legacy. Nearly all trailblazing works have unremarkable titles. My own, in the spirit of Lenin, would simply be called *Two Practices*. Thereafter I would dash off two or three popularizations for the bestseller lists (*Methods of Perversion, New Methods of Perversion, New Perversions*), map out some weekend seminars, and set up a worldwide network of branches equipped to give personal consultations. Just as Hollywood was the capital of the entertainment industry, so Berlin would become the metropolis of the perversion industry. Where was the true home of perversion, if not in a city with a "death strip" beneath which U-Bahn trains ran at five-minute intervals? If my business generated a turnover only one-tenth the size of Hollywood's, I would be awarded the Nobel Prize in Industry.

I didn't limit myself to one broiler—no, I bought one a week and put it to the test, experimenting with a variety of positions and fillings. All these perverted experiments are compiled and described in the Index of New Perversions. My research project for the salvaging of socialism was so secret that not even the Stasi knew of it. The Index of New Perversions escaped subsequent seizure and publication by civil rights activists when the Stasi's records became accessible. Although the nation marveled at, for instance, a *collection of sample scents* with the aid of which trained dogs could be unleashed to sniff out suspected dissidents, no one even guessed at the existence of my Index of New Perversions. Technically, I'm under a legal obligation to surrender my data to the Federal Commissioner for the Supervision of Stasi Records. His job is to sift through 180 kilometers of shelving, but my 12 centimeters of data would be a very special 12 centimeters; they even discuss the question "Are sexually abused foodstuffs edible?" The Index of New Perversions may not be the most explosive revelation—remember the Guillaume affair?—but it's still good for a banner headline: STASI'S SECRET SEX EXPERIMENTS! DR. SCHNABL: "LOATHSOME!"

My next perversion was a lip simulator known, in its development phase, as the Fellatiomat I. Two toy animals—miniature elephants composed of red foam rubber as soft as marshmallow—were heated on an electric hot plate, on the lowest setting, and kneaded into a pair of sausages that served me as an upper and a lower lip. If gripped between the thumb and forefinger of each hand, these formed a mouth whose lips moved when my fingers did. I used this contrivance to fellate myself a couple of times. Though easier than eating with chopsticks, it wasn't, somehow, the real thing—not a milestone in the history of perversion. My reach still exceeded my grasp. What gimmick must I offer the Blue World's masses? What did they expect? What would tickle their fancy?

George Bush had been elected on the strength of his pronouncement "Read my lips: No new taxes!" Was that how one became the Blue World's *numero uno*? I was tempted to follow suit. On the other hand, I balked at taking a leaf out of the White House book and was determined to develop my perversions on a staunchly socialist basis. Being by this time a student at Golm Law School, the Stasi academy, I spent many lectures mouthing the lecturers' words with a thumb to my lips. By conveying a tactile impression of my lip movements, this would—or so I hoped—enable me to identify phrases of a particularly stimulating and titillating nature. I was testing lip movements for the delectation of millions of Western penises. To no avail, alas, because the lecturers produced nothing but useless verbiage extruded through bared teeth. I found it an appealing notion that, from the hundredth anniversary of the *Special Theory of Relativity, Three Essays on the Theory of Sexuality,* and *Two Tactics* . . . onward, millions of men in the Blue World would be brought to orgasm by messages of socialist content.

Unfortunately, no suitable messages presented themselves. Read my lips, Mr. Kitzelstein: "subversive elements," "capitalist corruption," "Marxism-Leninism," and so forth—all staccato, all calculated to reinforce a subject's castration complex. "Impermissible contacts with the West" was the only semi-possibility: great lip movements but rhythmically inappropriate.

Then, while attending a psychology lecture on the character structures of unofficial informants, I found my thoughts straying to the only unofficial informant with whom I was in any way acquainted: UI Catalogue, the librarian whom I'd heard say "Simone de Beauvoir" into the phone. Read my lips, Mr. Kitzelstein: *Simone de Beauvoir.* Note the muscular dynamics of the lower jaw—positively acrobatic, no? Note the gentle, fluid rhythm, the subtle suction effect! That was it: a Quelle woman who performed *à la française*—I'd always dreamed of such a thing. I ar-tic-u-lat-ed "Simone de Beauvoir" in front of the mirror, studied my lip movements, and tried to reproduce them with my foam rubber simulators. For weeks I strove, with the two red foam rubber sausages between my fingers, to imprint "Simone de Beauvoir" on my muscular memory.

Realizing that this perversion transcended the Fellatiomat I, I christened my new project Fellatiomat 2005. Wunderlich had assured me before I embarked on my legal studies that I would always be welcome to consult the Accounts Department of the Periodicals Postal Subscription Service if I encountered any problems. I was therefore able to request the loan of a wire and a lapel mike with which I went to the library and made an original recording of UI Catalogue saying "Simone de Beauvoir." I wrote the name on a request slip and asked her to enlighten me on how it should be pronounced. By dint of saying "Eh?" and "What was that again?" I got her to record "Simone de Beauvoir" three times in succession. Then, selecting the version I found most sexually stimulating, I asked Wunderlich to issue written instructions to our Stasi recording studio to dub it onto an autoreverse cassette. My ostensible purpose was psychological intimidation: the AE, or antisocial element, would hear "Simone de Beauvoir" ringing in his head *ad infinitum* and think he was going mad. Wunderlich was delighted and prophesied a great future for me.

On weekends I would stretch out on the bed in my one-and-a-half-room, ground-floor apartment in Hellersdorf, lower my trousers, and listen to the autoreverse cassette, simultaneously mumbling my dick with the artificial lips. I also set a stopwatch and entered the duration in my Index of New Perversions. I could not exclude the possibility that the place was bugged—Minister Mielke might have instituted inquiries into my way of life, given the great things he had in store for me, and I didn't think it would enhance my career prospects if a surveillance log informed him that I spent twenty minutes every weekend listening to a tape that ceaselessly ar-tic-u-lated the name of a female French intellectual—so I always wore earphones when testing the Fellatiomat 2005. During the week I slept at the law school in a four-man dormitory equipped with two double-decker bunks. My roommates never guessed that they shared their sleeping quarters with an ace pervert-to-be.

According to Schnabl, most perverts make a socially well-adjusted, thoroughly unobtrusive impression. I myself was exceptionally well adjusted and unobtrusive. Did that prove me exceptionally perverted? I only know that I was feverishly preoccupied with devising new perversions. I even bade farewell to my long-cherished hope that Minister Mielke, Major Wunderlich, and some big gun from Intelligence would issue me with false papers, an air ticket to Brussels, and a cover story to be memorized prior to letting me loose on the NATO Secretary-General's microfish. The compiling of my Index of New Perversions allowed of no distractions.

To my great relief, my erstwhile hope and present fear of being charged with the abduction of fifty million NATO Secretaries-General evaporated completely. During a Law School lecture on detective techniques, the lecturer projected the word "microfiches" on the screen, and the pfennig finally dropped. What a misunderstanding! You sometimes hear of semen banks getting their test tubes mixed up, but only I could have confused the NATO Secretary-General's seminal fluid with his microfilms. If orally instructed to procure the Secretary-General's microfiches, I might have found some means of making off with a few drops of his semen. Think what a fool I'd have looked, standing in Minister Mielke's office when my mission was completed. Instead of the documents he'd hoped for, I would have deposited the ejaculatory discharge of NATO's highest-ranking official on his desk. I would have brought him fifty million dead. I would have been executed, and, worse still, punished. A judge would have looked me in the eye and addressed me as "Accused"!

More important, Mr. Kitzelstein, stealing the enemy's microfiches was a secret service activity of long standing, and what good had it done from a historical perspective? Had it resolved the worldwide conflict between Red and Blue? No, and I still firmly believed—to put it mildly—that I would not be entrusted with any run-of-the-mill secret service assignment, only with conspiracies of the most arcane and momentous nature. I was conscious of my historic mission, and all that happened to me accorded with it. Whatever I did was earth-shaking and epoch-making *because I did it.*

I previously likened Article 213 of the Penal Code to a perpetual motion machine. Everyone knows that perpetual motion machines don't work. Sooner or later the upper receptacle empties and all the water collects in the lower one. Sooner or later there would be no dissidents left to sell—at a rough estimate, in the year 2005. Thereafter, East German socialism would have to keep afloat with the aid of my perversions. Once the Iron Curtain parted in Hungary, however, my perversions had no further chance of shaping world history—even I sensed as much. The upper receptacle had been holed and the water was no longer playing over the waterwheel.

Despite this, I experimented with a new perversion. Day after day during the summer of 1989 I slipped away to a secluded pond near the law school and used a fine-mesh net to catch tadpoles, thousands of which wriggled near the banks. Having counted out as many tadpoles as East Germans had defected from our Republic the previous day, I stuffed them into a condom and put it on. How about *that,* Dr. Schnabl? My *mass sodomy,* too, belongs in your still-to-be-written Chapter 11! The violated tadpoles steadily increased in number. The bigger the exodus, the more agreeably they tickled my trumpet. I may have been the only member of the Stasi who thought kindly of the defectors.

My father took only a few days to die. My mother called me to say that "our father" was dying. He had just been discharged from the hospital, where his abdomen had been opened and promptly sewn up again because his case was hopeless: the cancer had spread to an inoperable extent and his intestinal tract was so badly obstructed by rampant tumors that he could no longer rid himself of the excrement he produced. Even the saliva he swallowed aggravated his condition. He would sooner or later have digested himself into a single bedridden, pajama-clad lump of shit weighing 110 kilos. His only recourse was to stop eating, with the result that he died of starvation. He did so without uttering a word.

Since his death I continually come across traces of him in the family apartment, elaborate little devices and contraptions made of key rings, fishing line, and washers. What is noteworthy about all these feats of DIY is that they were meant to be invisible—or to make things so. No trouble was too great in that respect. My father rendered 20 centimeters of telephone cable invisible by concealing it beneath the edge of the carpet, a task that necessitated the dismantling of an entire wall of closets. The door of another closet, which we used only two or three times a year, persisted in opening of its own accord. He remedied this, not by wedging it with paper, but with a magnet so skillfully hidden that you would have needed a metal detector to locate it. In my parents' bedroom I happened on some mysterious lengths of fishing line which must, I suspect, have formed part of a contrivance that enabled him to open and close the window from his bed. I still keep coming across things whose purpose defies elucidation: two nails dangling from a few inches of string concealed beneath the washbasin, or a shaving mirror affixed to the inside of a garbage pail lid. One of our central-heating pipes (which are covered, of course) has a lone piece of tinfoil wrapped around it. Any idea what purpose *that* could serve? I still don't know what my father did during the day.

Neither does my mother. When she tried to have him buried in the Socialist Cemetery at Friedrichsfelde, hoping to improve her chances of obtaining the additional pension to which state employees' widows were entitled, she knew too little about his activities to be able to substantiate her application. He earned good money. Long after his death a newspaper published the Stasi payroll for 1987, which listed approximately 100,000 salaried employees in order of income. My father was in the top three hundred, but don't ask me why. I assume that he had something to do with the print media. Strange items of propaganda appeared after his death. All our newspapers published page one articles on the magnificent achievements of our nuclear physicists and their alleged successes in the field of cold nuclear fusion. They also splashed the firsthand account of a frightened East German dining-car steward who had been abducted in Budapest—with the aid of a drugged menthol cigarette—and borne off to Vienna, where he was finally rescued in dramatic circumstances. No such lurid stories were published in my father's lifetime. Although this far from proves that propaganda was his job, I'd learned at summer camp that a certain person had got a certain Young Pioneer onto the cover of a certain magazine. There the wheel turns full circle, for summer camp information was always the most reliable. Besides, he must have done *something*. We all did *something*, after all.

It was on a Saturday in August, exactly one year after Yvonne had whispered "Hurt me!," that I finally received a summons from the Stasi—the *genuine* Stasi, I mean. It happened as suddenly as I had always imagined it would, not that anyone actually came to my one-and-a-half-room, ground-floor, all-mod-cons apartment in Hellersdorf. Why should they have bothered to come in person when I had a telephone? The caller, a staff officer who acted as assistant

to the principal of the Golm Law School, informed me that
I was wanted "forthwith" at the Ministry in Magdalenenstrasse. "That's an order," he concluded. He didn't say what
it was about—nor, in the case of such a vitally important
assignment, did I expect him to. I would be told all I needed
to know at the Ministry. I was instructed to report to the
Polyclinic's reception desk, where Dr. Riechfinger would be
expecting me.

This was the moment I had always dreamed of: they had
discovered me at last! Further work on my perversions could
wait. The situation was grave—very grave, because the flood
of defectors pouring across the Austro-Hungarian border was
increasing daily. I could live with that daily exodus, as you
know, but I was mystified by the authorities' failure to act—
or, rather, I surmised that they were holding off because their
think tanks had already devised some ingenious plan. It now
transpired that I was to play the leading role in their plan.
Why had they called me on a Saturday? Why couldn't they
have waited until Monday? Because we couldn't afford to
lose any time.

They were going to entrust me with a special assignment
of vital importance and extreme complexity. I was their chosen instrument, the repository of all their hopes. The die had
been cast at the biggest conference table of all: I was to be
given my instructions and sent on a dangerous mission. I
might not get a wink of sleep for the next four days, but my
place on magazine covers and in history books would be assured thereafter. I would address schools, open bridges,
smash bottles of champagne against ships' hulls. Dr. Riechfinger lived an hour and a half's drive from State Security
headquarters. If they had gone to the lengths of summoning
him there on a sacrosanct Saturday afternoon, purely to attend a medical examination, my physical fitness must be of

vital concern to them. They had set up the examination for a weekend, too, when the Polyclinic was deserted and the number of those who were in on it could be kept to a minimum. My mission was so important that any measures were justified. Everything had been planned, nothing could be left to chance: there was too much at stake.

But what of my perversions? Should I conceal them from the Minister? What if he sent me behind the lines on a Chekist mission to conquer the hearts of the enemy's secretary-receptionists? Was it permissible under international law to let a perverted agent loose on the other side's vulnerable womenfolk, or did it violate the Hague Convention? If I failed—if I were put on trial and *everything* came out—wouldn't the enemy's propagandists make a meal of it? HO-NECKER'S PERVERTED AGENTS: THE STASI'S LATEST DIRTY TRICK! Complete with photograph—*my* photograph, on the front page of the *Bild-Zeitung*! Our Republic's reputation ruined! The prestige accruing from Katarina's gold medal down the drain! Perversions that surpassed even Siegfried Schnabl's imaginings, and all of them devised by a brain dedicated to the socialist ideal. My daily mass abuse of tadpoles—that would be enough in itself, if the enemy got to know of it! Was it worth the risk?

Dr. Riechfinger, who was waiting for me at the Ministry, gave me a blood donor consent form to sign. Then we rode down to the basement, where a second doctor escorted us to another elevator, which gave access to the Polyclinic's air-raid shelter complex.

"We need your blood," he told me with a Stasi smirk as the elevator door closed.

My blood? Why, what was so special about it? Had I acquired an abnormal blood type from my sexual preoccupation in puberty, the quelling of hard-ons? Had it directly conduced to my perversions? Did I possess a typical *pervert's blood type*? Was the Stasi in need of a pervert's blood?

"I don't propose to blind you with science," said the second doctor. "Just look at it this way. Your blood is to be used as a form of medication. You'll be injected with a serum that will trigger certain metabolic processes in your system. Those, in turn, will alter the composition of your blood in the way we require for our purposes."

"We have selected you," said Dr. Riechfinger, "because of your unique blood type, which leads us to expect some superb metabolic processes."

Unique blood type, *superb* metabolic processes—the man certainly knew how to flatter. Oh well, I thought, this is what I've spent years training for.

Once I had been injected with serum in a subterranean chamber fitted up like Frankenstein's laboratory, I spent a couple of hours trying to figure things out. I couldn't discern any connection between my giving blood and the exodus of refugees. Maybe there wasn't any connection—maybe the whole business had something to do with *doping*? Were they developing some new performance-enhancing drugs with my assistance? Ever since the scandal at Seoul in 1988, when Ben Johnson, the Olympic 100-meters champion, was compelled to return his gold medal, the game had been up for those mathematical geniuses who prescribed dosages and times with the aid of tables they drew up themselves. Had they now discovered a drug that was wholly undetectable? Using an intermediate host for prohibited substances would surely be far more sophisticated than swallowing preparations designed to fatten calves. But whom would I be supplying? *For whom would it be my privilege to bleed?* A single star, the whole Olympic team, or just my own blood group? The weightlifters, the track and field athletes, the strength or endurance specialists? The swimmers, perhaps? If so, it meant that I, the last of the dog-paddlers, would ennoble our Olympic swimming team with my blood! My blood would swim its way to countless victories! If my swimming instructor learned of it, he would go down on his knees and beg my pardon for all the slights he'd subjected me to.

I was passionately interested in the future whereabouts of my blood, Mr. Kitzelstein. Even if only a few milliliters of myself became an Olympic champion, *I had to know it*! It was unthinkable that even the tiniest bit of myself should mount the top step unbeknownst to the rest of me. Would I, as a fourteenfold Olympic victor, feel that I had at last achieved true fame? Would I, the self-effacing hero, be invited to the celebration dinner and share a table with the medal-winners of my blood group? Or was I to bleed *for Kati*? Could she be planning a comeback? Would we mingle our blood? Would I be seated at dinner between her and her coach, Jutta Müller, *who got everyone to perform*? Would Erich Honecker join us for a chat? What a picture! A glossy, full-page, full-color photograph in the next Olympic program: the General Secretary and Kati, our gold medalist, plus coach and blood donor: *me*.

"Those blood cells will soon be standing on the top step," I told myself, profoundly moved, as Dr. Riechfinger stuck a cannula in my arm and I saw my blood flow out into a plastic bag.

What ludicrous, megalomaniac romanticism! What naïveté! I had blithely ventured into the deepest air-raid shelter in Berlin, Mr. Kitzelstein, although my parents had always warned me never to be lured into cellars by strange men. A few minutes later I was on a drip, a machine beside my bed was going beep-beep-beep, and there were tubes, wires, rubber sleeves, and electrodes everywhere. This was the genuine Stasi, no two ways about it. Nothing that happened in here would ever get out. I'd been duped.

A constricted sensation overcame me. What rules prevailed down here? Why were they monitoring my heartbeat—because it might cease at any moment? Was I undergoing some form of intensive care? What had I let myself in for? What were they doing to me? Why didn't they tell me anything? Attached to a drip, hooked up to a machine that went beep and festooned with tubes and wires, I was lying in the bowels of the earth with blood draining out of me. Not a window, clock, or radio anywhere. Why couldn't I be allowed to know what was happening to me?

"Will you be much longer?" I asked after an hour, when the beeping began to accelerate.

"That depends," said Riechfinger. "A couple of days at least."

"But I thought this was a blood-donor session," I whispered as defiantly as I could.

"So it is," Riechfinger replied. He bent over the bed and shone a light in my eyes. "You mustn't be alarmed if your vision deteriorates. When subjected to blood loss, the healthy organism is so constituted that it ensures its viability by temporarily shutting down any functions that are particularly well supplied with blood but not essential to survival. Temporary loss of vision is quite normal and does no lasting damage."

The other doctor cleared his throat. "But keep your eyes open for as long as you can. We'll need some indication of when you lapse into unconsciousness."

"Unconsciousness?" I repeated feebly.

"Oh, that's just another temporary loss of function that does no lasting damage."

"An entirely natural organic reaction."

"A defense mechanism."

"And, in the event that you remain unconscious for an exceptional length of time, we've made arrangements—"

"—to feed you intravenously, so please don't worry."

Everything went black before my eyes, and I did something I'd always put off: I perfected my last words. They had to be quotable and in the classical German tradition. Had I known I was to die so young, I would already have devoted some thought to them. Goethe's "More light" had always struck me as thoroughly apt, but present circumstances made it difficult to hit upon something equally quotable. I abandoned my quest for a message to posterity with the words "Oh, shit!"—hardly the summation I had always wanted carved in granite over my grave. Those botched last words preyed on my mind. I dreamed I saw Dr. Riechfinger filling out my death certificate at his desk and, under the heading "Last Words," making the entry "KING'S GAMBIT" in block capitals. The light that shone down from the ceiling was bright and intense but infinitely soft and *perfect*. It was simultaneously alluring and beguiling, exciting and soothing. All I had known in the way of light was merely illumination by comparison. Then it vanished, and I was holding Yvonne's kaleidoscope in my hand—she had suddenly materialized beside me. I gave it to her. She peered into it and said, "This . . . is . . . no . . . game."

I recovered consciousness to find myself looking up into the two doctors' faces.

"You made it," said Dr. Riechfinger.

"You'll soon recover," said his colleague.

When they left the room I really did find my death certificate in a slim folder on the desk. It was complete except for the date of death—they'd even signed it. Fine, I told myself, if they've already made out my death certificate, all they need do now is finish me off: I'm done for! You see, Mr. Kitzelstein, that's how I treated the subject of my death. I had so little self-respect that I even tried to joke at a time of deadly peril. I resolved to greet my murderers as if they were the movers' men: *Hi there, Drs. Riechfinger and A. N. Other, come to kill me because I know too much? Too bad, not a pleasant job, sooner you than me. Anything I can do to make things easier for you? Do you have a last wish before I die?* See what a first-class candidate for death I was? See how much self-esteem I'd acquired in my twenty-one years? I should have taken a leaf out of my mother's book—at least she'd yelled "Shut up and take my son to the emergency room at once!" But what did her son do when danger really threatened? Did he rant and rage? Did he pound the door with his fists and bellow, "Let me out!"? No, nothing of the kind. Lucie Uhltzscht's son, who had always been left to answer his own questions, did what he always did: he racked his brains in a decorous manner. Why had they done this? Would they kill me? What if they didn't come back? Would I starve to death or suffocate?

All right, I'll talk about death for once, but seriously, an octave lower. Let's see how desensitized I really am. I already guessed that it wouldn't be so easy to shrug off my father's death. I'd spent hours at the monster's bedside. He lay there exhausted, brimful of shit and barely conscious. He'd been through the torments of hell but he didn't show it. A real man. I was still afraid of him, and still I waited for some sign that I was his son, and that he trusted or acknowledged me or whatever. Even though he was *at long last* simply lying there, doing nothing but expiring, I couldn't banish my eternal feeling of inferiority, of immaturity and insignificance. Once, but only once, did he utter a gasp. He gave me a last admonitory look, as if to say, "That concludes this demonstration of how to die like a man." Then his eyes closed and his heart stopped beating. *No more father,* I thought with relief. I wanted to sing, but I couldn't.

There he lay. That lump of shit in human shape had shown me the ropes. He'd run to catch streetcars looking at the doors and not the driver. He'd transformed women into malign creatures who extorted confidential information by threatening paternity suits. He hadn't gone to the doctor until he was past saving because it would have made him feel soft. He'd gritted his teeth even on his deathbed. Oh yes, he'd shown me the ropes all right. He'd made and raised and influenced and dominated me, and now he was dead and I, the repository of all he'd drummed into me, was his residue. What could I do to avoid dying like him? I got up and opened the curtains. "Leave them!" he said, but I knew he was dead. I resumed my place at his bedside and savored the *no more father* sensation. No, I hadn't imagined it: he'd drawn another breath. It was part of the process of dying. His chest relapsed with a sigh that seemed to issue from every pore: the shit who was my father had actually succeeded in pretending that his body housed a soul.

I still don't know what he did, as I've said, but I know what *I* did as soon as he was dead: I pulled the bedclothes down and looked at what he'd always concealed from me: his *balls.* Having seen Riechfinger making out my death certificate while I was dead, I hope my father saw me take his balls in my hand and squeeze them. *Go on,* I thought, *if you're so damned omnipotent you'll sit up with a jerk, knock my hand away, and box my ears.* But he was too dead for that. I squeezed his balls for twenty seconds. He'd squeezed mine for twenty years, from the look of them.

There are certain things I've done that I'd sooner not have done, but that isn't one of them.

So now I'd stood on the threshold and had my near-death experience—no, let's be accurate, anyone can say "near-death experience." This had involved *light* and *levitation*. Slowly rising into the air, I saw Dr. Riechfinger making out my death certificate at his desk. I could also see myself lying in bed, cocooned in wires and tubes, but I was confident I wouldn't become entangled in them because I felt so weightless and so—how can I put it?—so *spiritual*. Then there was the *light*. It was a soft, lustrous light with an infinitely soothing quality, and as I floated upward, lighter than a leaf in the wind, I drifted toward it. The subterranean chamber suddenly became a shaft, and the higher I rose, the dimmer the light became.

Was I transformed by this experience? Not at all, Mr. Kitzelstein, so don't look embarrassed. It was only a matter of life and death—in other words, nothing serious. To be absolutely frank for once, I'd led such an apathetic existence that I was indifferent to my own death, and once I grasped that fact I carried on as before. A person of my kind deserved to be slaughtered if need arose. I returned from the realm of the dead and did what I always did: I pondered. With my own death certificate in my hand, I debated whether the doctors would come back or leave me to rot.

They did come back. I held the death certificate under Dr. Riechfinger's nose—a risky thing to do, because there was no guarantee he wouldn't clasp his brow and exclaim, "You're right, it's incomplete!" He shone a light in my eyes and said, "Excellent, we won't be needing that now." Then, very obligingly, he tore up the certificate, tossed it into the wastebasket, and strode out. If that isn't Kafkaesque, what is?

I survived. I fished the fragments of my death certificate out of the wastebasket, secreted them in my wallet, and stuck them together when I got home. I still carry my own death certificate around with me, a privilege that ought to arouse the envy of any true existentialist. Then there were the repercussions on my Index of New Perversions. Having sex with me, for instance, must necessarily be classified as *necrophilia*—I have it in writing. Furthermore, I'm a dead man with sexual urges. What should that be termed, *draculism?* No such perversion has ever cropped up before. Not even Sigmund Freud described the perversion I practice in his *Three Essays on the Theory of Sexuality,* nor did he even postulate its existence (as Einstein did the bending of light). Rise and applaud the first socialist perversion, as great a pioneering feat as Yuri Gagarin's in Vostok 1. I am the living proof of socialism's historic superiority in the field of perversion—I, the Gagarin of perversion!

I returned to Golm Law School after a few days' convalescence. The situation—it was mid-September by now—had become more acute. I seriously expected the whole of the State Security Service (some hundred thousand strong, as we now know) to be ordered to defect to West Germany, thereby engineering the latter's economic collapse. Instead, we scurried around on the athletic field, practicing the encirclement and detention of *troublemakers at riotous assemblies held without prior notice.* As you see, Mr. Kitzelstein, we believed our internal enemies capable of any enormity, even the dispatching of troublemakers to unannounced riotous assemblies. (What had happened in the past? Did people go to the police and say *Good morning, we're forty troublemakers and we want to hold a riotous assembly?*)

True to form, I headed obediently for the government hospital as soon as the second summons reached me. Once again, my instructions were transmitted by the Law School principal's assistant. I had every reason to mutiny, if I valued my life, but I refrained from doing so. What I did venture to do—

my most rebellious act while serving in the Stasi—was to ask what awaited me. The reply, uttered with a Stasi smirk, was "Nothing that could cause you to regret going there." "You mean like the last time?" I said. "Just go there," I was told, "and you'll see what I mean." Damn the man. Why did other people always know what was going to happen to me? Who made the plans that involved me? My next death certificate would not be torn up, but if I had to die I wanted at least to know what for.

Die? Did I say *die*? Was I a character from a Shakespearian tragedy? Shakespeare's characters *died,* or shuffled off this mortal coil, or departed from our midst. Whose midst could I depart from? Who would lay flowers on my grave? My kind *kicked the bucket.* "Let's get it over with," I would tell the doctor, and, "Oh, do me a favor and let me write out the death certificate myself; I've got a weakness for paradoxes."

I was awaited at the government hospital by Dr. Riechfinger's anonymous colleague, but his opening words sounded quite innocuous: a life had been saved, thanks to my donated blood, and the patient in question wanted to thank me personally. He also said something that promptly set my Nobel Prize antennae quivering: the therapy employed had previously been considered impracticable, and only my selfless and extremely hazardous contribution had made it possible.

An instant before I entered the patient's room I heard a faint clatter—someone had just cocked a pistol, I thought, until I perceived the source of the sound: the patient who owed his survival to my selfless and extremely hazardous contribution had just dropped a set of jackstraws on the table. Sunlight was flooding through the big windows. The nurse closed the door behind me, leaving me alone with the jackstraws player. I knew his face. Everyone did. It was an almost daily page one spectacle.

I smiled, glad that we had met at last. We had momentous matters to discuss. There were hard times ahead, but he hadn't forgotten me. We would have to devise some means of stopping the flood of defectors to the West. Things couldn't go on in this way.

He gestured to me to join him at the table. I did so, resolved to wait in patient silence. He, the grand strategist, must already have worked out what he proposed to tell me. While seeking the right opening—words of historic importance, no doubt—he concentrated on his game. This, I assumed, was his way of collecting his thoughts prior to issuing weighty instructions. He removed a couple of loose jackstraws, then tackled some trickier ones.

"This set," he said after a while, "was presented to me by a Chinese delegation. In those days . . ." He left the sentence unfinished and readdressed himself to his jackstraws. There was a record player beside his bed. The record had come to an end: no music, just thirty-three clicks per minute. The needle was lodged in the escape groove, but the switch-off mechanism had failed.

I stayed put and waited. Why didn't he turn the record over? Why didn't he say something? He must have had something, *something*, in mind when he sent for me. Our country's most eminent and important Cover Picture had received me in his pajamas. How informal, how intimate! I was ready to plunge into the fray and carry out my historic mission at his behest, but all he did was play jackstraws, a game you lose as soon as something moves . . .

So, Mr. Kitzelstein, to sum up the situation: Like the Little Trumpeter, I had died—if only on paper—to save my General Secretary. I wasn't a merry "young blood" in the Red

Guard; my blood was just a timid pervert's blood, but only you and I know that. Let me talk about *blood* for a moment—we Germans have always had a thing about it. Realizing as I sat there that we were *blood brothers*, I grasped what that signified—for me, for him, for our country and the history of the world. My rare and therapeutic blood owed its rarity to the fact that I drank almost nothing, as you know. I drank almost nothing so as to suppress my sexual urges. By suppressing my sexual urges, however, I had strayed into perversion. Ergo, only a pervert like me could have saved the jackstraws player and enabled him to go on playing.

A rather tacky *curriculum vitae*, perhaps, but also—whichever way you look at it—imbued with *meaning*. The historical context suddenly dawned on me: I'd wondered what "they" planned to do with my precious life, and it had transpired that my precious life was ensuring the survival of a General Secretary. The obvious inference was that the General Secretary was leading our Red World out of its current predicament. I was convinced of this. If it weren't so, I should have laid down my life for a bogeyman, and that was impossible. I was a near genius, after all, and geniuses don't get sacrificed just like that. Consequently—nations, take note!—this General Secretary would save the Red World.

Funny, the thoughts that run through your head when you've spent hours sitting in silence beside a pajama-clad man previously known to you only as a Cover Picture . . . My urge to explain the world to myself is a curse, I know, but the worst of an obsession is that it always finds evidence to support itself.

When no more jackstraws could be removed without disturbing the rest, the patient counted his haul again and again. He carefully arranged the garnered jackstraws in order of value, stared at the rest in silence, and studied the situation from every angle—he even moved from chair to chair, all around the table, in search of a solution. When none presented itself, he hoped for a miracle. He didn't speak or take a gamble, but he didn't give up either. He simply refused to admit defeat, just as I refused to acknowledge that I would have laid down my life—and had actually done so, according to my death certificate—for a hopeless old obsessive.

He sat there all that afternoon, a dogged, impotent figure with nothing but the click of the record player to listen to, staring at a heap of little sticks. As for me, I sat there all that afternoon filled with expectancy. I was his accomplice, his only intimate at a time of trial. At ten after six, when the nurse came in with his supper, she cleared away the jackstraws. "Now I can't prove I wasn't beaten," he said sulkily.

Afterward the anonymous doctor took me to his office and proudly spread out a selection of West German papers. "Today's," he announced, smiting a banner headline—HONECKER RUMORED DEAD—with the back of his hand. "Or what about these?" He indicated some more: CANCER OF THE PANCREAS—HONECKER NEAR DEATH.

Thinking of my death certificate, I said, "Men reported dead live longer." The doctor guffawed delightedly and promised to pass that on to his patient. Weeks later, when Erich Honecker reappeared in public, our newspapers splashed my *bon mot* on page one, like a schoolboy's impudent grin. Honecker's conduct of affairs was perceptibly affected by his transfusions of pervert's blood. At his last major appearance before undergoing treatment he had come out with a little rhyming slogan to the effect that socialism was on course and that nothing could halt its progress. This statement was so puerile but so typical of him that one couldn't take it amiss.

However, his transfusions of pervert's blood put an end

to such innocuous behavior. Wounded vanity prompted him to divert trains, close the last open frontier, and change our Republic back into the Soviet Zone. He celebrated the fortieth anniversary of its foundation with a torchlight parade a hundred thousand strong, shed no tears for his victims, ordered rifles to be loaded and aimed. Provoking demonstrators is a tactical device and gunning them down is a crime, but provoking them so as to gun them down is a perversion. I can't refrain from making up quotable inanities, as you see. I understand *everything* that happened at that time. I understood it so well that I was able to topple the Berlin Wall. I'm probably the only person for whom the turning point in Germany presents no mystery whatever. After all, I brought it about.

THE FINAL CHAPTER

René, my tent mate at Freienbrink camp, also shared a room with me at Golm Law School. During my year with the Accounts Department of the Periodicals Postal Subscription Service he had been obliged to sit in the basement of the radio station in Nalepastrasse and monitor all the phone calls that were broadcast live. Live phone conversations with random callers were first introduced in the middle of the 1980s, and everyone in the Stasi took it for granted that the enemy would exploit this attempt to inject a little "color" into our radio programs. René was under orders to ensure that listeners were never subjected to political agitation. It was his job to prevent "undesirable" conversations and, if necessary, to cut them short. He never once had to step in. When we arrested a handful of demonstrators on the night of October 7, therefore, he was utterly mystified. "But in theory," he protested on seeing them, "there shouldn't be any. They never phoned in." "Don't get worked up," I told him; "there aren't all that many of them."

At the Alexanderplatz U-Bahn station the following night we arrested any subversive-looking individuals coming from the Pankow direction. Demonstrations were then held mainly in the evening and at night, and homeward-bound demonstrators had to change at Alexanderplatz, where they were easy meat. Our squad commander played the civil war strategist. He set up his headquarters in the stationmaster's office, kept in touch with developments at other stations by phone, and gave us our orders over the public address system. His excitement mounted after midnight. "The rioters are dispersing. The next train will be full of them. It's an express train. They're getting on at Schönhauser Allee and they'll come straight here without stopping." He jumped down from the little rostrum on which the station announcer's microphone was mounted and strode along the platform, grinning broadly. "They're trapped," he called to us. "We'll get 'em— every last one of them!"

The train—a short one, incidentally—pulled in. It was empty. Having stopped at Alexanderplatz a couple of times in the course of his evening shift, the driver had seen the arrests in progress. When instructed to take his last trainload straight to Alexanderplatz without stopping, he had warned the demonstrators over his own public address system and stopped at every intervening station to let them off. It may well have been the very first time he'd used his public address system—and the very first time he'd defied authority. I couldn't help thinking of my father and his habit of waving at the doors, not the driver, when sprinting to catch a streetcar. It was probably an occupational disease of Stasi personnel to believe that streetcars and U-Bahn trains were creatures with a life of their own.

"Arrest him!" our squad commander bellowed over the station loudspeakers. "Arrest that driver!"

Raymund and I grabbed the man by the arms. He offered no resistance. "I suppose you're proud of yourself!" the squad commander barked. The driver didn't look proud of anything, but the squad commander barked at every detainee on principle. We escorted him to the station exit. "Let him go," I said to Raymund; "then we can shoot him while attempting to escape. I don't feel like driving him out into the woods." That tickled Raymund. He laughed so much he let go of the driver's arm. "Want to clear off?" he asked. The man didn't answer. "That's it, then," said Raymund. "You'll have to come with us." We escorted him outside the station and made him board a waiting truck. "You missed your chance" were Raymund's parting words. "We'd have let you go."

Why have I told you this? Everyone knows that only staunch Communists were shot by the Nazis "while attempting to escape," so what inspired my sudden suggestion? Why did I put myself on a par with the Nazis? If brought before a Party board of inquiry, I would have replied that my remark was meant to be instructive: *not* being shot would have shown our prisoner the fundamental difference between the Nazi dictatorship and our own socialist system, thereby reinforcing his gratitude toward the latter and his feeling of socialist solidarity. It was the negation of negation, or dialectics in general. One of our socialist system's indisputable advantages was that, except when defecting from the Republic, citizens were not shot while attempting to escape. How had Owl put it? *They don't know how lucky they are.* The train driver was supposed to breathe a sigh of relief and tell himself, "What on earth made me think I'd be shot while attempting to escape? That kind of thing doesn't happen here, not now. Once upon a time . . ."

You don't believe me, Mr. Kitzelstein? All right, hand on heart: Why did I scare that unfortunate train driver? Because I'm mean and nasty? Because I'm a Stasi rat? Remember my first kidnapping and the way I tormented Sara by beating her incessantly at Parcheesi? Why am I so rotten? Because I *want* to be rotten? Because it's part of my persona to do mean, lousy, odious things? Because my sense of guilt needs feeding? Given that children's laughter is "our most valuable asset" (or "our finest reward"—I can't recall the official phrase, but there was a superlative in it somewhere), only a contemptible character would claim to have relished a child's *tears*! Only the most abject individuals—only those who, like the Nazis and me, did not balk at snuffing out fifty million lives—are capable of cynical, shot-while-attempting-to-escape pleasantries. Yes, it's true: I'm a rotten swine. I deserve to be stoned to death!

It was, in fact, my *sense of guilt* that prompted me to defy an official ban and attend the mass demonstration in Alexanderplatz on November 4. Yes, Mr. Kitzelstein, it was my sense of guilt that impelled me to go there and court death. Perhaps Sara would recognize me and point me out. My fate would be sealed by her cry of "Mama, that's the man who made me play Parcheesi with him!" The game would be up, the day of reckoning would have come. I would be swinging from a lamppost within minutes.

But why should it have to be Sara who unmasked me— why not leave my Stasi ID dangling on its little cord? A chance encounter with the train driver would be equally effective. Well, now that retribution was inescapable, I made no attempt to escape it. Anyone who had a score to settle with me could go ahead: I wanted to get it over with—I didn't want to get away unscathed. Mark you, there were so many demonstrators in Alexanderplatz that I had little chance of bumping into any of my victims. It was the lead item in next day's newspapers: three-quarters of a million people! Incredible! Not long ago the Berlin protest potential could be accommodated in a U-Bahn train—a short one—and four weeks later Alexanderplatz was filled to overflowing. Hundreds of thousands of innocent citizens marched behind a street-wide banner inscribed PROTEST DEMONSTRATION. What had gotten into them? Discounting a group of people small enough to fit into a short U-Bahn train, all of them were fellow travelers. Had they forgotten that? How could I feel genuinely guilty, how could I reproach myself in their presence? Admittedly, I was the worst and most abominable of all—Honecker's Little Trumpeter, a resurrected zombie, a perverted Stasi, a kidnapper, and the rest—but I was one of them nonetheless. I had done nothing my teachers and TV programs had warned me not to do. I had always done what other people wanted. I had never done what I myself wanted, otherwise I would have been happy. Whether or not such thoughts were worth pursuing, then came *the speech,* and everything changed completely.

Every revolutionary movement emancipates language as well. That wasn't my mother engaged in a debate about linguistics; it issued from the loudspeakers. The very sound of that calm, admonitory female voice was as much as I could stand. Anyway, how could anyone talk about *language* on such a day? Why not about the weather and have done with it? That at least would have been consistently inconsistent! The woman at the microphone was too far away for me to see her face. Who was she? Any seminormal person would have accosted one of the three-quarters of a million people and said politely, "Excuse me, who's speaking?" Not I—not the son of a man who watched the doors while sprinting for a streetcar instead of trying to catch the driver's eye. No suspicion-ridden Stasi type who mistrusted everyone on principle would ever have asked a stranger something he could discover for himself—he might be told any old thing—so I elbowed my way through the crowd toward the microphone to identify the speaker with my own eyes. In so doing I made the twentieth century's most momentous mistake.

Dear fellow citizens, every revolutionary movement emancipates language as well. All at once, things that have hitherto been hard to express flow freely from our lips. We stand amazed at what was obviously in our minds for so long, and at what we now cry aloud: Democracy, now or never! By that we mean rule by the people. And we recall the stillborn or bloodily suppressed initiatives in our history and are unwilling to pass up the opportunity inherent in this crisis, because it is arousing all our productive forces . . .

I have problems with the expression "turning point." It conjures up the picture of a sailboat when the captain shouts, "Stand by to go about!" because the wind has veered or is blowing in his face, and the crew duck as the boom swings across. But does that analogy still apply? Does it still apply in this daily-changing situation? I would prefer to speak of revolutionary renewal. Revolutions proceed from below. Top and bottom are changing places in our system of values, and this change is turning socialist society upside down. Great social movements are under way.

Never have people in this country talked as much as in recent weeks—talked with one another, talked with as much anger and sorrow, but also with as much hope. We strive to make the most of every day, we sleep little or not at all, we make friends with people we didn't know before and are painfully estranged from others whom we thought we knew. That is termed "dialogue." We called for it, but now we can hardly bear to hear the word. And we still haven't really learned what it means. We stare mistrustfully at many a suddenly outstretched hand, at many a previously expressionless face. "Mistrust is good, control even better." We refurbish the old slogans that have constrained and injured us and send them back by return mail. We're afraid of being used and exploited—afraid, too, of rejecting a genuine offer. Such is the dilemma in which our entire country finds itself at the present time. We know that we must practice the art of not allowing this dilemma to degenerate into confrontation. These weeks and these opportunities are being given us only once—by ourselves. It puzzles us to see how skillfully those flexible individuals popularly known as "wrynecks"— birds that the encyclopedia describes as adapting themselves swiftly and easily to any given situation—contrive to operate within this new situation and exploit it. They, I believe, are the chief obstacle to the credibility of the new policy. We're not yet at a stage where we can accept them with the sense of humor we already manage to display in other instances. "No free rides!" I read on some banners, and demonstrators chant, "Get changed and join us!" at the police. A generous offer, I'm bound to say. We also think in economic terms— "Legal security saves on State Security!"—and today I saw one banner bearing a quite incredible slogan: "No more privileges for us Berliners!"

Yes, language is breaking free from the officialese and journalese that swaddled it and recalling its emotive words. One of those is "dream." Let us, therefore, dream with alert common sense: Imagine if this were socialism and no one were leaving! But we see pictures of those who are continuing to leave, and we ask ourselves: What can be done? And, like an echo, we hear the reply: What can be done! That's what happens now, when demands are becoming rights, in other words, obligations. Fact-finding committees, a constitutional court, administrative reforms—there's much to be done, and all of it in addition to our work—on top of reading the newspapers! We won't have time for any more patriotic parades or officially decreed demonstrations. This is an authorized, nonviolent demo. If it remains that way to the end, we will know more about what we can do. And then we will insist on it.

Here's a suggestion for May Day: let our rulers parade past the people. None of this is my idea—it's part of our national literary heritage. An incredible transformation: the citizens of the German Democratic Republic are taking to the streets in recognition that they are the people. And these are the most important words to be heard in recent weeks, the thousandfold cry: "We are the people!" A simple statement, and let us not forget it.

There the speech ended. I was within eighty meters of the platform by this time, close enough to identify the speaker. It was Jutta Müller, the figure-skating coach, my mother's idol, and—in her capacity as the woman who always got her students to "perform"—the doyenne of my sexual fantasies. What lay in store for us if someone of *her* caliber had been engaged to speak? Who would speak next—the Sandman?

Every revolution gets the speeches it deserves, Mr. Kitzelstein. I've reproduced this one in full because it's still regarded as the point at which the fall '89 situation crystallized—something immediately apparent, believe it or not, to myself. A genuine figure-skating coach's speech, don't you agree? Studied elegance and purple passages guaranteed to earn good marks for artistic impression, coupled with a breathless, short-term political program in which a few botched or omitted jumps remain unnoticed by the besotted audience. Don't ask me what I was *for;* I only knew, when I heard Jutta Müller's speech, what I was *against.* I was against her demands-into-rights-i.e.-obligations nonsense. Perhaps one can only expect a figure-skating coach to speak like a figure-skating coach, but where does the "emancipated lan-

guage" come in? Take her voluptuous toying with the term
"turning point" and the way she ar-tic-u-lat-ed "We're afraid
of being used and exploited." Oh, Mr. Kitzelstein, I felt I was
back home with my mother, who had consulted the encyclopedia's article on → GREECE when what interested me was
penises. → WRYNECK . . . An ingenious idea.

But what really enlightened me was when Jutta Müller,
my mother's idol, began to dream: *Imagine if this were socialism and no one were leaving!* Having carefully picked
holes in the term "turning point" early on—having cited the
ornithological dictionary's definition of "wryneck," and all
in the interests of emancipated speech—she came to this: her
dream, which was called socialism, slipped through un-
checked without so much as a glance at the encyclopedia—
without being probed from all sides like the term "turning
point." Suppose, just suppose, that she *had* consulted the encyclopedia: she might have come across → SOCIALISM: *a social system founded on the collective ownership of the means
of production.* Could *you* dream of that—dream of it in a
truly visionary manner, I mean? "Imagine if production were
collectivized and no one were leaving." Sorry, Jutta, it doesn't
make my heart miss a beat. I wouldn't have anything against
collectivized production if it didn't occasion a mass exodus,
but as a *dream* it's two sizes too small for me.

It would be funny if it weren't so tragic, Mr. Kitzelstein,
but these mothers and figure-skating coaches are genuinely
attached to socialism. They crawled from the ruins of the
Thousand-Year Reich with such an ingrained fear of air raids
that, even today, fireworks remind them of anti-aircraft fire.
They were hungry. The more principled among them were
ashamed of being German. Their past was unpresentable and
their present existence bleak.

But the future—ah, that would be different! When the

youngsters of that generation sat around the campfire at night, bones aching after an eleven-hour day spent building dams or draining marshes under the auspices of the Free German Youth Movement's reconstruction program, they probably felt proud of themselves for the very first time, and they all got blind drunk on the contents of a capacious bottle labeled SOCIALISM. It kept them warm, and even today they still rhapsodize about "true socialism" when what they really mean is their campfire emotions.

I'm not being deliberately arrogant—I'd have acted no differently—but before we allow Jutta Müller and her friends to signal the next round of *Imagine if this were socialism* let us consider, *with alert common sense,* that socialism is an abstract idea, and that everything worthwhile can be expressed more concretely—as long as we take care to use "emancipated language." Even today, when everything suddenly "flows freely from our lips," people speak of socialism and not of our need for unrestricted access to the world at large.

Anyway, I wanted to fight my way onto the back of the open truck and seize the microphone, eager to put an end to this socialist hocus-pocus. I, the Stasi swine, Honecker's perverted Little Trumpeter, wanted to display myself to three-quarters of a million people as a deterrent object lesson in socialism taken to extremes. What also alarmed me was a word association, namely, that *Jutta* and *Mutter* rhyme, and that all that differentiates *Mutter* from *Müller* are two little cross-strokes. Jutta Müller, the mother of all mothers! The figure-skating coach was right to wear WE ARE THE PEOPLE! in her buttonhole. Heavens! If my mother's son had become a pervert, what would become of a country revolutionized by figure-skating coaches and sanitary inspectors?

The speaker's truck was parked a few meters from the

entrance to a pedestrian subway. I decided to take that route because it would be easier than forging a path through the crowd. Hurriedly, I made for the subway entrance, so preoccupied with the opening sentences of my fierce, inflammatory speech that I failed to notice what some demonstrator had abandoned upside down at the top of the steps: a cardboard placard mounted on a broomstick. I not only failed to notice it but tripped over it, dislodged it with my foot, stumbled, lost my balance, and would have fallen headlong but for the broomstick between my legs. I speared my balls on the end, lurched forward, and pogoed onto the next step down, and scored a third bull's-eye. Not until this circus act was complete did I somersault and crack my head on the steps, which, compared to what had gone before, was positively relaxing. Just to complete the picture, the poster was inscribed *Self-determination for all!*

I was stretched out on the landing halfway down when I recovered consciousness. Four or five crouching figures were peering anxiously into my face. A woman with wonderful brown eyes was gently, tenderly, slapping my face.

"Can you hear me? Are you conscious?"

"Yes," I said feebly.

"I'm a nurse," she went on, brushing a strand of sweaty hair out of my eyes. "Do you know what happened?"

"Yes," I whispered. "Jutta Müller, the figure-skating coach, gave a speech. I was trying to get to the microphone because I'm in the Stasi, I'm afraid. I wanted to—"

"Ssh," said the nurse. "Don't excite yourself."

"What I wanted to say was 'Imagine if this were socialism and nobody gave a damn.' "

They exchanged worried glances.

"He's delirious," said a woman's anxious voice from somewhere near my feet.

The nurse stroked my forehead, a gesture that finally enlightened me on the difference between *maternal* and *motherly*.

She continued to gaze at me with her warm brown eyes while waiting for the ambulance to arrive, then gave a sudden, involuntary sob. "Oh, my God!" she said hoarsely, looking away to curb her emotions. "Oh, my God, to think I should live to see the day! Would you have believed it possible that there were so . . . so *many* of us, and that we've got ideas of our own and know what we want. And you"—she laughed through her tears—"you have to go and split your head open on this of all days. Never mind, though, everything'll be all right." It was a uniquely moving moment. If I hadn't been almost dying of pain, it would have been too good a moment for a scumbag like me. *Never mind, though, everything'll be all right.*

My true identity caught up with me on the operating table, when the surgeon pulled his mask down and started talking about the Stasi. My "busted balls," as they were jocularly called, necessitated an immediate operation. My gruesome injury had been inspected by the entire staff of the emergency room—a grossly overmanned department, incidentally, because preparations had been made to receive an influx of wounded rioters. "All I did was fall downstairs," I told any doctor or nurse that risked a look, but when I was lying on the operating table, waiting to be anesthetized, a nurse came in, called to the surgeon, and whispered to him briefly. Returning to the table, he stared at me suspiciously and dangled something in my face. It was my Stasi ID card.

"How did you say the injury occurred?" he asked through his mask.

"All I did was fall downstairs," I whispered back.

"Really?" he said. "I'd like a demonstration sometime."

"No, honestly," I whispered. "I fell downstairs."

"I only ask," he said, "because we so often get patients who have come straight from your . . . your *institution* and claim to have fallen downstairs. We've never been able to figure it out." He gave a supercilious smile. "Some stairs you must have—really intriguing." His surgical team had gathered around expectantly. He pulled his mask down with a sudden, angry gesture. "You wouldn't be joking, I suppose?" he said sharply. "Are you interested in what it says on your admission form? 'Cause of injury: falling downstairs.' Presumably so the Stasi can testify in court that even one of their own people, e.g."—he consulted my ID—"Officer Cadet Klaus Uhltzscht, State Security Service, was stupid enough to fall downstairs and injure his head and genitals."

"No," I said feebly, cold sweat breaking out on my forehead, "I really did fall downstairs. It happened in the middle of Alexanderplatz."

He gazed deep into my eyes. What did that look imply? I was so helpless. His knife awaited me—his *scalpel,* to be exact. What had I let myself in for?

"Will you operate on me like any normal patient?" I asked timidly.

"Of course," he snapped. "What do you take me for?"

I was in terrible pain when I woke up after surgery. Sleeping with an erection was an old habit of mine, but now, fresh from the operating table . . . My *intimate reflex* was exacting its ultimate revenge. I couldn't help thinking, as I gnawed the corner of my pillow and prayed for relief, of my father and the poker face he'd maintained in his death throes. I, being a total failure, was cut from a different cloth. My blood ran cold when I finally saw what the surgeon's knife had done to me. It was a spectacle reminiscent of a squashed frog. This, so I'd always imagined, was how a wounded soldier looked when a hand grenade exploded in his pocket. I found it incomprehensible that such a mess could manage an erection.

But at night, when I woke up racked with pain, I began asking myself some other questions. Where had I gone so wrong that fate should subject *me* to such pointless torment? Why had all this happened? Why, why, *why*? At last I had a reason to hate my life. I was so manifestly washed up and done for, so far down the road, that I finally repented. I'd survived my death certificate in the belief that I was the greatest, one of the elect, but this pain had smashed my rose-colored spectacles. It was there, it was real, it filled every part of me, and it mortified me so much that no future prospect could console me.

It was so humiliating. Pain was my whole existence. Chewing on my pillow like a dummy and groaning at each uncontrollable erection in the nights that followed, I cursed myself for having to lie there, for falling down the steps, for winding up in the Stasi, for living in a way that precluded me from cheating my destiny, and for the fact that it all made sense. I discovered that I had a past, and that my present pain and the squashed frog were not fortuitous irruptions into my life, merely a continuation of all that had gone before—that everything was following a logical course and had *had* to end this way. My pain was the harbinger of truth. I acknowledged it to be a form of punishment and became a seeker after guilt and responsibility.

That may sound sanctimonious, Mr. Kitzelstein, but—verily, verily, I say unto you!—I was undergoing a Job-like ordeal. I refused to take any drug that might have alleviated my sufferings. Damned painful, but damned creditable of me, don't you agree? Why do you think I'm now able to talk into your microphone with such absolute candor? What kind of person would I be if those nights had wrought no change in me—if the pain had borne no fruit at all?

Aside from the fact that every hard-on drove me well-nigh insane, I was unable to walk for three days. The first time I got up to go to the bathroom I didn't *walk*, I *crept*. The bathroom was situated at the far end of the passage. Barefoot and attired in a far too short elf's costume open at the back except for a tie at the neck, I had to shuffle all the way, four centimeters at a time. Although the series of humiliations that now made up my life seemed to be perpetuating itself, I noticed something in the john that fascinated me no end: my dick was bigger than it had been. How come? Postoperative swelling? Inflammation? *Transplantation?* Had the surgeon carried out an organ transplant? I mean, what better source of body parts than the emergency room? Had he taken receipt of a fresh corpse with intact genitalia? Why had he done it? Out of pity? Compassion? Forgiveness?

But, to revert to my spiritual awakening in the hospital, I soon felt an urge to read a book. Apart from their newspapers, the men in my ward possessed just one book apiece, if that, and were naturally unwilling to part with their only reading matter. Courageously, therefore, I set off for the women's ward—an act that might easily have provoked a sex scandal because my elf's costume was so short that it put me in mind of Siegfried Schnabl's exhibitionistic window-cleaner, who had mounted the windowsill of his ground-floor apartment wearing a jockstrap and nothing else. In the very first cubicle of the women's ward I saw a whole bedside table stacked with books. Their owner was eating yogurt. She reminded me of my former music teacher, a diminutive woman who felt insecure unless entrenched behind her piano accordion. I wanted to ask the woman for a book that took account of my condition, but I waited for her to finish her yogurt in case my elf's costume was so short that it made her lose her appetite (consideration has always been one of my salient characteristics). Finally I ventured inside and asked if she would lend me a book. Which book? Not just any old book, I replied. "I'm searching for something."

"Aren't we all, one way or another?"

"I need to get a few things straightened out."

"I understand. You'd like to quit the Party but you don't dare?"

"There's more to it than that."

"That's what they all say. Help yourself."

Among the books on the bedside table was one by Christa Wolf. I had hitherto avoided reading Christa Wolf in spite of my five library cards. She was reputed to be "difficult," which you, Mr. Kitzelstein, should construe as "sophisticated."

"There's something else," I said. "It mustn't . . . well, *arouse* me."

She smiled. "So I see," she said, and handed me the book. "It's a love story, but"—her eyes twinkled—"quite *innocuous.*"

Back in my bed I opened the book. It was dedicated *"For G . . ."* "G" for what? Gustav, grandmother, greenbacks? Was "G" monosyllabic and, if so, did Gerd Grabs know the dedicatee's full name? For G . . . "G" for G spot? A love story dedicated to the G spot? Ouch, and I'd wanted a book that wouldn't arouse me! I'm still of the opinion, Mr. Kitzelstein, that anyone desirous of understanding Christa Wolf could do worse than ponder the dedication of her first major novel. It sparked off a literary controversy in which hordes of East and West German intellectuals forged themselves a variety of interpretations. Christa Wolf wrote a novel and dedicated it to someone. She could have made it clear to whom, but she didn't, and I've no idea why. The potential implications are legion, and perhaps that's what they were meant to be. Don't expect clarity. You won't get any, not even at the simplest level.

The novel in question opens with a horrific scenario for which the author requires but a few short sentences. What a picture she paints in the space of a single paragraph! A city is overwhelmed by the stench of a chemical plant. The filth from a hundred factory chimneys blots out the sun, the inhabitants can scarcely breathe, the river is contaminated, the local water undrinkable. *What an opening!* I thought, ready to forgive her nebulous dedication. *You can tell she's a master of her craft!* Such is the setting, and all the action takes place in a stinking city never penetrated by the sun's rays. Every cup of coffee has to be gulped down with distaste, every conversation is interrupted by fits of coughing. A love story? Boy (conjunctivitis) meets Girl (eczema).

I had to read the concluding sentence of the first paragraph three times: "But the earth still bore them up and would continue to do so for as long as they existed." *Huh?* Was Christa shutting the toy box already? *Dear Readers, ghastly though life in our cities may be, let us never forget that the earth bears our weight. That's something at least—* was that her true meaning? Discounting a grammatical ambiguity that made it uncertain whether what the earth would continue to bear was the city or its inhabitants or both, the thing that puzzled me most was: Why such an elaborate opening paragraph? Had Christa deployed all her artistry only to retract everything in a single sentence, or was it the essence of her artistry to retract every statement she made? That needed some getting used to even for a reader who, like me, had joined five libraries.

You see? Only half a page into the book, and I was more interested in the author than in her story. *What sort of person had written this stuff?* After roughly twenty pages I pictured her as a thirteen-year-old girl afflicted with palpitations while waiting for the teacher to return her essay on "My best vacation experience"—an essay in which she has taken something of a gamble: instead of "An Evening by the Campfire," or "Out Hunting with Uncle Hubert," or "A Visit to Berlin," she has produced "Sunrise beside the Sea," so she's infinitely relieved, not to say overjoyed, when the teacher smilingly informs the class that "our Christa" has once again written "the best essay of all." That settles "our Christa's" literary hash—irrevocably so. She's destined to remain the girl desirous of writing the best essay of all. *But the best novel of all was written by our Christa . . .*

I hadn't finished the book when the inevitable happened: *she* materialized beside my bed. I felt shattered. How had she found me?

"Klaus," she sobbed, "I knew it. *A mother senses these things.*"

You see, Mr. Kitzelstein? That's what I've been talking about the whole time. My mother and her maternal instincts had succeeded where the Stasi's entire Missing Persons Bureau had failed. I was her child all right. I could read the mute reproach in her eyes: *Why didn't you let me know where you were?* and *How on earth did it happen? Why can't you take better care of yourself?* Hadn't she always, and with considerable success, kept me away from all potential sources of danger? Had we ever traveled by subway train without my hearing *Stand away from the door?* And hadn't I been warned, even in my early teens, never to put a plastic bag over my head for fear of suffocation? Had I ever been allowed on the street after 4 p.m. on New Year's Eve— *those stupid fireworks can so easily blind a person!*—and hadn't I been told never to play in derelict buildings for fear they might collapse? Hadn't I been forbidden to eat mushrooms, sit in the front passenger seat of a car, or travel in the first four cars of a train, not to mention climb trees? And all to no avail. Hadn't I learned a thing? How was it that, since casting off her aegis, I'd passed up no opportunity to fall down flights of stairs—stairs, moreover, which I'd trodden for the purpose of masturbating or crossing swords with her idol, Jutta Müller? I should have listened to my mother and Jutta, those two implacable purveyors of divine judgment.

"Mama," I said, reaching—much as I hate to admit it—for her hand.

"I don't know what things are coming to," she said, wagging her head. "We sacrificed ourselves for people, quite ordinary people. That's why we're heroes."

"Heroes?" I said bemusedly.

"Of course," she said. "Heroes like us have nothing to be ashamed of."

How could I have contradicted her? Before long, she and her kind would be recounting their heroic deeds. And I? What feats of heroism should I recount? I was Honecker's Little Trumpeter, I had saved his life, I was the author of *Men reported dead live longer*! But I'd never collaborated with my elders in total innocence or shared the naïve enthusiasm that inspired them during the years of reconstruction. I couldn't claim to have sacrificed myself for other people, nor could I dream of socialism, and if I'd said so to my mother she'd have bent my ear: *We were quite different in those days. Not so materialistic . . .*

No, those things were as impossible to discuss with her as anything else.

"All right," she said at length, "let's take a look." She started to pull the sheets down, but I grabbed her hand. Every inch my father's son, I hid my dick as the Communists of Eisleben did their red flag.

"Well, well," she said, "what a shrinking violet! Don't tell me you're too shy to show your mother where you hurt yourself?"

That was her all over, Mr. Kitzelstein. If I'd let her look and confronted her with my hard-on, I'd have been *playing with it again;* if I didn't, I was a *shrinking violet.* Given half a chance, she'd have gone at it with *baby powder.* What impelled her? Where did it spring from, this ingrained thirst for action?

"Mama!" I pleaded, hanging on with all my might.

"Don't be so silly. I'm medically trained, remember?" When I continued to cling to the sheets, she folded them back from the bottom up. The sheer horror on her face suggested that she'd made some gruesome discovery—a charred or mutilated corpse, perhaps. She let go of the covers and hurried out. "Doctor, Doctor!" I heard her calling in the hallway. Then I took a look myself.

Peacefully curled up between my legs was a species of animal. It couldn't be, could it? Imagine waking up one day and finding that your familiar little dick had been replaced by the biggest *membrum virile* you'd ever seen. What would your reaction be? The first thing that shot through my head was a snatch of Jutta Müller's speech: *Incredible transformation.* My next thought was of my jeans, which I'd worn only once and would never fit into again.

This isn't my son! Thus the reproachful message in my mother's eyes as she dragged the duty intern to my bed and folded back the sheets for his benefit. The intern, who couldn't have been thirty, briefly inspected my mother's discovery, clicked his tongue, and winked at me. "Enough to give a man an inferiority complex," he murmured. Penile swelling was not uncommon after an operation in which the lymphatic duets had been severed, he explained—more to my mother than to me. These things happened, and when the lymphatic drainage had stabilized itself *after a few weeks, three months at the most,* the penis would revert to its normal size. He did, however, concede that he'd never seen a penis become distended as rapidly as mine or assume such vast dimensions.

Please don't look like that, Mr. Kitzelstein; this isn't just callow bragging on my part. If I'm parading my dick in public, I'm doing so for a legitimate purpose. You see, the reasons for my unique and gigantic expansion were elucidated some months later. The serum injected into me at the Polyclinic was intended to transform my blood into a medicament for subsequent extraction. Fair enough, except that my remaining blood became subject to unsuspected "cumulative interactions" that didn't manifest themselves until my lymphatic drainage system was obstructed. This explained the unique speed with which my penis attained its unique dimensions and retained them for a unique length of time—far longer than the intern's "few weeks, three months at the most" prognosis.

And now, Mr. Kitzelstein, take a deep breath, because I've another little sensation for your newspaper to impart to the world. As you know, I wasn't the only patient with blood of a novel type in my veins. The other patient defied a prognosis—which expert witnesses discreetly gave in court three years later—to the effect that he had only *a few weeks, three months at the most,* to live. There must be a handful of doctors in Germany who now grasp the significance of this genuine blood brotherhood, to wit, that my outsize dick and the former General Secretary had something in common: the blood they shared enabled them to confound all prognoses.

Men reported dead live longer. Had the expert witnesses known of the serum and its effects (which could have been studied with the aid of my genitals), their predictions would have been less pessimistic, the Honecker trial need not have been adjourned *sine die,* the sensibilities of innocent citizens would have been sufficiently catered to, and Honecker would have been internationally regarded—after Nelson Mandela's release—as the world's most eminent political prisoner . . .

But at that time, while I was still in the hospital, I knew nothing of these circumstances and had no idea what the future held in store. The intern assured my mother that he would raise the subject when the senior consultant did his rounds the next day. I tell you, Mr. Kitzelstein, the size of my dick threw a dozen doctors into confusion—the kind of problem I'd always dreamed of!

"I suggest relieving the strain with an elastic support, Professor. The organ's weight will exert abnormal downward tension, with unpredictable consequences." "I'm sure you're right. However, gentlemen, what if the process continues unabated?" "Another two weeks, and that appendage will restrict his freedom of movement like a ball and chain." "Four weeks, and his erections will induce unconsciousness. They'll consume so much blood that his brain will be starved of oxygen—not to mention the consequent visual impairment." "Six more weeks of this, and the patient will have become metamorphosed into a giant penis. This bed will be occupied by a ninety-kilogram penis resembling a dead seal." "Would it still be capable of an erection?"—"Of course, except that the thing in the bed would then resemble a *deep-frozen* dead seal."

I was a prey to mixed emotions. On the one hand, I wanted to witness this scholarly debate and savor the perplexity of the Gods in White; on the other, I had no wish to surrender my new acquisition—not immediately, anyway, and certainly not at my mother's insistence. Every man would like to have the biggest, and I *had* it. Why should I let the doctors tinker with it when, for the first time ever, I had no quarrel with my destiny, or the size of my dick, whichever? I decided to abscond, dick and all.

I also owed my chances of escape to the fact that I wasn't wearing jeans on admission. Otherwise the Wall would still be standing, because I could never have escaped in tight pants. You've guessed it: I fled the hospital on the evening of that historic November 9—not that I had any intention of toppling the Wall. My sole concern was to save my monumental thing.

As soon as it was dark I squeezed into my pants and returned the Christa Wolf to its owner.

"Well?" she asked expectantly.

"Well . . ." I replied.

"My sentiments exactly," she said. She pointed to a newspaper. "And as for this speech of hers!"

What speech? I thought. The answer dawned on me a moment later: *But the best speech of all was given by our Christa.*

Everything went black before my eyes. It was a mistake! It was all a big mistake: I'd confused Jutta with Christa. The orator had been Christa Wolf, the novelist, it said so on page one. Imagine my feelings, Mr. Kitzelstein. That a figure-skating coach should deliver a revolutionary speech was conceivable, given the general excitement, but that an author should have harangued the crowd like a figure-skating coach—no, that was too innocuous to be innocuous! It now transpired that I'd acted on an entirely false assumption. I would *never* have run down those steps to cross swords with an *author;* the son of Lucie Uhltzscht, with his five library cards, was far too much in awe of the creative artist. I would have listened politely and applauded like all the rest, not elbowed my way toward the speaker's truck, fallen down the steps, and hurt myself. No surgeon would have had to wield his scalpel, and my dick would never have assumed such enviable dimensions. I would not have suffered all that pain or asked myself so many unanswered questions . . .

Once I had laid the Wall low and begun to grasp the magnitude of my achievement, I was haunted by the question leveled at every naughty boy by his bewildered mother: "What on earth were you thinking of?" Yes, what *had* I been thinking of? The truth is, absolutely nothing. The question *What did I do wrong?* has always given me the craziest complexes, as you know. When I couldn't get it up I became a pervert for safety's sake. Such is my sensitivity I find it hurtful to be scolded even for minor misdemeanors, so now I can't help censuring myself for having toppled the Wall *with no firm end in view.* What on earth had I done? If Christa Wolf, the mistress of the written word (or whatever her surrounding aura was), had refrained, despite her "emancipated language," from inciting people to breach the Wall on November 4, she must have had her reasons. And I had breached it notwithstanding! I had done it by myself, without seeking her consent! I had inadvertently provoked a political opponent of alarming stature, for what is a woman whose vocation consists of teaching other people how to slide around and jump on the ice compared to an intellectual heavyweight in the field of contemporary German *literature*? What had I done? What indeed!

These tormenting questions prompted me to sift through Christa Wolf's oeuvre. Had she failed to advocate the breaching of the Wall in her November 4 speech because she'd already done so a dozen times on paper? Had she simply forgotten to do so in the excitement? If so, I would still be the person who had breached the Wall, but I would at least have acted in tacit collusion with my country's best-known literary figure and proved myself worthy of my five library cards. I resolved to comb her books until I could find a justification for *my* action in *her* words. I was bound to find it somewhere; then I could rest easy again—then I need not fear excommunication by our writers and intellectuals. Perhaps Christa Wolf had been greatly in favor of breaching the Wall. Perhaps she had even used "emotive words" like *Imagine if the Wall weren't there anymore*, etc. I would no longer be branded with sole responsibility for the end of history: I could claim to have acted in concert with our society's most enlightened minds!

Filled with hope, I delved into Christa Wolf's collected works. All I found at first were *intimations*, which got me nowhere; only unequivocal statements could dig me out of my hole. Christa Wolf had written a *love* story—which, as you will recall, served me well as an erection suppressor—and her politically intended writings were just as passionate. After I had spent six months exploring her oeuvre with no appreciable success, she published *What Remains,* a story set in the 1970s. This finally yielded something tangible. I've marked the place—mind if I read it to you?

She's talking about the departure hall at Friedrichstrasse Station, *popularly known as "the Bunker of Tears," in which the transformation of citizens of various countries, my own included, into transients, tourists, emigrants, and immigrants was accomplished in a light reflected by greenish tiled walls* . . . Oh, Mr. Kitzelstein, how extravagantly descriptive of light and color! Will she ever forget her essay "Sunrise beside the Sea"? The passage goes on: . . . *a light that issued from very high, narrow windows in which henchmen of the master of this city, attired as policemen or customs officers, exercised the right of restraint or release. Had its outward appearance matched its function, this building would have been a monstrosity* . . . There, Mr. Kitzelstein: *that* was what I'd been looking for all the time, an injunction to erect a monstrosity rather than demolish the Wall. I'm regularly afflicted by attacks of thoroughgoing anti-intellectualism at such moments. "The Wall must go!" would have said it all, but that stemmed from Ronald Reagan, the voice-test President, not from Christa Wolf. Absolute simplicity: no greenish light, tiled walls, or high, narrow windows.

I had read in *Neues Deutschland* a few weeks earlier that Christa Wolf had actually been commissioned to draft a constitutional preamble. Her eventual creation was a single sentence kept alive for four paragraphs with the aid of an ambitious participial construction. Were the participles intended to celebrate the noble democratic concept of *participation?* Was this *subtext* or *metalinguistic structure?* Who knows? Like my name, in which consonants proliferate and trample on one another's toes, this preamble was one big *Uhltzscht,* if you know what I mean. Everything in the way of nobility and veracity, everything exalted, edifying, and so forth, was crammed into it and linked by participles—present participles, naturally, because they pack more punch.

I know this style from my mother: in favor of compulsory bathing caps but liberal in other respects. *Demands are becoming rights, in other words, obligations* . . . Anyone who believes that the emancipation of language is compatible with that statement would naturally invest a constitutional preamble with the charm of a landlady's house rules. What sort of people want to live in a society governed by a constitution whose very preamble spells constraint? Figure-skating coaches? If you're going to use emancipated language, do it

properly. *Whoops!* would make a good constitutional preamble, or *Doo-wop-a-loo-bop*, or *And now for something
different*, or *Monday is washday*, or *Toodle-oo-doo-doo,
toodle-oo-doo-doo.*

But something else happened during that crazy, topsy-
turvy year, Mr. Kitzelstein. A few weeks later I took Christa Wolf under my wing in the course of—you've guessed
it—the so-called *deutsche Literaturstreit* or German literary
controversy (not the same thing as the German literary *competition*). Thanks to my enviable anatomical development, I
was by then a pornographic movie star of whom part, at
least, had received widespread page one treatment. Christa
Wolf sparked off the literary controversy with a story in
which the Stasi unnerve a woman writer by staring at her for
weeks on end, so much so that she eventually devours an
entire box of candy in half an hour. The story may have had
another theme as well, for all I know, because my primary
purpose in reading it was to find an answer to my question:
Did Christa Wolf support my breaching of the Wall? I knew
nothing of the German literary controversy, nor had I been
expecting it, so I was staggered when I learned of its existence. I mean, how can one fairly assess the politics of a
writer who has seldom if ever made an unambiguous political
statement? Know what she says about Budapest 1956? That
we sat in front of our radios filled with "concern." Meaning
what? Did anyone sit in front of his radio filled with *relief*?
Did Ulbricht? Did Adenauer? And where was the box of
candy? Those who express themselves equivocally are open
to wide interpretation, but what rendered this debate so absurd was that everyone could make of it what he chose.

To draw attention to this paradoxicality, I made a serious
attempt to place a wholly inappropriate gloss on Christa
Wolf's work. What if one regarded her—the author whose

first novel had been lent to me in the hospital as an erection suppressor—as a pornographer? No problem: the requisite material was to hand in *The Quest for Christa T.*, of which two pages describe how Christa T. uttered a very special cry: *Hooohaahooo—something like that . . . I wanted to share in a life that brought forth such cries as hooohaahoo, a life that must have been familiar to her.* Just letters on paper, but what did the cry really sound like? Why is the cry spelled with three concluding o's in one passage and only two a page and a half later? Is there an audible difference between "hooohaahooo" and "hooohaahoo," and, if so, what? How should one set about uttering this cry, however many "o's" it contains? Christa T., at all events, began *to blow, or shout—there's no apt expression for it . . . Hooohaahooo—something like that.*

That was quite enough dialogue for a pornographic actor of my caliber, Mr. Kitzelstein. Whenever one occurred to me in the course of my duties, I enlivened the proceedings with a Christa Wolf quotation: either *Hooohaahooo* or *Hooohaahoo.* Unfortunately, this imparted a definite slant to her sentence *I wanted to share in a life that brought forth such cries,* but what could I do? I had to demonstrate that Christa was, if not a man for all seasons, a writer for all occasions. You'll see what I mean if you take the trouble to browse through the adult section of your video library.

How relentlessly ir-rep-roach-a-ble our mothers are, and how many merit marks they can claim! They've won Olympic medals and written preambles to draft constitutions. They raised our country from the ruins or at least watched others doing so from their baby carriages. Their *curricula vitae* fill me with such awe that I go weak at the knees: war, devastation, air raids, mass expulsions, weekends spent as construction workers . . . Tired of sitting down, Sunday after Sunday, to roast pork with mashed potatoes and red cabbage? Try complaining about it to a housewife reared on ration cards! "We'd have been glad of it . . . boiled rutabagas . . . slates in school instead of notebooks . . . You don't know how well off you are!" Oh, sure! And they can't conceive how *badly* off we are—how could they? How, surrounded by Olympic mothers, can we talk about it in our own halting words when *they* have staked an exclusive claim to emancipated language, even if the first thing that "flows freely" from their lips is the statement that demands are becoming rights, in other words, obligations? And when, as if scaling the ultimate pinnacle of virtue, they present us with a preamble to the draft constitution designed to tell us in black and white whom or what to mourn in the aftermath of 1989? Future generations of historians will pay them homage, of that they can rest assured. What a brilliant swan song!

My own contribution to the debate is the story of my perversions, my little trumpet, my snooping and informing, my impotence, my abnormal masturbatory fantasies, my combination of megalomania and staggering naïveté. Hardly a success story, yet I'm almost glad I was in the Stasi after all. I can ask myself the relevant questions. I can get at the root of my turpitude. I've absolutely no need to begin by making deplorable excuses: "I never harmed anyone . . ."; "On the other hand, I was able to . . ."; "Even in those days, I . . ." A complete distortion, and nobody notices! How could our society have endured for decades if all its members had been as discontented as they claim? That's not a rhetorical question, Mr. Kitzelstein, so take it seriously. They were all against the system, yet they integrated and collaborated. Were they pusillanimous, besotted, or just plain stupid? I'd like to know for sure, because I think that *all* modern societies are in the same quandary.

For as long as millions of failures fail to face up to their failure, they'll remain failures. *Their* fate may leave me cold, but how am I to change *my* fear-and-submission-ridden life if no one is prepared to talk about fear and submission? It's all true, what I've told you, but does that apply to the way I've told it? Hard to say. It only adds to my feeling of help- lessness, because I *know* we East Germans owe it to the world and ourselves to hold a debate. Although what I've told you, and what your paper will print, is far from initiating that debate, it does at least draw attention to the need to launch one. I should have liked to paint my story as black and de- pressing as it really is, but if all the rest do nothing but justify themselves, self-justifications are all that occur to me, too, and all my attempts at candor fail.

"Even in those days, I . . ." Any statement prefaced by those words can be dismissed. "Never again will I . . ." would be more interesting, but that they can't manage. They all "did, even in those days," which is why they've no need to change. "Things are just the way they were!" they grumble. "Worse, in fact!" No, they themselves are the same as they were, and they don't even realize it. Having demolished a wall, they think they're sanctified to all eternity. That's why I'm going to put an end to all this humbug and tell you what really happened on the night of November 9, 1989.

A man went forth into the night—a man and his appendage. (I'm referring to myself, as you may imagine.) I was the pos- sessor of a penis that merited such a description. No more little trumpet for me. The weight of my balls imparted a new sensation as I went on my way. I no longer scuttled along like a roach on a hot plate; I walked with measured tread, conscious of myself, my balls, and the ground beneath my feet. Wow, what a holy trinity! This would be my persona from now on, this and no other. I felt an urge to call Bogey and exchange a few gruff, macho words with him, except that he was dead (too dead to answer the phone, as Raymond Chandler might have said). Besides, I didn't have his number.

My first thought on escaping from the hospital was to call on the Sausage Woman. She had sneered at my little trumpet, so I had a score to settle with her. I didn't know exactly what I would do when I got there, but the proper course of action was bound to occur to me in time. With a dick like mine in my pants, nothing could go wrong . . .

I never got to her place. She lived in Isländische Strasse, a side street running off Bornholmer Strasse. Yes, *that* Bornholmer Strasse, the one with the checkpoint at the far end. Milling around in front of it were members of the so-called masses, who, for reasons I then found incomprehensible, were hoping that the gates of heaven would open right away and enable them to stream westward. There were thousands of them, and confronting them were a few border guards who opened the gate a crack whenever a Westerner appeared and flashed his papers. The masses would begin to shove at such moments—only symbolically, of course, but what could one expect of revolutionaries who publicly claimed credit for having ensured that their protest demonstrations were officially sanctioned? They didn't want to get "mixed up in anything," after all. The border guards had a hard time shutting the gate again, but they managed it. (They managed it because they were *supposed* to manage it.) They threw their full weight against the gate and bolted it, and the masses continued to flatten their noses against it.

Although I did not know it, the masses' expectations had been aroused by a cryptic remark of Günther Schabowski's at his press conference. What Schabowski meant to say was that those wishing to travel to West Germany need no longer take the roundabout route via Czechoslovakia, but could go there directly. Being a true Party functionary, however, he made such a rigmarole of that simple statement that it might have meant anything. Within minutes, a sitting of the Bundestag broke up amid scenes of excitement—"We have just learned that . . ."—and a number of deputies spontaneously rose and sang *"Deutschland über Alles"* in the belief that the frontier was open. The TV newscasters thought so, too, with the result that tens of thousands of East Berliners set off for the crossing points, only to discover that their hopes were misplaced. Anything seemed possible in those days, however, so they stood there and waited and shouted *We are the people!* And that was how we encountered each other: they wanted to go West *just like that,* and I and my outsize dick were en route to the Sausage Woman.

It was a pathetic sight, Mr. Kitzelstein. There they stood, thousands of them confronted by a few dozen border guards, and they didn't dare to make a move. They shouted, "We are the people!," the principal slogan of recent weeks, and somehow it hit the nail on the head. They were indeed "the people." Who but "the people" would have stood there in such a docile, diffident way, shuffling from foot to foot and hoping against hope? This was how I knew them of old: timid and tractable and programmed to fail. I pitied them, somehow, because I was one of them. I *was* one of them. People who accept that the emancipation of language is a revolutionary achievement when told so from the back of a truck, people enthused by the information that they're protesting with official consent, people nonplussed by a handful of border guards—people of that kind have undersized dicks, take it from one who knows. It wasn't tanks that deterred them, it was ten or a dozen white-faced, trembling border guards who did their duty by bracing themselves against the gate. They also seized and marched off some of the more vociferous rabble-rousers in the forefront of the crowd to resentful cries of "No violence!" from the nearest bystanders. A strange ritual. The missing feature was an outburst of righteous public indignation.

But before that public could go home again, as I feared they would, and half a century hence, with romantically transfigured expressions, tell their grandchildren how they "almost" set foot in the West on November 9, 1989 ("even the border guards' knees were knocking, there were so many of us")—before it could come to that, I, the redeemer with the outsize dick, decided to act. The next time the border guards opened the gate a crack I looked them firmly in the eye and, when they threw their weight against it to repel the symbolically shoving crowd, shouted at the top of my voice, "Go on, shove harder, damn you! Give it all you've got! You can do it, I know you can!"

The crowd heard my cry of "You can do it!" and thought, "If *one of us* is brave enough to risk a battle cry in the very front row, eyeball to eyeball with the border guards, we can't not back him up. What was that he shouted? 'Shove harder!'? Well, why not?" But they shoved so symbolically that the border guards were able to force the gate shut by degrees, even though—and here I'll let you into another closely guarded German secret about that night—even though they no longer *wanted* to shut it. When I shouted to the crowd and, for safety's sake, looked at the border guards as if exhorting *them* to shove harder, the guard commander merely shook his head resignedly. He expected the pressure to increase and refrained from making a final effort to counteract it. At that moment, Mr. Kitzelstein, nobody wanted the Wall anymore. Even the border guards were sick of guarding it and rejoiced at the belated appearance of someone determined to sweep the thing away.

Just then the proceedings were interrupted by the sort of person who always intervenes on such occasions: the circumspect rebel whose opening words are "I'd like to speak to whoever's in charge!" A man of around thirty, he looked like an experienced moderate who had learned his trade in countless debates on grass-roots democracy. He was also run to earth by the media, but long before me. "*Someone* must be in charge here!" cried Aram Radomski, for such was his name. And, turning to the crowd: "Surely there must be someone in charge!" Eager to know how his quest for someone in charge would end, the crowd waited. Someone did, eventually, admit to being that someone. Radomski proceeded to try to persuade him to open the gate at once.

That was when I had an idea, a kind of inspiration: the border guards might also be sons of mothers of the *Have-you-been-playing-with-it?* type. It *was* an inspiration, there's no other word for it. Slowly and deliberately, I unbuttoned my coat, undid my belt, and unzipped my trousers, looking the border guards full in the face as I did so. They'd paid particular attention to me ever since my cry of "Give it all you've got!"—in fact they'd never taken their eyes off me. So much the better. Grinning, because I'd known that grinning was *de rigueur* ever since encountering the flasher in the S-Bahn, I lowered my underpants. And, while Aram Radomski continued to argue with the man in charge in lucid and committed language, unaware of what I was doing beside him, the border guards stared spellbound at my display. When all of them were standing at the gate, transfixed, I turned to face the man in charge. His flow of counterargument ceased abruptly. "Then you can let us across!" said Radomski, still unwitting, and the man was too bereft of energy to contradict him—too flabbergasted even to cite some regulation or other. He simply stared at me with ever-widening eyes.

So much of what happened then seemed incredible that I felt confident of success: if *that* didn't floor him and the other border guards, nothing would. Never having seen such a phenomenon before, they couldn't credit it. The spectacle confronting them was so fantastic, they would never be able to talk about it because no one would believe them. I took my time. I gazed at each man in turn until one of them, as if mesmerized, unbolted the gate. Before they could have any second thoughts—Radomski was still arguing, still *reasoning* with them—I gripped the bars of the gate and pushed it open. "There," I cried, loudly enough to be heard by the crowd behind me but reluctant to turn and face them with my fly open, "the rest is up to you!"

However sardonic my account of this episode, it did pave the way for some of the happiest moments in German history, rare moments of *innocent* joy. You know the pictures: champagne parties at the Brandenburg Gate, horse-riding on top of the Wall, happenings with hammer and chisel. Everyone was ecstatic, no one grasped what had really happened. The latecomers and the ones at the back felt sure they would have pushed the gate open if they'd been at the front, and the ones at the front thought they *had* pushed it open because it really had opened. If I had claimed sole credit at the time, no one would have believed me. Those border guards weren't toy soldiers, after all. It's only now, with the passage of time and in the light of subsequent developments in Germany, that my version of how the Wall came down becomes so thoroughly plausible. I mean, look at the East Germans today: as passive now as they always were. How could *they* have demolished the Wall? Never mind, I thought at the time, their experience of freedom, dignity, and self-assertion may prove infectious and strike a lasting chord. Let them believe in a strength they never possessed, just as they went in fear of a power that never existed.

Yes, Mr. Kitzelstein, I, too, rejoiced that night. I was half-demented with happiness, and it was at one of these moments of exultation that a camera crew stationed itself in front of me and held a microphone under my nose. *Every revolutionary movement emancipates language as well*, so listen carefully to what I, the veteran composer of aphorisms and quotable pronouncements, *burbled* to the international media. I was incapable of *speech*, having lost control of my *ar-tic-u-la-to-ry apparatus*, but no matter, my utterance sufficed to become "the word of 1989": *Cra-a-a-zy!* Yes indeed, I was the person that uttered it on the Bornholmer Bridge on the night of November 9, 1989, and its status was officially confirmed, three months later, by the German Language Association in session at Darmstadt. No more of those laborious, disciplined, didactic turns of phrase from the mother of all mothers; burbling was the rule from now on . . .

I simply couldn't go wrong that night: I'd preserved my dick, ended the Cold War, and coined the word of the year. Even when I caught sight of a familiar figure in the throng and yelled "Hey, Sausage Woman, it's as big as a rolling pin these days!"—she couldn't hear me, of course—my effort wasn't altogether wasted because a West Berlin photographer slipped me his business card. "If you'd like to earn a few marks . . ." he said, clarifying his offer with a jerk of the hips. That was how I'd always imagined the West: hardly across the Blue border and already involved in blue movies.

My feelings of triumph abruptly evaporated when the driver of one of the Trabants crossing the bridge, alarmed by the revelers wildly drumming on his roof, offered them a copy of *Neues Deutschland* as a form of toll. Not just any old rag but the Party's mighty central organ, the newspaper was summarily torn to shreds amid cries of delight. I found it comical to see seven or eight people scuffle for the privilege of tearing up a newspaper until I heard the comment of a West Berliner near me: "The lynch mob is going berserk." He meant it as a joke, but the zeal and fervor that attended the newspaper's destruction reminded me of my bosses' warnings. They had told us countless times that the enemy—"everyone is a potential foe"—wasn't squeamish and wouldn't balk at murder. Days earlier a revolutionary speech had enjoined the people to "read the newspapers" instead of pulling down the Wall. *Read* the newspapers, yes, but I had suddenly become a witness to outrages committed against the Party's central organ! The days of nonviolence were over; *violence against things* was the thin end of the wedge, everyone knew that. What would become of me? What would become of *my* mighty central organ? I wanted to survive. I had regained my love of life and found it immature and stupid of me to have thought, as I had done only a few days before, that my kind deserved to be hanged from a lamppost. I wanted to get away, I was frightened, and when another camera was thrust in my face I blurted out a word that emanated from the deepest quagmires of my soul: "Germany!" I half croaked, half whispered it—out of fear. The West Germans took it literally, of course, though they subjected it to a small but vital distortion: they behaved as if all who said "Germany" meant the "Federal Republic." How unimaginative! All they lacked in their spick-and-span republic, where even the rivers have been straightened out, was the feeling that they led a life for which others envied them. What's so good about the Federal Republic, aside from the fact that it produces the best BMWs in the world? It isn't that I consider the Federal Republic a horrific institution, but it's not so perfect that one can't conceive of anything better. How could I have known that the whole East German nation would suddenly feel called upon to take up my bewildered cry of "Germany!"? Don't go telling me that *Germany* was the only still-inconceivable thing at a time when people were enjoying the fact that inconceivable things were happening every day. If so, you'd have to explain why they didn't abolish the army. Perhaps we'll get somewhere, Mr. Kitzelstein, if we try something along these lines: *Language is recalling its emotive words, and one of these is "Germany."* "Germany" was my verbal talisman against the fear of what I'd done, against my fear of the consequences and the possibility that officially decreed rights and obligations were a thing of the past. It wasn't as clear to me that freedom ensues upon emancipation. I was the first whose fear reduced him to that single word "Germany." My God, can you think of anyone apart from Leonardo da Vinci who was so far and so perceptively ahead of his time?

But why should I trouble to explain Germany to you? Take a look at the country for yourself. Knowing as you do how reunification came about, you won't be surprised at what has happened since. I've no illusions, Mr. Kitzelstein: no one will believe a social outcast and Stasi pervert, kidnapper and rapist *manqué* like me, but so what? No one who dismisses my story can possibly understand what's wrong with Germany. Why not? Because nothing makes sense without me—because I'm recent German history's *missing link.*

Was that what you wanted to know?